SONS OF THE STEPPE

HANS BAUMANN

SONS OF
THE STEPPE

*The story of how
the Conqueror Genghis Khan
was overcome*

LONDON
OXFORD UNIVERSITY PRESS

Oxford University Press, Amen House, London E.C.4

GLASGOW NEW YORK TORONTO MELBOURNE WELLINGTON
BOMBAY CALCUTTA MADRAS KARACHI KUALA LUMPUR
CAPE TOWN IBADAN NAIROBI ACCRA

© Oxford University Press 1957

First published 1954 under the title

STEPPENSÖHNE

by ENSSLIN AND LAIBLIN VERLAG, REUTLINGEN

First published in English 1957
Reprinted 1959

Printed in Great Britain by Richard Clay and Company, Ltd.,
Bungay, Suffolk

Translated by

ISABEL AND FLORENCE McHUGH

Illustrated by

HEINER ROTHFUCHS

CONTENTS

Contents

PART ONE

The Inseparables

An Encounter on the Edge of the Desert

IT was about a hundred thousand strong, the horde of horsemen which had been pressing southwards for weeks already through the eastern part of the Gobi Desert; and the Desert offered it no particular difficulties. The apparently endless cavalcade did not seem to disturb the Gobi, a region which is normally so notoriously hostile towards all who dare to tread it. Often, provoked by a mere handful of horses or camels, it would silt up the infrequent wells on the caravan track, or attack the merchants and outriders with sandstorms. For this stretch of desert between the grasslands of the Mongols and the Garden of China was not kindly disposed towards traders.

The hundred thousand horsemen were under arms. Many of them bore scars—reminders of battlefields which lay several months' ride distant the one from the other. To many of the older warriors the riding tracks through half Asia were as familiar as the lines on their own palms. News of each coming battle had always filled them with greedy longing, and caused their narrow slits of eyes to flash dark fire, visible signs of their invincible craving to bring more strange lands under the hooves of their small, nimble horses.

But this time their faces were gloomy. There was no fire in their eyes, and their glances did not leap ahead. Even the horses seemed to move forward reluctantly. The rough, dishevelled beasts, which understood the slightest hint, missed the hidden play of the riders' legs against their flanks, by which they were used to being encouraged.

3

Far ahead of the hundred thousand rode a solitary man on a horse whose white coat was marked with dark flame-coloured flecks the size of a hand. It was a 'tiger' horse, and its hooves struck the sand so quickly that a tiny dry wave leaped up at each step. The horse could feel through the saddle the pressure of the hard knees, and it pranced ahead with arched neck, straining at the reins. For the rider was pressing it, and in his deportment there was no hint of weariness. His face was full of uneasy shadows, and his eyes searched the distant horizon. In endless waves the desert lay ahead of him, one wave of it just like the next. And the man had but one thought, and he thought it a thousand times over—each time that a sand-dune rose above the flatness of the desert—though the thought hurt him. He rode bolt upright, with squared shoulders, like a man who is trying with all his might to hide that he is wounded.

It is *my* wound, thought the solitary man, but it is not my fight only to which we are riding. The enemy who is waiting for us beyond the Gobi is the concern of all the People of the Steppe; and it is more important than ever that we win. I know well that the hundred thousand behind me do not think as I do, but once they see that the others, who are riding out against us, are riding side by side with Chinese hirelings—with the cage people who were vanquished by our fathers; that, despite having faces like ourselves, these faithless men who have forgotten that they were once Sons of the Steppe, face us as defenders of rice-tilling peasants—oh, then my horsemen will rouse themselves from their gloomy doubt and avenge their mother, Mongolia, on the traitors who look upon a vanquished people as equals and no longer see that the Eternal Blue Heaven has raised us Mongols above all the peoples of the earth! My hundred thousand will no longer recognize as brothers those men over there on the Great Wall who pose as friends of the Chinese, any more than I will recognize as being still my brother the man who is their leader. My warriors will be even more pitiless towards those renegades than towards any enemies they have encountered up till now . . .

'You are asking too much of your people,' a quiet voice said suddenly beside the solitary man, who, turning round, found himself face to face with Adar-Kidai, the leader of his best *tuman*.

Adar-Kidai was nearer to him than any other of his officers, and it was almost always he who acted as spokesman when the army had some request to make. Moreover, he was one of the few permitted to address the man on the tiger horse by name.

'They will never last it out with so little rest, Arik-Buka,' said Adar-Kidai. 'It is too much for the horses also,' added the young leader of ten thousand, after waiting in vain for an answer. And he thought to himself: He has ears only for his own thoughts; he did not even hear me riding up to him, so far is his mind from us.

'Once you men have them before you,' said Arik-Buka excitedly, 'you will forget the long road you have covered.' Then he added with a touch of mockery: 'It is indeed something new that my men should find the ride to a war too much for them!'

'If it were against enemies . . .' said Adar-Kidai hesitantly.

'It *is* against enemies,' interrupted Arik-Buka, 'against enemies of the worst kind—traitors!'

Arik-Buka urged on his tiger horse with a hard pressure of his thighs. Adar-Kidai remained by his side. 'Many of us, and also I myself, have a brother over there—beyond the Great Wall,' he said earnestly. 'It is not easy to ride to war against your own brother.'

Arik-Buka's face grew still darker with anger. 'You call *those* brothers!' he cried. 'He who renounces his mother also renounces his brother. They have broken the Law of the Steppe, which bade them rule over the people of the South. They have made Chinamen their brothers. How, then, can they still be our brothers? Their country is no longer Mongolia, but China. The rice-fields are more to them than the grasslands. They no longer dwell in yurts, but in palaces!'

'Leave China to them!' cried Adar-Kidai. 'They cannot take the Steppe from us! Kublai, your brother, has declared . . .'

'Do not speak his name!' shouted Arik-Buka angrily at the leader of his horsemen. 'Moreover, has he not himself renounced his Mongolian name? Does he not call himself Tshe-Tsu now? Why should I not ride to war against a man named Tshe-Tsu, the more so since that same Tshe-Tsu lays claim to the throne of Genghis Khan in declaring that China, which Genghis Khan, the father of our father, wished to annex to the Steppe, is the Middle Kingdom, and not Mongolia our Great Mother?'

With flaming face Arik-Buka continued: 'I will overthrow that man who became another man while I remained what I was: in striking him I will be striking at the man who led him into treachery, the astrologer from the South, the renegade Yeliu, who wormed himself into the favour of the Khan, the Lord of the World, in order to destroy him, and my brother, and all the Sons of the Steppe! It will be a good fight, Adar-Kidai! Nothing is more necessary than to destroy those who are false to their own. Kublai is no longer a Son of the Steppe.'

'Now you yourself have named him by his name,' said Adar-Kidai.

'It was for the last time,' cried Arik-Buka. And he turned round in his saddle. 'Let the *tumans* ride faster!' he ordered. 'Tell them that I, the true successor of Genghis Khan, expect them to be more eager when they are on their way to exterminate traitors.'

Adar-Kidai saw that any further argument was useless. Silently he turned and rode back to his *tuman*. His heart was full of grief, and he thought without ceasing of his brother Yung-So, who was leader of a *tuman* in the service of Kublai. We shall soon meet, thought Adar-Kidai to himself. And when the order to ride faster reached the *tumans* many thought as Adar-Kidai did, for many of them had a brother on the other side, and it was bitter to every one of them to have to urge his horse to go faster.

By the Dolon-Nor, the Seven Lake, the *tumans* of Arik-Buka came on the army which Kublai had stationed there to guard the northern frontier of China. Thrice Arik-Buka tried to break through into the land of rice-fields. Twice his *tumans* were defeated, but Kublai gave orders to spare the retreating force and not pursue it. When they met for the third time it did not come to fighting. Before Arik-Buka could launch an attack single riders on white horses detached themselves from Kublai's ranks. They bore no arms, but only gigantic silken banners. The banners were white like the horses, and had written signs on them in dazzling blue. Utterly dumbfounded, the warriors of Arik-Buka watched Kublai's standard-bearers approach. They could not read the written signs on the white flags, but they stared at them as if they were magic symbols. For how could these few men have dared to ride forward against thousands unless some mighty magic was protecting them?

One of the standard bearers rode straight up to the spot over which the standard of Arik-Buka was fluttering. The ranks parted before him. Only when he reached Arik-Buka did the standard-bearer halt his horse. Arik-Buka, enraged at his horsemen for falling back, shouted: 'Drag the traitor down from his horse!'

For the first time his horsemen did not obey him.

'White flags!' raged Arik-Buka. 'Flags of traitors, as at Samarkand! Yeliu's flags! And he dares to try that on me!'

The silken banners spread full in the wind, and the horsemen continued to stare as if bewitched at the writing. Arik-Buka turned to the standard-bearer: 'Does this Tshe-Tsu believe, then, that we have learned to read in the meanwhile?' he asked. 'What has he written on the flags?'

Thereupon the standard-bearer cried in a voice which all could hear: 'You and we—sons of the same Heaven!'

'What nonsense!' cried Arik-Buka. 'We are Sons of the Steppe; you are vassals of the Chinese!' And once more he gave the command: 'Drag him from his horse!'

No one stirred. The great silken banner stood silent and motionless in the wind. All who saw it now knew the message which it bore. And all knew who the man was who held the standard. It was Yung-So, a leader of horsemen, who was renowned among all the Mongols for his courage. Arik-Buka foamed with rage. 'So you will not obey, you who have twice retreated!'

Arik-Buka fixed his angry eyes on Adar-Kidai. 'Your *tuman* retreated, do you hear? You fled, you were afraid—afraid!'

'Should we fight those who are not our enemies?' asked Adar-Kidai.

'They are worse than enemies!' shrieked Arik-Buka. 'They are traitors who would infect us with their treachery!'

And he seized hold of Yung-So and dragged him, still grasping the banner with both hands, from the saddle.

'Why do you not defend yourself?' he asked him arrogantly.
'I have orders not to defend myself,' said Yung-So.

With both fists Arik-Buka forced him to the ground, but
Yung-So remained kneeling and held the white flag high above
him.

'Put down the flag of the astrologer, or you will be trampled
in the dust! Down with the flag of Yeliu!'

Yung-So held the white flag high above his head. Arik-Buka
took hold of his whip. At this Adar-Kidai stepped between him
and Yung-So. His face was pale as he said: 'If you do that, I am
no longer your man!'

Arik-Buka stepped back a pace. 'What do you mean, you rebel,
you double-dyed coward?'

'He and I have the same mother,' said Adar-Kidai. 'You shall
not strike my brother Yung-So!'

'I will horsewhip him! I will slash you both with this
whip until that accursed white flag is dyed red!' raged Arik-
Buka.

Red flames danced before the eyes of Arik-Buka. As he raised
his arm to strike the first blow he could see neither Adar-Kidai
nor Yung-So. But before his whip could swish down, his own

people had seized him. They bound his hands with the sharp-edged thongs of the whip.

'Take those fetters off him!' ordered Kublai when Arik-Buka was led before him. 'Why have you done that?'

'It was his own people who did it, not we,' answered the officer who had led Arik-Buka into Kublai's presence. 'He tried to horsewhip Yung-So and Adar-Kidai.'

'Leave us alone!' ordered Kublai, when Arik-Buka's hands had been freed.

Kublai gazed intently at his brother, who stood morose and silent with his back to the ermine-covered wall of the tent. Arik-Buka's gaze was fixed on the magnificent carpet which covered the floor of the spacious tent. Only when Kublai came nearer did Arik-Buka raise his head with a jerk and look at his brother out of his narrow, slanting eyes with such an expression of ill-will that Kublai, taken aback, stood still.

'How could you do that to me?' asked Arik-Buka in a hoarse voice. 'White flags—as Yeliu did to the Western People!'

'I wished to stop the senseless murder,' said Kublai. 'I did not wish that Mongol blood should be shed by Mongols, and that brother should slay brother. I did not mean to offend you.'

'Everything about you offends me,' replied Arik-Buka, without a moment's consideration. 'Your clothes are the clothes of a Chinaman. Your yurt is the luxurious tent of a Chinaman. You speak Mongolian, it is true, but you speak as no Mongol speaks. As you stand there, no Mongol stands. And your smile—it is the smile of a Chinaman. You are no longer a Son of the Steppe. They have made you into one of themselves—into a conquered man!'

Kublai saw that no word or look of his could reach Arik-Buka's mind until the embittered man had come to the end of his indictment, so he resolved to make no reply.

'I hear that you now call yourself Tshe-Tsu and claim to be the founder of a new Chinese dynasty,' continued Arik-Buka, with biting scorn. 'You have cast off even your name!' He made a threatening step towards Kublai. 'How did you dare to absent yourself from the *Kurultai*, the Great Council of the Steppe, after

B

Mangu our brother, third successor on the throne of Genghis Khan, remained behind on the field of battle?' Without allowing the other time to answer, Arik-Buka continued scornfully: 'Oh, yes, I know, you were too busy. You had so to distribute the tax-levies that not a handful too much should be taken from any one of your rice farmers! You had to build canals so that your town-dwellers should lack for nothing in their markets! You had to attend to your imperial kitchen, lest any of the idlers who lounge about your residence should go hungry . . . You see, I am well informed about the man on the Dragon Throne! I know that he has spent many nights regulating the calendar—for his Chinese; that he is building schools and observatories—for his Chinese; that he is laying down post roads and trade roads—for his Chinese. How could he come to the *Kurultai* in the Steppe when the Steppe is no more to him now than a miserable strip of grass-land beyond the Gobi, an insignificant frontier region in which camel herds live in poor and wretched dwellings? This Tshe-Tsu aspires to make the country which we wanted as pasture for our horses into the Middle Kingdom! And I am not to hate this man, who would bar us from our conquests!'

'You are my brother, Arik,' said Kublai quietly. 'Your hatred cannot change that.'

But Arik-Buka stood there as if he were deaf.

'All have left you,' continued Kublai, 'even Adar-Kidai, your closest friend and the commander of your best *tuman*. Whom have you got left, except me?'

Arik-Buka stared before him into space.

'Why do you look past me?' asked Kublai, with emotion. 'No one is nearer to me than you are.'

'No one is nearer to me than you are.' Arik-Buka put himself on the defensive against the invitation so plainly contained in those words of his brother. I dare not listen, he thought des-perately—not to him. And he tried to steel his heart, and he searched for words; but all the bitter words which he had pre-pared had already tumbled out, and he felt nothing in himself but a terrible emptiness.

'Sit down beside me,' said Kublai, 'and let us have a talk. Do not be distressed by what is strange to you here. What does it matter whether the yurt is lined with felt or with ermine? This yurt, too, has a window at the top, and the Eternal Blue Heaven is looking down at us. He knows how everything has come to pass, and has forgotten nothing. It seems to me that in our situation there is nothing more necessary than to recall the past.'

Arik-Buka made a movement of displeasure, but he did not oppose his brother.

'Did we not live many years one for the other?' asked Kublai. 'Remember those things again, Arik, and then we may perhaps find a way out of our conflict.' In a still more urgent tone he continued: 'And then it is possible that your hate might prove to be only . . .'

'To be only what?' interrupted Arik-Buka distrustfully.

'Love which has been disappointed,' said Kublai, without hesitation, 'or a love which has grown blind to many things. Perhaps we shall come to understand each other again if we try to look back the whole way. In this hour it seems to me that nothing is more important than that we should look back.'

Arik-Buka stood irresolute, but Kublai took him by the hand and drew him down beside him to a seat. 'Do you remember how we used to ride side by side in our first *yagun*, and the fun we used to have with that wild camel stallion? Do you remember when we rode to the Feast of the White Monkey in the mountains, and to the panther ground? Do you remember, Arik, how you carried me out of the ice after we had lost our horses on the Roof of the World?'

'I remember all those things very well,' said Arik-Buka gloomily, 'for nothing was ever more important to me than the things which were between us—those things which bound us to each other and those things which threatened to part us. I have forgotten nothing, not even the smallest detail. But I do not understand why you want to bring up all this now. Does not the whole way which lies behind us speak against you? You, too, were once a Son of the Steppe, and now you are one no longer.' With still more vehemence he continued: 'Oh, yes, let us recall everything which once was. Nothing can serve better to show us that it is you who have gone the wrong way and I who have remained on the right one; that it is I, not you, who have persevered in the path of Genghis Khan, the greatest of all the Sons of the Steppe. Let us place before our eyes once more how it all began—how we rode side by side, the one the shadow of the other, on our tiger horses, neither of which would take one step without the other, to the sacred *Tobu dolo gam*, the Holy Mountain of Five Peaks, in the heart of the Steppe . . .'

'Oh, yes,' said Kublai, a happy smile spreading over his face. 'Let us begin with the ride to the *Tobu dolo gam!*'

CHAPTER ONE

The Ride to the Tobu Dolo Gam

Two little clouds were flying over the Steppe, up alongside the Kerulen River, which, swollen with the melted snows, had flowed out beyond its accustomed bed in many places. It was a curious thing that the two little clouds were flying directly over the sands of the Steppe from east to west, though the light wind which had come up with the sun was blowing from the west.

Along the edge of the mountain twelve horsemen were galloping, a troop of six men apiece north and south of the river, and they were keeping at almost the same level as the two little clouds. The riders were trusting to their horses to be wary of the treacherous ground underfoot. Their own eyes were following the two little clouds which were often lost to sight when they dipped into green hollows. When they emerged into sight again the squads of horsemen would signal across to each other: they were making fine speed and keeping their direction well, steering straight for the *Tobu dolo gam*, the sacred five-peaked mountain of the Mongols. And the horsemen laughed: It will not be difficult to come up on them undetected there . . .

The twelve horsemen all had the same thought. At the foot of the *Tobu dolo gam*, where the sand ceases and the overhanging scar-like strips of grass begin, there will no longer be two little clouds but only two exhausted horses and on their backs two horsemen with boys' faces.

Even yet the two horses were hardly to be distinguished, though they were no longer leaving a flying cloud in their wake. The twelve horsemen could see only two bright spots streaking

along, but every man of the two troops knew with absolute
certainty that these two spots were two tiger horses flecked with
dark, flame-red spots the size of a man's hand, with strong necks,
and rough black hide shoes on their hooves—horses such as only
the royal princes of the Mongols were permitted to ride. The
riders also knew the names of the horses. They were Bosa and
Fabo, and on them sat Kublai and Arik-Buka, sons of Tuli, the
youngest son of Temuchin, otherwise known as Genghis Khan,
who since the Year of the Panther had reigned as Lord of all the
Peoples of the Steppe.

By the time the sun was at its height Kublai and Arik-Buka had
climbed one-third of the mountain. Their horses were grazing,
with their forelegs loosely tethered, in a ravine which was easily
surveyed from above. The two princes had quenched their
thirst with mares' milk. The longish hide bags, made of leather
hard as stone, hung half-empty on the saddles. The boys had
not got even bows and arrows with them. In the belts which
fastened their buffalo-hide jackets were stuck their *purbus*,
curved daggers with which even a spirit could be stabbed, if the
shaman who whispered his magic formula over the blade was not
greatly mistaken.

The ascent to the middle peak was steep, but the princes
climbed like cats. The May sun could not reach them as they
clambered up the northern wall of the mountain. When they
stopped to rest for a few moments they could hear the wind
blowing the grains of sand against the knee-high *deresen* grass.
The thorny blades made a sound as if little metal sticks were being
beaten together. The climbers had to beware lest they tore their
hands. Everything that grew up there had spikes, and in the
crevices grew a grass called *dara*, which is the Mongolian for
hedgehog. Bolduru birds flew up frequently; the frightened
swarm would rise with a long-drawn-out whistle. The princes
could also hear the warning whistle of marmots, and they could
see wild sheep here and there on the slopes. But Kublai and
Arik-Buka were not on the look-out for wild creatures to hunt
now. It did not even trouble them when they set a stone rolling
by a careless step; they behaved as if they had no need to guard

against any kind of danger. They seemed intent on only one thing: to get up as quickly as possible to the summit, from which they could survey the whole country far and wide.

After two hours they were up.

Meanwhile the twelve horsemen looked for cover for themselves and their horses in the ravines, which were quite near. There they dismounted and each man tethered his horse with the *arkan* or lasso in such a way that it could graze but could not stray into range of the young princes' eyes.

Compared with the ice-capped giants of the Altai and other high mountain ranges which surrounded the pasture-lands of the Mongols, *Tobu dolo gam* was not particularly high, yet the middle peak offered a wide panorama. To the south-east lay the so-called panther ground, a veritable paradise for wild animals of every kind. According to hunters, so many lizards flitted about the ground in summer that horses were nervous to walk; *derezon* antelopes were at home there, as also lynxes, bears, and that most bloodthirsty of all beasts of prey, the snow panther ... They two would track down one of those panthers one day—of that they were certain. And it would be a great day for both of them, because neither of the two princes ever undertook anything of importance without the other.

They had ridden out from the east with the first rays of the morning sun. The great procession, of which they felt themselves to be the far-advanced vanguard, must soon emerge into view out of the broad dale through which the Kerulen River seeks its way eastwards.

Kublai and Arik-Buka looked down towards the south. There lay the Gobi, that vast desert which hid beneath its surface salt and gold, and in the sands of which precious stones— jasper, onyx and cornelian—glistened. The princes knew all about the desert, for they had plied with questions every rider who had come from the south. They had been told that no trails grow old in the desert because of the sand which wanders under the wind; that the skeletons of camels stick out from the sand drifts which fill the valleys between the dunes, and that many stretches of the desert were called *Tshar tshi tray*—the yellow place of horror—by those who knew the Gobi.

It was said, moreover, that the Gobi was more than a month's journey across—if a man rode hard, and if his beast could survive the journey, and if he reached the water-holes in time. There before them lay that terrible desert, with its wild, deeply cleft ridges of rock, stretching away to the horizon. The eyes of the princes could not see to the end of it.

'There are said to be a lot of old wells in it,' said Arik-Buka, without looking at Kublai.

'They say camels from very far away travel across it,' added Kublai.

'It would be the first time we'd leave our horses at home,' said Arik-Buka hesitantly.

'Perhaps it could be crossed on horses too. No horses could be tougher and faster and could do on less food than Bosa and Fabo.'

'That would be much better. You should see how I could make Fabo do the ride!'

'And I Bosa.'

'To reach the Khan on camels . . .'

'That wouldn't do,' said Kublai firmly. 'And go into our first battle on strange horses? No!'

'We won't go without our horses!' said Arik-Buka, looking blissfully at Kublai.

'And neither of us without the other,' replied Kublai, answering Arik-Buka's look.

'It's a good day,' said Arik-Buka.

'And a good place, high up over everything, and so near the Gobi.'

'It will be our longest ride yet, Kublai.'

'A ride through the desert, into our first battle, Arik!'

'I'll go into no battle without you, Kublai!'

The sun was reflected on the desert, making it look as if it were on fire in many parts. 'It's a good place to make a promise in,' said Arik-Buka suddenly. 'Let us promise never to part, Kublai!'

'It's not necessary to promise that to each other.'

'But I want us to,' said Arik-Buka. 'I promise it to you, and I want you to promise it to me.'

'No one will ever be nearer to me than you are,' said Kublai passionately.

'If we were not brothers we would have to seal our pact with our blood.'

'I'm glad that you're my brother,' said Kublai. He started to look for something in his pocket with a somewhat embarrassed air. 'I'm hungry,' he remarked.

'I'm terribly hungry too,' said Arik-Buka. And he turned his gaze away from the desert and drew his hand over his smarting eyes. Together the princes devoured some dried meat which they took out of their bags, and with it they ate some wild leeks. Again and again their eyes turned southwards and tried to penetrate beyond the Gobi to the mountains behind which was the country they dreamed of as they lay in the yurt at night, and even by day as they rode over the Steppe.

Kublai nudged Arik-Buka and pointed to the east. The head of the procession, as yet too far distant for anything to be distinguishable, was now visible. The princes knew exactly what it was, however. It was a line of yurt-carts, with axle-beams as long as ships' masts, each cart drawn by a team of twenty-two yaks, two abreast. And behind these were camel-carts loaded with boxes of provisions, and treasure-chests, and little arks, in each of which sat an idol with its mouth smeared with fat.

It was Genghis Khan's *Ordo*, the women and children and aged people of the tribe of the Burtchigin Mongols, to which Kublai and Arik-Buka belonged. The *Ordo* was escorted by half a *tuman*—five thousand horsemen—all of whom were recovering from wounds. All the other men of the tribe fit to bear arms were far away from the *Ordo*, beyond the Gobi. The five thousand rode at the head and tail of the procession, but kept swarming out beyond it again and again. The man who was leading it had given Kublai and Arik-Buka a day's leave for the ride to the Mountain of Five Peaks. The two princes knew exactly where the procession was going to. They calculated the distance to the place where the 'town on wheels' would halt and the yurts would 'dismount'. Kublai and Arik-Buka were to be there by the time the sun touched the crest of the mountain-chain to the west. They glanced up at the sun, then began to climb down.

The tiger horses had recovered, and during their rest had devoured with bared teeth quantities of green 'hedgehogs'. Yet

expert though they were at saving their mouths, the foam which hung from them was flecked with blood.

When the princes had drunk their milk bags empty, loaded the saddles and loosed the tethers, the horses immediately began to prance eagerly. On the homeward ride the two boys had the sun at their backs. They were not dazzled, but it did not occur

to them to scan the foothills at each side of the valley ... The
two squads of horsemen who were riding along by these now
kept a little behind.

The nearer they came to the new camping place, the more
frequent the patches of green became, and the softer the grass.
Yet this place had been sought out by a man who was blind, and

he had not sent scouts out first. The man who commanded the half *tuman* of men and was responsible for Genghis Khan's *Ordo*, knew the Steppe thoroughly. From many hunts and expeditions of the past he knew every nook and cranny of it. What difference did it make that he had been blind for more than ten years now? The Steppe did not change—in a hundred years its face did not alter.

The princes knew that this blind old man had never lost 'sight' of them the whole day. They were certain that he already detected their coming. He had a more acute scent than a steppe fox.

It was still daylight when Kublai and Arik-Buka reached the *Ordo*. Meanwhile the five thousand men had done nearly everything that was necessary to make a town on wheels into an encampment on firm ground. The yurts were lifted from the wagons and, with their open doorways facing south, were pegged down well apart and so firmly that even fierce storms could not shake them. The wagons were left standing between the yurts. The horses, yaks and camels were already out on the pasture. The princes passed through the widely scattered herds before they caught sight of the tribal standard which fluttered at the entrance of the encampment.

Goats and sheep were being slaughtered in the lanes between the yurts. Smoke was rising from the hole in the middle of each yurt roof. In front of the yurt of Sjurkuk-Teni, their mother, a man was just in the act of slaughtering a goat—rapidly slitting open the skin under the ribs a hand's breadth wide, and striking through at the heart, all in one instant. The beast had not even time to utter a cry of pain. Kublai and Arik-Buka hurried past. They had no business in their mother's yurt, since the old man had taken over charge of them.

The sun was setting. The blind man was standing outside his yurt as if on the look-out. A gleam passed over his face as the princes dismounted from their horses. Two servants took the sweat-covered beasts away. The old man went on ahead into the yurt and signed to the boys to follow him.

As soon as the two princes had reached the grazing herds the twelve horsemen had turned aside into lower ground from which they had a good view into the encampment. From two sides they continued to watch the two light-coloured spots until they had disappeared between the yurts. Then they withdrew deeper into the hollow, and let their horses loose, after which they kindled a fire and ate their evening meal. Afterwards one of them sang some songs. They were tired, but they had carried out their orders well for that day: they had watched and not been seen.

Half an hour later they lay down to sleep, wrapped in skins. They did not post any sentries. As they dropped off to sleep their minds wandered to a blind old man.

CHAPTER TWO

The Burnt Kang

THE blind old man's name was Sorgan-Shira. He was an *Orluk*, which means a prince, and was one of the nine men whom Genghis Khan had raised to this highest of all ranks. To lead the *Ordo* was considered the greatest honour which could be attained; for one of the duties of the leader of the *Ordo* was to instruct the young chiefs in riding. No one was more expert at this than Sorgan-Shira, the great silent horseman. He had already instructed five grandsons of the Khan in horsemanship. Batu and Borke, Kajuk, Mangu and Hulagu had become expert riders under his direction. They galloped like the wind through the Kingdom of Chin with the Khan's warrior hordes, winning fame by their skill and caution, their courage and endurance. Now, of all the princes, only two, Kublai and Arik-Buka, still remained in the *Ordo*. The *Orluk* shared a yurt with them by night.

The three were now sitting at the little fire which was burning in the middle of the yurt, and the princes, hungry after their ride, were looking at the splendid metal dishes of steaming meat, and even more eagerly at the mares' milk in the china bowls which glowed in the firelight. Sorgan-Shira took his time. Obviously he did not consider a ride of seven hours and the climbing of the middle one of the five mountain peaks to be a special reason for being hungry and thirsty. He bent his head as if he were examining the food or the little table of coloured wood which stood in front of the pearl-embroidered cushions. Then he deftly dipped his fingers into a dish and lifted out a piece of meat dripping with fat. He stood up. Kublai and Arik-Buka stood up too. He walked over to a table which was decorated with many carvings. On this table, which stood in front of the red, silk-lined wall of the yurt, was a wooden figure with a protruding stomach and open mouth. The *Orluk* bowed before it. The two princes also bowed, and remained reverently bent forward while Sorgan-Shira smeared the thick wooden lips of the statue with the piece of meat. He muttered some words as he did so, then flung the piece of meat out of the door of the yurt. With this the ceremony ended: the lord of the yurt had made a sacrifice to the Lord of Heaven by offering the first bite to the house-god Natigay. According to the Mongols, Natigay kept the Eternal Blue Heaven informed regarding the piety of the occupants of the yurt.

Without speaking a word, but with increasing cheerfulness, the *Orluk* and the two boys now ate the remaining 'bites'. The food on the tables in front of Kublai and Arik-Buka disappeared much more rapidly than the *Orluk's* meal, and the servants whose duty was to refill the bowls were kept busy. The food and drink were served in strict rotation; Sorgan-Shira did not have to grope about. Between the meat courses the princes devoured several bowls of *ʒamba,* yellow millet cooked in salty Mongolian tea. But their favourite drink was *kumiss,* fermented mares' milk, which they drank from china bowls. The china was as thin as a dry tea-leaf, and made them feel as if they had nothing at all in their hands.

These fragile bowls, with flowers and birds painted on them, looked odd in the boys' rough hands with their strong nails. But the contrast between the splendid furnishings of the yurt and the plain attire of the blind prince was even more striking. The *Orluk* wore grey riding-breeches and a long jacket—a leather coat of mail—such as all the warrior horsemen of the Mongol armies wore. The leather was scratched and smeared with grease, and it stank. But Sorgan-Shira seemed to feel comfortable in the jacket, for he hardly ever took it off. On the other hand, he had only once thought it worth his while to feel hurriedly over the sumptuous furnishings of his yurt. He had never yet opened the chests. He seemed almost to dislike the magnificence. Perhaps he tolerated it only because the Khan had sent all those things to him.

Only one present from the country of china and silk really pleased him, namely, the Chinese rice beer. The Khan had sent good brewers to the *Ordo*; they enjoyed the special favour of the *Orluk*. In the past Sorgan-Shira had drunk only beer and brandy made from mares' milk, but ever since rice beer had passed his lips he seemed to have forgotten *kumiss* and *karakumiss*. After the third or fourth tankard of rice beer he would always say that the Chinese had invented this drink specially for him, and after the fifth tankard he would make the surprising declaration that it was only for him that rice was grown in the southern country.

Sorgan-Shira was now at the third tankard, and still he had not said one word about the climbing of the mountain. But at a sign from him the servants brought in a roasted rock-pheasant for each of the princes. And after that the tit-bit which was given only after unusual fatigues, the fatty tail of a steppe sheep, was placed before them. Only after the fourth tankard, when the speech in praise of the rice beer had been made, did the *Orluk* say suddenly: 'If I'm not mistaken, you can see right over to the Altai Mountains from up there.'

The princes were somewhat embarrassed. They had not looked over very carefully to the Altais, which lay in the west. They were only able to give a vague description. Their information about the view towards the north and east, about which Sorgan-Shira inquired, was also scanty. The *Orluk* knew enough now, and asked no more. Why does he not say a word about the south? thought the princes angrily. The silence was too long for them. But they did not venture to speak their thoughts. Through their slits of eyes they gauged Sorgan-Shira's face. It was a hiding-place with many nooks and crannies. Not a movement betrayed what was going on behind it. No one could perceive that love was hidden there, an uncannily watchful love which discerned exactly what was going on in the minds of the princes.

Sorgan-Shira had known long since that they were rebelling inwardly against him—because by his silence he stood between them and the South, the kingdom into which the wolves of the Steppe had broken, amongst them Batu and Borke, Kajuk, Mangu and Hulagu—grandsons of the Great Khan just as they,

Kublai and Arik-Buka, were. The *Orluk* detected the burning questions: Why may we only ride in three directions, when, after all, everything which matters to us is awaiting us in the fourth one? What right has this old man to keep us back in the *Ordo*, in a safe retreat?

Sorgan-Shira knew the questions perfectly, though they had never been uttered. But never before had he felt them so much an indictment as today. He was overcome with the temptation to answer them, but he shook it off.

Only when he had drunk a few more tankards did he let himself be induced 'to stroke the young wolves'. It seemed a suitable evening to fulfil a promise which he had made the princes a long time ago. Again and again they had begged him to tell them how he had become what each of them wanted to be, namely, one of Genghis Khan's men.

Kublai and Arik-Buka noticed a movement pass over the face of the *Orluk*. Sorgan-Shira took a drink, then leaned back as if he wanted to observe something from a greater distance. Then he suddenly asked: 'You know what a *kang* is?'

The princes knew quite well. A *kang* is a heavy yoke into which criminals are shut—or prisoners who have to be specially carefully guarded. The neck is pressed into the *kang*, the yoke lies heavily on the nape and stands out over the shoulders. The wrists are chained to the ends of it. No one who is put in a *kang* can escape far. Every Mongol knows all about it; therefore the princes did not regard Sorgan-Shira's question as a real question, and did not answer it. But they listened, because the *Orluk* began to speak of a fetter . . . and they felt themselves fettered whenever they thought of the South.

'You know it of course,' said Sorgan-Shira, 'but you do not know that he once had that heavy yoke on his neck.'

The princes, startled, turned towards the *Orluk*. He—why that could only be the Khan. 'The Khan in a *kang*?' asked Kublai incredulously.

'He was not yet Khan at that time,' continued Sorgan-Shira thoughtfully, as a deathly silence fell in the yurt. 'He still bore the name of Temuchin, and he was scarcely older than you are. But even at that time I was his man, though I only got to know

c

him later on.' It was again breathlessly quiet in the yurt. Suddenly Sorgan-Shira began to laugh uproariously.

'I'm laughing at myself,' he explained, 'at the steppe hare, Sorgan-Shira! For at that time, you two young wolves—at that time Sorgan-Shira was afraid. He was afraid of the young wolf Temuchin. He was also afraid of Targutai, the chief of the Taichute Mongols, to which tribe he belonged, though to tell the truth he was pretty well the most miserable of them. It was long ago! Now, at that time things were such that in spite of his youth Temuchin, as the early orphaned son of Yessugai, was head of an *Ordo*. And a miserable *Ordo* it was! A yurt in which his mother Hoelun and his brothers Bektar, Kassar and Belgutai dwelt! Eight horses and so few goats and sheep that they could hardly be called a herd. Yessugai, the father, had been lord of many yurts; but at his death everything went to ruin. Each of his followers had thought only of himself at the time and forgotten the oath with which he had bound himself to Yessugai and his clan. The Mongols in those days were not what they are today. Each one was for his own advantage. They did not want to have for chief a boy who would not be a man for several years. They regarded Temuchin as just an ordinary steppe wolf.

'But Targutai, the Taichute chief, thought otherwise. After Yessugai's death he had made himself leader of all the Mongol tribes and had claimed the pasture-land between the Onon and the Kerulen for his own tribe. No one disputed his claim, for Targutai had many warriors. Temuchin alone continued to graze his few horses, sheep and goats on the hereditary land of his tribe.

'Targutai called his warriors together and said: "I did not expect otherwise, for he is made of even harder wood than his father. And that is just why he must either be broken—or made so docile as to forget what he was and choose to become a Taichute."

'The horsemen understood very well what Targutai meant. When darkness fell they rode forth. But Temuchin slept with his ears awake, and so it was that before the Taichutes had surrounded their yurt Hoelun and the sons of Yessugai had escaped to the woods on the upper Onon. Hoelun, Bektar, Kassar and Belgutai were soon run to earth. Targutai asked them about

Temuchin. They did not answer. Targutai saw that they knew nothing, so he let them free. He only wanted Temuchin. He could not be far away. The region in which he must be hiding was surrounded by horsemen. At midday the following day they ran him to earth. His face was scratched, for they had dragged him out of a narrow hole in the ground. His reddish hair was clotted with clay, but his grey eyes had not lost their icy brightness.

' "You have the choice," said Targutai, and he ordered a Taichute horse and also a *kang* to be brought along. "Either you swear loyalty to me or go into the yoke!"

'The fearless grey eyes did not flinch. The lips had a mocking expression. Then Targutai had young Temuchin fastened into the *kang*.

'A feast was prepared in the Taichute *Ordo*, and there was great rejoicing in Targutai's yurt. In order to insult Temuchin the chief put a boy sentry to watch him. The sentry watched carefully for a few hours. Then he turned his ear more and more to the sounds of revelry which were wafted on the wind from Targutai's yurt. Temuchin crouched on the ground with all the appearance of exhaustion. The sentry turned his back on him for a moment and looked over towards the chief's yurt, where a cheerful fire was flickering. Suddenly the sentry felt himself enveloped in darkness. Temuchin had thrown himself on him and felled him to the ground with the *kang*.

'When the horsemen found the sentry unconscious and the prison yurt empty, they became sober in a flash. And so did Targutai when he heard of Temuchin's escape. He had horses saddled forthwith to ride out in pursuit. The camp was very close to the Onon. Temuchin could only be hiding in the reeds, for the steppe offered no cover. Or could he have crossed the river? But no one could cross the Onon with a *kang* fastened on him.

'A little moonlight made the search easier, but the horsemen were unable to find anything. They searched for three hours. Then Targutai called his Taichutes together and said: "We need not bother about him any more; the Onon has relieved us of the trouble. He tried to get across and now he's eating mud at the bottom of the river. Let us get back to the camp and go on drinking!"

'The horsemen were long since tired of the search, and they immediately turned back their horses.

'I alone remained by the river-bank,' said Sorgan-Shira, looking up. 'My horse stood still while I stared spellbound at a dark round spot among the reeds. And when the other horsemen were at a safe distance I said in a low voice: "I cannot do any more for you, you grey-eyed wolf!" Then I galloped after the others.

'But I was mistaken. Temuchin, who had crouched for hours with the water up to his mouth, was not to be shaken off. When I returned to my yurt the following night with a heavy head, the skins which lay in a corner began to move, and Temuchin appeared. I thought I was seeing a ghost. And then I began to get frightened. When the ghost began to speak, not at all in the manner of a ghost but with the voice of young Temuchin, my fear became so great that all the blood went from my face and all the spittle from my mouth. I could not utter a word. But Temuchin said with as much confidence as if he were suggesting a very advantageous barter: "If I'm found here, Targutai will roast you alive. And if they find out why you remained behind on the banks of the Onon after the others, I'm afraid he will have you tied to the tails of two horses. Therefore it would be better for you to feed your yurt fire with my *kang* and give me one of your bows instead of it, and perhaps an *arkan*. Then I'll get a horse for myself."

'Each one of these words struck me like an arrow. But it was strange: the longer I looked into the grey eyes, the more did my fear leave me. Something else rose up hotly within me. It was shame. The blood returned to my temples. The dryness left my mouth. I could have spoken again. I did not waste time with words, however, but silently opened the *kang*. I no longer had any fear, not even of the young, grey-eyed wolf in my yurt. I hid him, and only when no sound but the snoring of drunken men could be heard in the camp, I gave him a bow and arrow, a sword and my best *arkan*, and told him where the sentries were posted and where he could most quickly lasso a horse.

'I did all that because I saw that he was a hundred times stronger than Targutai. I did it because through him I had become a man instead of a coward. He who had been fettered with a *kang* had turned a frightened hare into a warrior who dared to do something which seemed like treason, but was actually a feat. The grey-eyed wolf had seized me with his teeth and taken me into his pack. You know that in time that pack became Genghis Khan's army, that army which no power on earth can stop. It began with me.'

The *Orluk* drank the tankard empty and stood up. He walked with steady steps to the door of the yurt towards the cool draught of air. Every night he walked through the camp before lying down to sleep.

Kublai and Arik-Buka went to their sleeping-places which lay side by side. When they had lain down they noticed how heavy their arms and legs felt. They lay awake for a long time, nevertheless.

Sorgan-Shira had not succeeded in his purpose. His story had only stirred up still more the longing in the hearts of the two princes. They wanted to go to the man who had made Sorgan-Shira what he now was ... The thoughts of the two princes returned again and again to the same point: That time when Sorgan-Shira had freed Temuchin from the *kang*, had he not also taken a yoke off his own neck and exchanged it for the freedom to serve the strongest man in the Steppe? Was not shaking off a fetter always a matter of having courage? Kublai and Arik-Buka tossed uneasily in their beds. Only when they heard Sorgan-Shira coming did they keep quiet and pretend they had fallen asleep long ago. They did not wish to betray in any way the fact that their first and last thoughts each day were of arrows speeding southwards.

CHAPTER THREE

Blunt Arrows

THE sun was just emerging over the edge of the Steppe when the twelve horsemen unwrapped themselves from their sleeping-skins. The distant stamping of hooves had awakened them. Down in the plain they saw a whole crowd of flitting clouds flying in all directions, suddenly wheeling about and sometimes re-coiling. It looked dangerous. The twelve horsemen nevertheless behaved as coolly as if the strange cloud game, which was accompanied by constant thunder, did not concern them in the least, and as if they had nothing to do but to wait and see if two small individual clouds would detach themselves from the dust storm raging around the *Ordo*.

The twelve horsemen waited in vain the whole day long.

The bigger clouds, too, were again and again swallowed up by green patches as the two little ones had been the day before. Then horses and horsemen emerged, every ten an *arban*, every hundred a *yagun*—and sometimes ten *yaguns* joined together, making a *guran*, and one *guran* attacked the other or detached itself to flee. It was Sorgan-Shira's school, in which many divisions of a thousand men each were manœuvring.

The riders guided their horses without reins, and only by the pressure of their legs and the shifting of their weight in the saddle. They used their hands to manipulate their bows and arrows, to pull in front of them the shields which hung on their backs, or in the case of close fighting, to grasp their clubs or daggers. They were allowed to wield their clubs only against the leather-covered shields, and the daggers with which they were thrusting

30

were wooden ones without points. When arrows whizzed towards the horsemen in an attack they ducked behind their shields, and the horses which were hit tried to make off—yet there were only blue marks and no wounds. The arrows were blunt.

The boys also rode in the *yaguns*. They had known how to ride from infancy. They had grown up with bows and arrows and clubs. It seldom happened that one of them failed to get his shield in front of him in time and let himself be marked by an arrow, or was thrown from the saddle through failing to intercept the blow of a club cleverly enough. After a hundred or two hundred clashes such a thing could not possibly happen again.

The sons of the Steppe sat on their horses as if they had grown up on them. Shooting and striking out seemed inherent to them. Only one thing had they to learn from the beginning: to flee. That there were occasions in battle when it required more courage to turn one's back on the enemy than to jump at his throat—this they could not believe. Therefore, an attack which turned into a retreat was the one practised most often. Sorgan-Shira called this the 'two-way switch of the banner'. In the first move the *yagun* rode up to within twenty lengths of a horse of the opposing ranks, dodged along in front of them, spraying them with showers of arrows, and fled in a headlong gallop. Then, just when the enemy felt certain of victory, they gathered their forces for the second move and, switching round, attacked him in the flank. Now the *arkans*, the leather lassoes, swished down and encircled the breasts of the enemy horsemen with unerring aim. The *arkan* throwers pulled back their horses, the lassoes were strained to breaking point, and the prisoners were dragged from their saddles. The horsemen, who had changed so suddenly from pursued to pursuers, galloped over their adversaries who were lying in the dust—and were later 'dispatched'—and attacked the rear of the enemy ranks, which had already been broken by the riderless horses. This 'two-way switch of the banner' could only succeed if horseman and horse made every movement with the utmost precision. There could be no hesitation, for in the terrifying seconds while the enemy was confused the decisive move had to be made instantly.

Besides the 'two-way switch of the banner' there were many other manœuvres by which the Mongol warriors were able to terrify and confuse their opponents. They always charged in such a way that it was impossible to know whether they were about to apply the 'simple tongs', the 'kettle', the 'two-way saw', or some other form of attack. This became clear only when they were so near that the arrows were already flying and one had to hide behind one's shield.

Kublai and Arik-Buka were assigned to a *yagun* which was distinguished from other *yaguns* only by the fact that it included two tiger horses. The princes had but one privilege—they were always allowed to ride in the very front line.

During the manœuvres Kublai and Arik-Buka were unable to indulge in their dreams. As long as the Steppe was vibrating with the hoof-beats of twenty thousand horses, they were in a constant fever, and so were the other horsemen. Only when the 'vanquished' enemy had mustered again and the 'fallen' had remounted their horses, did the princes come to themselves. How often more must they sham being victors? When would they at last be allowed to strike in such a way that their opponent would remain down for ever? When would the time of blunted arrows come to an end? They had already swept old warriors out of their saddles with a blow of their clubs—only seldom did their arrows, sped as they stood up in the stirrups, miss their mark. There was no exercise in which others surpassed them . . . A school in which there was nothing left to learn—was not that even worse than being in a *kang*?

In the afternoon they practised attacking wooden 'walls' as if they were fortresses. Siege engines, protected by movable covers, were pushed in front of the walls. The fire-snakes, guns which spat molten metal over the walls from long tubes, were great fun. The besieging warriors were equipped with rope ladders instead of with *arkans*. There were many surprises during these 'siege' operations. The attackers had always to be on the alert to catch those who were flung down.

The most exciting of all were the man-to-man encounters on the wall. Only five attackers and five defenders were allowed to take part at a time. They attacked each other with wooden daggers or went for each others' throats with naked hands. Referees announced the winners by shouts. Then the fight had to stop at once. In the beginning most of them found this cessation of hostilities in the midst of the most wonderful hand-to-hand fighting just as hard to understand as the enforced flight in the 'two-way switch of the banner' manoeuvre.

There was a man named Haltsundoriki in the *yagun* to which Kublai and Arik-Buka belonged. He had distinguished himself for extraordinary daring in several campaigns, but had been severely wounded in the South, and when lying on the ground had got a further blow on the head with a cudgel. Genghis Khan had honoured him with gifts and sent him home. Sorgan-Shira knew the man, who was a good silversmith, and he had not the heart to exclude him entirely from military service. But he was not allowed to take part in the man-to-man fighting on the walls, for during cavalry fighting he had often lost control of himself and forgotten that he was only practising and was not on the field of battle.

On that first afternoon on the new practice ground Halt-sundoriki was the cause of an incident. He was standing directly beside one of the rope ladders up which the five assailants, among them the two princes, had climbed on to the plank wall, which was twelve feet high and nine feet thick.

The attackers were in the act of overpowering the five defenders. The battle was being fought through with lightning speed. Kublai and three of his group 'dispatched' their opponents decisively after a few seconds, and the referee declared the attackers to be the victors.

Everyone found the decision right—everyone except Halt-sundoriki. He had eyes only for the man who was fighting hand-to-hand with Arik-Buka. This man had been in the South at the time that Haltsundoriki had been wounded, and it was he who, despite his own wounds, had snatched up the prostrate Halt-sundoriki and brought him to safety. Since then Haltsundoriki had regarded him as his *anda*, which means 'brother'. Now, there was no doubt that his *anda* had been getting the better of Arik-Buka. Haltsundoriki saw how, on hearing the referee's call, he immediately let Arik-Buka go. But the prince had hardly got to his feet again when he sprang at the throat of his retreating opponent. The *anda* hit out fiercely, heedless of the shouts of protest. Haltsundoriki could restrain himself no longer; within a few seconds he was up on the wall. He threw himself upon Arik-Buka, pulled him away from his *anda*, and doubtless would have flung him over his head down from the wall if Kublai had not come to his brother's rescue at the last moment. He gave Halt-sundoriki such a heavy blow on the head with his wooden dagger that the man tumbled over and fell from the wall, together with Arik-Buka, whom he would not let go.

Kublai, who tried to hold the two, was flung down with them. They were caught below by many hands. But while the princes quickly got to their feet again, Haltsundoriki remained lying unconscious.

A crowd surrounded Haltsundoriki, for all liked the wild warrior. Kublai, too, had always liked him specially, for though he could behave so savagely, he was a merry fellow and a comrade who was always ready to help. Kublai wore a broad silver band on his left arm which Haltsundoriki had made for him.

Haltsundoriki's *anda*, who had come down the rope ladder, went to look after the unconscious man. The two princes gazed in perplexity at the face from which all the blood had vanished. Then they glanced around at the bystanders. They saw no reproach in their faces, but rather, satisfaction at witnessing at last a fight in which one of the party was put out of action, at least for a time.

'Such things happen,' said the captain of the *yagun*. 'But it must be reported to the old man; that is the order.'

'It is our affair,' said Kublai.

Haltsundoriki was carefully carried away. Kublai and Arik-Buka walked back slowly and reluctantly to Sorgan-Shira's yurt.

'It was my fault,' said Arik-Buka.

'It was I who hit him on the head,' protested Kublai, 'and with the hilt of my sword too.'

'But I had driven him into a frenzy first.'

'Anyone can fail to hear the referees sometimes.'

'I heard them—but I was down at the moment, and that drove me wild.'

'You didn't throw him roughly.'

'But it was against the rules in any case.'

'Rules! Am I only to be allowed to hit this way or that way?'

'If we had to weigh every blow in the balance . . .'

'Well, it's orders.'

'How long is this to go on!'

As they neared the tent Kublai said: 'I will tell him how it happened—but I will also tell him that I'm sick of the wooden swords.'

'And I'll tell him I'm sick of the blunt arrows.'

'It's about time. After all, we're not just horse-herds; we're princes, and our place is where the other princes are.'

'That's what I think too,' said Arik-Buka. 'Here in the *Ordo* there's no longer anything new for us to learn.'

Soon afterwards they entered Sorgan-Shira's yurt. The *Orluk* listened quietly while Kublai and Arik-Buka described the incident on the wall. Each reported his own part, without sparing himself. The princes defended Haltsundoriki so fervently that Sorgan-Shira interrupted them.

'He always flared up very easily.'

The princes were going to continue defending him, but Sorgan-Shira signed to them to desist. Then he looked up.

'You have something else to say?'

'Yes,' said Arik-Buka.

And Kublai, intensely excited, began to tell in passionate words what was in the minds of both of them.

'How much longer are we to be kept from the South? We are tired of life in the camp!'

'Indeed?' said Sorgan-Shira, when Kublai had finished his complaints. 'And why are you tired of the *Ordo*?'

'Because there's nothing more for us to learn here,' said Arik-Buka.

And Kublai added: 'Because we, too, want to strike one day in such a way that the opponent does not stand up again.'

There was an ominous silence in the yurt after Kublai had said this. Then footsteps could be heard through the wall of the yurt, and these soon came nearer. The captain of the *yagun* appeared at the entrance and asked if he might enter.

'What is the matter?' asked Sorgan-Shira.

'Haltsundoriki is dead,' said the captain of the *yagun*.

The princes stared at him. The man shrugged his shoulders, embarrassed. Kublai opened his mouth, but there was no use in saying what was in his mind: that it simply couldn't be true . . . that bear of a man, Haltsundoriki, who had held Arik-Buka in the air only an hour before . . .

'He has been a broken man since he came back from the South,' Kublai heard the *Orluk* saying behind him. 'Any trifle could have finished him off. It was an accident. He had no business up on the wall.'

The captain of the *yagun* went off. Sorgan-Shira's face was impenetrable. In an unconcerned voice, as if nothing had happened, he said: 'Take your bows and come with me! We shall see if there's nothing more for you to learn.'

They went to the shooting-stands. There were many blind-alleys there, separated from each other by walls of trellis-work. At the end of the alleys were targets made of dressed skins held in large frames. The skins had the shape of horses seen from the front, or of running or crouching human beings. The skins were stretched as taut as kettle-drums on the wooden frames. When one of the blunt arrows hit one of them it made a sound like a drum being beaten.

Sorgan-Shira made the princes shoot from a great distance. After each shot there was the sound of a drum-beat. Then he led them up to a length of ten horses distant from the target.

'Blindfold yourselves,' he said. 'You are now going to learn to shoot by sound, as is necessary at night.'

Sorgan-Shira went to the top of the alley and stood behind the target. He gave a sharp command. Kublai shot. The arrow hit the trellis-work.

'Again!' cried the *Orluk*.

At each call Kublai shot his arrow, but always into the trellis-work. Then Arik-Buka tried. He did not succeed any better.

Now the *Orluk* ordered Kublai to stand behind the target and call out. He took Kublai's bow; Arik-Buka passed him one arrow after another.

Kublai gave a start at each shot. Not an arrow was sped which did not hit the transparent wall in front of his breast. They hit without ever a miss: Bang! Bang! Bang! . . . Kublai was pale when the blind old man called him out of his cover. In silence they left the alley in which Sorgan-Shira had given them such a peculiar lesson.

During the evening meal the *Orluk* had little to say. They retired to bed early. As usual, Arik-Buka went to sleep at once. Kublai found no rest. He saw Haltsundoriki's face in the darkness. The dull thud of blows never left his ears.

CHAPTER FOUR

In the Gorge with the Sheep

THE fire in the middle of the yurt had long since burnt out. After midnight a little moonlight came through the open door. Kublai could see his brother's face. Arik-Buka was sleeping the sleep of the horseman, which, like the sleep of the beast of prey, admits any sound which announces danger, but shuts out like a wall any sound which does not concern the sleeper. Kublai, too, usually slept in such a way as not to be easily wakened by anything, even noise, which did not closely concern him. But tonight . . . The dull thuds did not cease. The walls of the yurt oppressed him, and when he shut his eyes it was even worse, for then the walls seemed a glaring red, as if fire or blood was reflected on them.

Kublai groped his way carefully out of his sleeping-place. He wanted to go out and call his horse with a whistle, and then ride on and on, so that the beating of the horse's hooves would drown the dull thuds. When he was almost at the door of the yurt the *Orluk* moved. Half aloud he said: 'Come over here!'

Kublai went over to his sleeping-place.

'Sit down!' said Sorgan-Shira, turning over on his side. 'Sit nearer!'

Kublai sat so close that their faces were no more than an arm's length apart.

'Could we not talk outside?' asked Kublai.

'Why outside?'

'So that Arik doesn't hear us,' whispered Kublai.

'He's sleeping,' said Sorgan-Shira. 'What we have to say won't waken him . . . Otherwise he would be awake already.'

'I cannot sleep because the thuds won't stop.'

'It's good that the target stays in your mind.'

'It's not the target.'

'The thudding will remind you that there's still something for you to learn.'

'The thuds remind me of something else.'

'He had orders to keep away from the wall,' said Sorgan-Shira harshly.

'I should not have hit him from behind.'

'You had no time to lose.'

'And not on his head.'

'You hit exactly the right spot.'

'But he's dead.'

'His time had come.' The *Orluk* paused and then continued tensely: 'Any *shaman* who knows his business could have told you that. The time comes one day for every one of us.'

'But I killed him, and he was not an enemy.'

'You were only the tool. That death was intended for him.'

Kublai tried to grasp what Sorgan-Shira had said. But after a while the thumps began again.

'You still have a lot to learn,' said Sorgan-Shira.

'After a few practices I shall be able to hit the target blind-folded too.'

'I'm not thinking of the target now.'

Kublai looked at him puzzled.

'You still have to learn to do nothing that is unnecessary.'

'What unnecessary thing have I done?'

'You are dwelling on something which is past.'

'May I not mourn for Haltsundoriki?'

'No.'

Kublai was startled by the decisiveness of that 'no'. Only after a while did he venture to ask: 'But, after all, wasn't he one of us?'

'Others will take his place,' said Sorgan-Shira. 'We will not forget that Haltsundoriki was a good warrior. The whole tribe is proud of his deeds. But he must not hold us up now that he can no longer ride with us. What you have to learn in your situation you can learn from that wolf. No wolf ever lets himself

be held back by a dead wolf. And no wolf ever repents of anything. Whoever repents, thinks back. A horseman has to think
of what is nearest—what lies in front of his horse's hooves. How
can you be on the alert if something is hindering you? You will
have to learn to leave the dead behind you . . . to let none of
them cling to you.'

Kublai looked into Sorgan-Shira's face, in which all was im-
mobile except the lips, but when the words ceased Kublai saw
Haltsundoriki before him, just as he had seen him for the last
time. The thumping did not cease.

Then the *Orluk* began to speak in a whisper. 'You grieve me,
Kublai. I always thought you were like your brother—a wolf
of the Steppe. Arik will never be hindered by doubts. Up on the
wall he had occasion for such, when he sprang at the other's
throat. He does not brood. Listen to him—he's sleeping as
peacefully as ever.'

'It was not he who killed Haltsundoriki.'

The *Orluk* jumped up. The faces of the two were now but a
hand's breadth apart, and Kublai felt each word striking his face
when the *Orluk* said: 'I command you never again to think of
this.'

How can he ask that of me? thought Kublai. He felt for the
silver band on his wrist. Sorgan-Shira sank back on his bed. He
seemed to be listening to Arik-Buka's quiet breathing, which was
the only sound to be heard in the yurt. But Sorgan-Shira was
waiting for a word from Kublai.

'It is unfortunate that this is so difficult for you,' said the
Orluk. 'It is unfortunate that it is necessary to help you to overcome it. But there is nothing more necessary for a warrior than
that.'

The *Orluk* paused again; now he was really listening to Arik-
Buka's breathing. Then he said: 'Bend down to me, Kublai!
What you are about to hear now only two other persons besides
myself know: the Khan and his mother, Hoelun; for Kasser and
Belgutai, who also knew it, are no longer living. The Khan entrusted the secret to me when he laid upon me the task of training
his grandsons. "If any of them ever shows himself to be too soft,"
he said, "tell him what I did when I was still a boy—a deed which

D

did not prevent me from rising to be lord of all Mongolia." '
The *Orluk* whispered: 'The boy Temuchin killed his brother
Bektar. And he did it because he meant to do it.'

Kublai tried to jump up, and stared, horrified, at the old man,
but Sorgan-Shira caught him by the arm and held him tight. In
a passionate voice he continued: 'Temuchin had to look after the
Ordo. At the time when Targutai was not to know that he was
alive he had to stay in the mountains with his family. There was
not enough there to feed them all sufficiently—there were too many
mouths in the one yurt. Hoelun, Mother Cloud, dug with a juniper
stick for roots of *sudun* and *tchidchina*, and gathered rowan and
moilka berries, and fed the sons of Yessugai with garlic and onions.

'Yessugai had two sons by a concubine. These sons were
called Bektar and Belgutai. Hoelun treated them like her own
children Temuchin and Kassar. But the two pairs of brothers did
not get on well with each other, and as each pair was equally
strong, the quarrelling never ceased. Temuchin ordered Bektar
and Belgutai to go fishing; they went hunting. He gave the order
that all four of them should surround a badgers' burrow and dis-
lodge the badgers; Bektar and Belgutai went down to the Onon.
Whatever they killed they ate themselves and then came home
empty-handed. They refused to eat roots, and once they
slaughtered one of the sheep in secret. One day when Bektar
boasted that Belgutai and he could not complain of being hungry,
for each of them had a *yeluga* and a *sokosun* fish in his stomach,
Temuchin was more silent and grim than usual. And a few days
later he said to his brother Kassar: "It seems to me they do not
understand that I am in command here, and no one else."

' "They'll never understand that," replied Kassar.

' "Not as long as they feel they are strong enough to compete
with us," said Temuchin.

' "They are as strong as we are."

' "They are at present," said Temuchin, "but they won't be so
for long."

' "What have you in mind?" asked Kassar.

'Temuchin gave him a searching look. "Do you think that
I'm to be in command or not?"

' "You are to be in command," said Kassar. "You alone."

' "Then I order you to take your bow and come with me. Belgutai has gone fishing, Bektar is up in the gorge with the sheep. Perhaps he is going to kill one of them again. We will get before him. Bektar is the most refractory of the two. In our position it is necessary that we be united."

' "And Belgutai?"

' "He will join forces with us when he sees that he can do nothing against us alone," said Temuchin.

'Then they went up to the gorge.'

'Did they do it?' asked Kublai, shaken with horror.

'And they never regretted it,' answered the *Orluk*. 'From that hour onwards there was no more disunion in the *Ordo*, and no more hunger. After that Temuchin and Kassar and Belgutai did everything together. They had but one will.'

'And Hoelun?' groaned Kublai. And he felt as if Sorgan-Shira's breath would suffocate him.

'In order not to offend against custom, she sang the dirge,' said the *Orluk* harshly. 'She cried: "You beasts, who know not what you do! The one, Temuchin, born of me with a clot of blood in his hand! The other, Kassar, like a he-camel who bites his foal in the heel! You are like Kablan tigers which rush wildly towards the abyss; falcons which collide with their own shadows. . . . And yet, except for your shadows, you have no helpers; and no whips but the tails of your horses—— If one of you destroys the other how are you to avenge the outrage which Targutai has committed against us?" Thus did Hoelun lament. Then she spoke no more about it. The tears she shed did not blind her. She saw that it was for the best.'

'Did she not mourn for Bektar?'

'As a Mongol woman she knew that the clan matters more than the individual. Before Yessugai took her by force she had been the wife of another. She advised that other man to flee when he had to choose between her and certain death. She said to him: "Only if you save your life can you take another girl, and you may even give her the name of Hoelun. Go quickly!" Such was Hoelun. If she were here now she would say: "What is for the good of the tribe is right. What does it harm, is bad." You still have to learn not to overvalue human life.'

Kublai again gripped the silver armband. The tips of his fingers hurt, so tightly did he grip it. There was a pain in his heart as if a dagger was plunged in it. The *Orluk* grasped him by the shoulders. 'You came to your brother's aid—nothing more than that. Now go and sleep! Tomorrow you're to be on sentry duty!' The *Orluk* shook him gently. Then he pushed him away. Kublai swayed like a wounded man.

Arik-Buka did not wake up when his brother crept into the sleeping-place beside him. Kublai was dead tired, but he fell asleep only when dawn was already breaking. He was tortured by terrible dreams.

When he woke up his face was no longer the face of a boy.

CHAPTER FIVE

The Festival of the White Monkey

THE next day was just an ordinary day in the *Ordo* of Genghis Khan. The twelve horsemen in the valley at the edge of the plain watched the *yaguns* doing their riding exercises. For a whole week nothing unusual happened. In the morning there were riding exercises, in the afternoon siege operations. Kublai and Arik-Buka rode in their old troop of a hundred. The *Orluk* had transferred a man to this *yagun*, so that it numbered ninety-nine horsemen and the captain once more. Haltsundoriki's *anda* still belonged to it. But even he did not notice that Kublai's face had changed. The service was hard. One had to keep to the task in hand; there was no time for useless brooding.

Kublai applied himself more ardently than ever to all the exercises. He returned to the yurt in the evenings utterly exhausted, and fell asleep as soon as he lay down. But Sorgan-Shira often heard him groaning in his sleep.

During meals the *Orluk* was more talkative than he used to be, and one evening he said to the two princes: 'It just occurs to me that the Dsaimans who live in this neighbourhood, about a day's ride farther up the Kerulen River, celebrate their great festival about this time. If it is not yet past and if you would like to——'

'We would love to go,' said Arik-Buka at once.

'And what about you?' asked Sorgan-Shira, turning towards Kublai.

'Why not?' said Kublai.

He did not sound enthusiastic. But Sorgan-Shira at once sent someone to the *shaman's* yurt. The man came back with the news that the festival would begin in two days. The *Orluk* knew that already. Now he began to crack all kinds of jokes about the Dsaimans. He knew of no people who were more entertaining than these mountain folk, of whom every second one had the goitre.

'Merry people,' he said, 'very clever at making beautiful shoes and sable-fur hats, drums and all kinds of instruments. They're cowards in the face of an enemy, but very useful in the camp. But they're most useful when left in their mountain nests. They are extremely hospitable and withdraw to their neighbours' yurt in order to leave their own yurt entirely to the guest. When they are playing their drums, flutes and cymbals not a word can be heard within the radius of an arrow shot. I attended one of their smaller festivals, a long time ago. There was such an uproar that I feared it might split the sky. They laughed when I told them my fears, for that was just what they wanted to do—to loosen the blue clouds so that rain would come down at the right time. Funny fellows!'

Arik-Buka was all enthusiasm for the plan, and his ardour carried Kublai away.

'Very well then, you shall start as early as possible in the morning,' said Sorgan-Shira. 'The festival lasts three days; you can cut out the third day, because by then they will all be so drunk that there will be nothing but rowdiness. It will be more worth while for you to turn aside into the panther ground on your way home.'

The princes could hardly believe their ears. Into the panther ground . . . the paradise of wild animals!

'Perhaps you will meet *kulangs* there and be able to make them do a roundabout,' continued the *Orluk* cheerfully. 'You only need to harry them well.'

The princes knew that *kulangs* were steppe asses. But a *kulang* doing a roundabout?

'You shall see!' said Sorgan-Shira. 'How big an escort do you want with you?'

'An escort?' asked the princes, with one breath.

'Well, after all, you will be several days away,' said the *Orluk* slowly. 'But if you wish . . . nobody need be there to keep a watch on you. Now that all the Mongols have one lord over them the Steppe is a paradise; the steppe wolves no longer bite each other.'

Never before had the *Orluk* been so jovial; the princes heard him still laughing to himself after they had lain down to sleep.

When the sun rose the princes had already been a long time on the road. The steppe grass sparkled in the first light, and the fact that they were allowed to ride alone made the morning all the lovelier. 'Flowering pasture'—those were the words which the Mongols used to express the things which were specially dear to them—three-year-old horses, girls in bridal attire, and the battle-field after a victory. They rode over flowering pasture; Arik-Buka began to sing a song in his clear voice, and Kublai joined in. They frolicked, and out of sheer high spirits chose the most winding paths of the Kerulen country. The horses would have two full days' rest grazing on the pastures of the Dsaimans if the merry fellows did not drive them mad with the deafening noise which they called music. The princes enjoyed the sound of cymbals, shrill whistling and drums. They, too, liked noise. During all the ride they thought of the funny people who were so clever at making sable-fur hats and the like but were cowards in face of an enemy, and who were at best just harmless fellows ... And as on the journey to the Five Mountains, the princes never suspected that twelve well-armed horsemen were riding along, too, at the edge of the plateau. They had leaped into their saddles some time after the princes had set out, but they had almost imperceptibly drawn nearer, until now they were riding almost level with them. When the pasture-lands became narrower they held back a little, and in the side valley which led to the Dsaiman people's country the two troops joined together and sent two of their men to ride out in advance as scouts. The two scouts rode at a distance which made it unlikely that they would be noticed by anyone glancing back hurriedly.

It did not occur to the princes to look around. They had rested in the valley for a short time. Now they did not allow themselves any further rest. They were thinking of the festival. Towards evening they arrived at the principal camp of the

Dsaimans. The twelve horsemen sought cover in positions which would make it impossible for any rider to leave the mountain valley in the direction of the Kerulen River without being seen by them. Every two hours the two advance scouts were relieved.

The next day began with a thunderstorm—at least, the princes thought so when they suddenly woke up with aching heads. It was not easy for them to find their bearings straight away. The yurt in which they were sleeping was not lined with red silk, but with brightly coloured felt. By degrees they remembered that they were guests of the Dsaimans, who had received them with immense jubilation and made them drink huge quantities of honey-mead and *karakumiss*, with the result that hardly any of the delicious meal which followed had remained in their stomachs. It had all been very jolly, and in honour of the princes the Dsaimans had sung a long song about a strange victory of Genghis Khan. The princes had understood little of it, because everything —Dsaimans and yurts—was going round and round about them, and the drums were thundering. Even yet they were booming in their heads, and the thunderstorm outside the yurt was nothing but the beating of drums to announce to the princes that the festival procession was now ready and only waiting for the princes to appear.

When Kublai and Arik-Buka stepped out of the yurt, instead of the blue sky they saw an animal's skull, the height of a man, with gaping jaws, staring down at them. The jaws were red and set with white, dagger-like teeth, and the whole skull was white with the exception of a few red lines around the eyes and nose. In place of ears it had big tufts of feathers.

It was Tsagan-sara, the White Monkey. It was composed of a head and a tail, the tail being the length of five horses, and made of white felt. Tsagan-sara was a whole procession in itself, for twenty men were required to move it. They were all hidden down to their waists under the white felt. Only their legs were to be seen three feet above the ground, for all these monkey-bearers were on stilts. They must have practised walking on stilts for a long time, for they did it perfectly.

After the White Monkey had greeted the princes it was ridicu-

lously funny to see the men stepping back to make way, at a call from the *shaman*. The princes could not help laughing. But no one took that badly. Tsagan-sara was a spirit who liked laughing at everything, indeed he lived on laughter, as the *shaman* explained to them eagerly when the noise had abated somewhat. The *shaman* also introduced the other spirits who were taking part in the procession. Every one of them was in the form of a bird. The heads, with their projecting beaks, which clapped at every step, had been fitted up with great trouble. Less care had been given to the wings. They looked plucked to bits like old besoms, and were fastened to the arms of the carriers. Instead of feathers the spirit-birds were draped with coloured rags. The birds came along on even higher stilts than the White Monkey, but the monkey was the principal figure and was carried in the middle. Only one of the birds, who answered to the beautiful name of Garudi, had a special place. It opened the gay procession. Huge flags, made of strips of silk joined together, were carried after the bird Garudi, then came a few more birds, again some flags, followed by the White Monkey and finally a whole forest of flags, four birds bringing up the rear of the procession. It was a feast for the eyes. And the drums, horns made of shells, and pipes saw to it that the ears too had their feast. Drums and horns were all painted, and when the procession began to wend its way through the lanes of the encampment, between the yurts, the princes, who had arrived when it was dark, noticed for the first time how brightly coloured the yurts were, even outside. Patches in all colours were sewn on to them, representing birds, and animals, and camels. They were quite different from the yurts of the warrior horsemen, which inside were of princely splendour but outside were the colour of the Steppe.

As soon as the *shaman* at the head of the procession began to strike the rattle which he held between his hands, something happened which first made the two princes numb with astonishment, and then made them throw themselves on the ground. The thunderous noise of the drums burst forth again, and the Dsaimans, who had been waiting between the yurts, stormed shouting into the lanes, threw themselves on the ground and pressed their faces into the sand. The men on stilts stepped over them. They did it

very skilfully. Seldom was anyone trodden on. Occasional cries
of distress were drowned by the uproar. The procession passed
through the whole encampment over innumerable 'humps' of this
sort.

Kublai and Arik-Buka were lying in a line with the others.
They furtively turned over on their backs. When the White
Monkey passed over them Arik-Buka nudged Kublai and pointed
up to the loosely hanging slit belly. The princes shook with
laughter. Seen from underneath, the stilt walkers looked anything
but dignified.

The procession was a kind of hiding game; some had their
heads in the monkey's skin, others in the sand.

Sorgan-Shira would never do that with us, thought Arik-Buka.
He always said: 'Look carefully, then a thing is seen in its true
dimensions. Never shut your eyes to anything—that would be
the beginning of fear!'

The *shaman* is a sly fox, thought Arik-Buka; he knows
exactly why he makes the people 'eat sand' and why he makes
them lie with their faces on the ground. If they lay on their
backs as we are doing, and saw what we see, perhaps they would
get some doubts about the power of the White Monkey.

Kublai did not think nearly so much as Arik-Buka did while
he laughed. He laughed because to him what the Dsaimans were
doing was so funny that it made him forget everything else.
The sound of blows which he had been hearing again and again
for days had been drowned in the tumult of the drums. It's a
good thing that Sorgan-Shira sent us here, thought Kublai. And
so the first day with the Dsaimans turned out just as the *Orluk* had
promised himself it would for his two steppe wolves. Both boys
were merry, and Kublai had no time for brooding. He saw this
strange world with the same eyes with which Arik-Buka saw it,
and he was proud to be a warrior horseman.

CHAPTER SIX

The Way of the Clouds

THE ceremonies which were carried out the following day were even stranger than the procession on stilts. Again Kublai and Arik-Buka had trouble in waking up when they were called early in the morning. Their resolution to keep to *kumiss* and not to drink either mead or spirits had been shaken towards evening by all the merriment, and had not held for long. That was why their heads ached. But at least the mask of the White Monkey did not grin at them again as they stepped out of the yurt. A procession of magnificently dressed people was standing ready. Even the children had been dressed up. The girls had jewels hanging from the lobes of their ears, and the boys were wearing their *buchulechi*, pretty fur caps. The men and women wore hats of sable fur with deep turned-up brims; from the middle of the hats rose little silver filigree towers. Filigree ornaments hung over the temples and held the hair, into which coloured ribbons had been plaited, so that it stood out over the neck. The women's dresses were of silk and richly embroidered.

Today, instead of flags many of the men were carrying long poles from which cords were hanging. Sheeps' shoulder-blades, over which the *shaman* had prayed, were attached to the cords.

'The Eternal Blue Heaven hears the prayers when the wind makes the sheeps' shoulder-blades rattle one against the other,' the *shaman* explained solemnly to the princes when he had greeted them; and he told them that a wedding was being celebrated that day. When Kublai asked where were the bridal pair, the *shaman*

pointed up to the sky. Then he led the princes to the head of the
procession and showed them what had been erected there. It
was a yurt hardly as high as one's knee but more beautiful than
any the princes had ever seen before. Behind it were horses,
camels, a few yaks, goats and sheep, none of them bigger than a
hand, made of every possible material. Even more striking were
the tiny sable-fur hats and *buchulechi*, silk dresses and household
articles, pans and dishes and fire-implements, which hung on
coloured strings.

Toys for girls! thought the princes. What have these got to do
with a wedding?

At a sign from the *shaman*, children took up the yurt, animals
and household goods, and the procession started to move. For a
moment the princes feared they would lose their tiger horses,
for the procession approached the pasture where the horses were
grazing. But the herds of the Dsaimans were used to noise, and
as they did not get excited the tiger horses remained quiet too.

This time all the Dsaimans were allowed to join in. The procession proceeded to the hot springs which were an hour's
journey away, far down the valley. From a long way off the
princes could see the white vapour rising up in three columns.
The *shaman* led the procession towards these three columns, and
it made the round of the three hot springs three times. Then the
shaman stood in the space between the floating columns of steam
and called the parents and near relatives of the bridal pair inside
the circle which the Dsaimans had formed. Kublai and Arik-
Buka were surprised that dolls were not carried in now, but that
real Dsaiman people came forward. And now they also learned
the names of the bridegroom and the bride, and that they had
been betrothed as children but had died before the wedding, the
bridegroom at the age of eleven and the bride at seven. The
shaman announced that he was ready 'to walk the way of the
clouds' and to seek out the engaged couple, who were now of
marriageable age, and join them in marriage up there in Heaven.

At this declaration the parents of the couple gave eager signs
of consent. Then there was silence. Walking with ceremonial
dignity, the *shaman* went up to one of the hot springs, threw himself on the ground and propelled himself forward like a lizard

until his head was thrust into the steam. He began to murmur prayers. The drums, horns and pipes immediately chimed in. The men who were carrying prayer-poles shook them, making the sheep's shoulder-blades clap against each other. The Dsai-mans knew that many prayers were needed before the *shaman* would be able to 'walk the way of the clouds'. The beating of the drums and rattles became wilder and wilder. Success did not come at the first spring. The *shaman* got up; his face was shining. He walked unsteadily to the second spring. There he repeated the attempt to find the ascent into the column of steam. But he had to give up at the second attempt too. With eyes shut he walked up to the third spring, from which the largest column of steam was rising. A few steps led up to the spring. The *shaman* mounted the steps without hesitation, and while the noise rose to a crescendo he disappeared into the column of steam.

Later they all asserted that they had seen the *shaman* up at the top of the column of vapour, where it passed into the sky. And no one doubted that up there, in the Eternal Blue Heaven, he had joined the betrothed in marriage for ever.

When the *shaman* reappeared, 'his soul was flowing from all his pores'—in other words, he was dripping sweat. The parents of the bridal couple took this as a sure sign that he had successfully 'walked the way of the clouds'. The relatives of both parties surrounded him and made him tell them in detail how things were going with the newly married couple.

'Oh,' cried the *shaman*, 'they are well and happy!'

All the people clapped their hands. But suddenly the *shaman* looked serious and said: 'There's only one thing amiss with them—they do not know where they are to live and what they are to eat. Their supplies are used up.'

The relatives looked at each other dismayed.

'Do not worry,' continued the *shaman*. 'There is a way of bringing everything to them. Just as the soul can find the way of the clouds, so also material things can go the way of the smoke. So come now, let us make a fire!' The relatives set to work, and in a short time a fire was blazing up between the three columns. And the pretty little yurt, the yaks, camels, horses, sheep and goats, and all the household goods were surrendered to the flames and, transformed into smoke, rose up into the Eternal Blue Heaven. So the newly married pair did not have to go without hearth and home. The bridegroom's relatives and the bride's relatives embraced each other; their faces shone with happiness. Now they were related by marriage for ever.

Arik-Buka was immensely amused. The whole thing was a huge joke to him. He noticed with some surprise that Kublai was looking on like someone who was taking the matter seriously. On the way home they fell back a little behind the procession, and Arik-Buka asked his brother ironically: 'Perhaps you also saw him ascending into the Eternal Blue Heaven?'

'They all believe it,' said Kublai evasively.

'Yes, the Dsaimans do,' said Arik-Buka. 'Why, they even stick their heads in the sand when the *shaman* tells them to.'

'He didn't look like a swindler,' said Kublai. 'And the fact that he came out of the column of steam alive and didn't suffocate in it . . .'

'People like that can stand anything,' said Arik-Buka, contemptuously. 'They live by mystifying others.'

'If only it did exist——'

'What?'

'The way of the clouds.'

'I don't understand how you can worry yourself about such a thing,' said Arik-Buka crossly.

Kublai remained sunk in thought. Arik-Buka, remembering how intently Kublai had watched the *shaman* and how he had stared at the third pillar, eyed his brother uneasily. 'Why are you so concerned as to whether there is a way to the clouds or not?' he asked.

'Let it be!' said Kublai brusquely.

'I want to know,' said Arik-Buka. 'Up to now we have always told each other what we think.'

Kublai did not want to confess it.

'I will give you no peace until I know,' persisted Arik-Buka.

'Do you not think,' said Kublai hesitantly, 'that it would be a good thing if one could send a message?'

'What kind of message, and to whom?' asked Arik-Buka, bewildered.

'Well, to someone who is up there now,' said Kublai.

Arik-Buka suddenly realized that Kublai had been thinking all the time of Haltsundoriki, and he said angrily: 'Those *shaman* humbugs! It's time for us to be off to the panther ground. There's no swindle about hunting *kulangs*!' And he thought to himself: How much longer is a third party to be present when we two go riding together? I hope the snow panther will frighten away the ghost!

CHAPTER SEVEN

The Battle of the Green Reeds

ARIK-BUKA was firmly resolved to ride away the next morning even before sunrise. He was fond of Kublai, and it pained him to see how he was torturing himself. He was going to make sure that they would leave the place with clear heads.

On the second evening of the festival, when the Dsaimans were feeding the White Monkey with more and more fun, Kublai and Arik-Buka kept to *kumiss* and did not touch either mead or spirits. They wanted at last to hear, with ears in which everything was not topsy-turvy, the song which had first been sung the evening before in their honour.

The Dsaimans did not have to be asked twice. They were proud to have grandsons of the Great Khan as guests in their camp, and they did everything possible to amuse them. The leader of the singers placed his barrel-shaped drum, which was painted in brilliant colours, right in front of the princes. The rest of the Dsaimans squatted round in a great circle, close together, and waited, their heads stretched out eagerly, for their turn to join in the song. The leader sang for the most part on one note, but his voice would suddenly jump many notes higher or lower, or would break from a humming into a wild shout, or a tremulous bleat, according to what his song had to tell. His face reflected so much of what he was relating that even someone who did not understand the words could guess what they were about.

First of all he chanted in a quiet voice about Temuchin, who rallied the Mongol tribes around him.

'The wolf with the burning fur drew the other wolves about him—'

Before the chanter began the second stanza his narrow eyes roamed around and looked more slanted than ever. In an unnaturally high key he told of a man named John who believed himself to be a great priest and a mighty king and, above all, very clever, and who tried to rob the Mongols of their herds.

'And the head fox led his foxes,
His ten times ten thousand, a hundred times a thousand foxes
To tables—to tables laid for others . . .'

The Dsaimans now joined in with loud 'he-hes!' and the drum beat more boldly. The princes distinctly heard the drum-beats calling to battle, and they expected the wolves to fall on the foxes straight away and thoroughly rout them. But instead the drumming ceased. The voice of the chanter now sounded mysterious, but because of the murmuring going on among the Dsaimans the princes could not make out the words. Only now and then could the drum make itself heard. The chanter fell into a plaintive note. Kublai and Arik-Buka heard with increasing astonishment how the wolves suddenly had the idea of counting the foxes, and when the count showed a predominance of thirty to one, they became irresolute . . .

'When they smelled how many foxes there were . . .'

A Dsaiman song! thought Arik-Buka, in a fury. He was about to jump to his feet and knock over the drum when the chanter beat it sharply and began to sing in a voice which seemed to rise up from the ground on which he was standing:

'But Temuchin, the wolf with the burning fur,
got Heaven on to his side.
He broke two reeds, two green reeds.
He cut on one reed the sign of the wolves,
he cut on one reed the sign of the foxes,
he ordered the shamans to speak the magic words,
so that one reed would fight the other.
The shamans took the green reeds,
the blood of their souls dripped from their foreheads.
They called upon the Eternal Blue Heaven.

And He forced the reeds to come to life,
and the one to attack the other.
The reeds fought, and no one guided
the reeds but the Eternal Blue Heaven.
Green blood flowed from each reed.
The green reeds fought for long.
Then the reed with the sign of the wolves
jumped up and stood over the reed of the foxes,
and danced on it until the reed broke.
Temuchin, the burning wolf, saw it,
and every wolf began to burn
and they singed the foxes' fur.
Temuchin vanquished Prester John,
the foxes vanished, the wolves remained,
the burning wolf and the Eternal Heaven . . .'

As the Song of the Green Reeds came to an end, the 'blood of his soul' was also flowing from the singer's brow; but he went on beating the drum, and the Dsaimans began a wild dance of joy. And then they started drinking as if they were celebrating a great victory. They went on celebrating until late into the night.

Arik-Buka was reconciled. As he lay in the yurt with Kublai he was full of praise for the *shamans*, who had given the blood of their souls to move the green reeds to fight.

Kublai listened quietly to his ardent words. Then he said: 'So it seems these *shamans* can be of some use, after all.'

'Yes,' admitted Arik-Buka reluctantly, 'but only when they have to do what the Khan wishes.'

Then he turned over on his side. He felt annoyed because, contrary to his habit, he had allowed himself to be led into a loud outburst of talk, an outburst, moreover, in praise of the *shamans*. He was filled with the deepest suspicion of these people who needed the help of sheeps' shoulder-blades, and prayer-wheels, and columns of steam in their functions. The mere fact that they advised men to change their names often in order to escape harm from evil spirits prejudiced Arik-Buka against them. If the evil spirits were really so stupid as to be taken in by such a crude deception, why should they be feared at all? The *shamans* infected others with fear, and that was why one must be on one's guard against them. If they had preached courage once upon a time, that was due to Temuchin.

'Temuchin . . .' Arik-Buka fell asleep as his lips whispered that name.

Kublai did not remain awake long either. His thoughts were on the swaying columns as he fell asleep. That night he dreamed many strange dreams. Towards morning he dreamed that his tiger horse was carrying him away across the valley into mountains of cloud. The walls of cloud shone like bare white rocks fresh with rain. Haltsundoriki came out of a rift in the clouds riding a reddish horse. He beckoned from far off.

'How are you?' Kublai asked him.

'I'm well, I'm in good health,' replied Haltsundoriki.

'But have you enough to eat?' asked Kublai, pointing to the naked walls of cloud.

'More than enough,' said Haltsundoriki, laughing. 'Shall we catch a couple of wild sheep?'

Only then did Kublai notice that the walls of cloud were covered with wild sheep. They rode up the steep slope without difficulty, and Kublai watched Haltsundoriki seizing a ram by its crooked horns and throwing it over himself high up in the air. He caught it and let it go again with one hand. The ram did not run away; it remained standing between the two horses, and shook its head.

CHAPTER EIGHT

A Kulang *Roundabout*

KUBLAI had to laugh aloud. Arik-Buka woke up.

'What are you laughing at?' he asked.

'It's too funny,' said Kublai, still half asleep, 'the way it's shaking its head.'

'What's shaking its head?'

'The ram.'

'A ram? Where is it?'

Kublai opened his eyes, blinked towards the door of the yurt through which light was streaming, and said: 'I've had such a funny dream!'

Arik-Buka did not believe in dreams, but he was delighted that Kublai had started the day with a laugh.

'It's already daylight,' said Arik-Buka, 'and time for us to ride off. It's quite a good stretch to the panther ground, and there's something better to be found there than just rams.'

'Yes,' said Kublai, getting up. 'There are lynxes and bears.'

'And snow panthers,' said Arik-Buka. 'That's what the place has got its name from.'

'I hope there are.'

They both listened and heard snoring from all sides. The Dsaimans had not kept only to *kumiss*. Kublai searched in his jacket pocket, and taking out a pretty little box, opened it to show Arik-Buka the precious stones which it contained.

'The *Orluk* gave me these for those wild topers. I think we should just leave the box lying here in the yurt.'

'That's certainly the best thing to do,' said Arik-Buka. 'If we

waken them they'll only try to keep us. But we must show our
gratitude, at least for the song.'

'Yes,' said Kublai, 'for that too.'

He placed the box in the little hollow which his head had made
on the skins. Then they took their weapons and saddles, and
crept out of the camp. It was quite easy to reach the pastures
without being noticed. Though they peered around keenly, they
could not catch sight of a sentry anywhere. The Dsaimans had
posted no guards.

'They do not need any,' said Arik-Buka. 'Genghis Khan holds
his hands over them. Who would dare to break the peace of the
Steppe?'

'They probably trust that the White Monkey is watching over
them,' said Kublai, 'or one of the magic birds.'

Arik-Buka was pleased to note the mocking tone in his
brother's remark. That's the old Kublai again, he thought. No
more of this white-vapour business, and the way of the clouds;
and no more ghosts. He is firmly on the earth once more, observing sharply and thinking keenly, as a hunter should. That is
because we are on the way to the panther ground.

Bosa and Fabo, the tiger horses, came at their first whistle.
The mutual greetings were boisterous. The horses were quickly
saddled, and the princes were even more quickly on their
backs. They left the Dsaiman pastures behind them at an easy
trot.

They were riding on about the same level as the gorge in
which the twelve horsemen had taken cover and were lying
watching when Arik-Buka's horse, Fabo, stumbled on putting
down his right foreleg, and came down. Arik-Buka fell expertly
without letting himself get under the horse. Kublai was out of his
saddle in an instant, and together the princes tended the fallen
horse. Both breathed a sigh of relief when Fabo was again on his
feet and had quieted down.

'It could have turned out badly,' said Kublai.

'If only I had kept my eyes open!' lamented Arik-Buka. 'And
for some time past I had noticed that it was dangerous here and
that we should watch out.'

He pointed to the spot into which his horse's hoof had slipped. '*Tabargans*', he said, 'or perhaps whistling hares, have undermined the ground here.'

He examined the ground in all directions and discovered more holes.

'Pitfalls,' he said, 'and they couldn't be more treacherous. There are weapons against tigers and panthers, but against these underground vermin . . .'

Arik-Buka was greatly excited. Again and again he felt the horse's foreleg, and then he patted him gently on the neck when he had assured himself that he had suffered no harm. He called over Kublai's horse, Bosa, and held the heads of the two horses together.

'Listen, you two!' he said to them. 'One of you must never get into trouble alone; better both of you together! One without the other! That won't do with you any more than with us!'

'Come on! Enough of that!' said Kublai, trying to calm his brother. 'Look how attentively they listen to you with their long ears!' And his eyes rested on the shell of his horse's ears. They were a wonderful pure white.

'They can't be reminded too often,' said Arik-Buka. 'And now we'll be a little bit more careful.'

They rode on together in step as long as they saw there were holes in the ground. Their eyes searched the ground unceasingly for five paces ahead of the horses. Again and again they came upon suspicious-looking spots, and they even saw the mark of horses' hooves. But neither Kublai nor Arik-Buka ever thought of even glancing over to the gorge where the twelve horsemen had taken cover.

But it would have been quite useless in any case. There was not a sign of life there. The twelve horsemen had remained only one day hiding there. Then a thirteenth horseman had arrived bringing them the order to lie watching in another place. The twelve horsemen had ridden into the panther ground and formed themselves into four groups, each of three men, and manned the boundaries of the panther ground so as to form a trap, as it were, which stood open towards the Dsaiman pastures. By the time the princes emerged from the upper valley, happy to leave the undermined ground behind them, the panther ground had long been encircled.

As soon as Kublai and Arik-Buka reached the plain they broke into a gallop. Fabo flew along with just as little effort as Bosa. Arik-Buka clasped his arms around the horse's neck and pressed close to him. Then he held on to his mane with his left hand and let himself hang down over the horse until his right hand touched the ground. He scooped up a handful of sand, threw it behind him, then swung himself back into the saddle. Fabo continued to gallop on unperturbed. Arik-Buka was wild with joy because his horse had not been upset by the fall, but seemed, on the contrary, in the mood for difficult feats, and as usual he responded to the slightest hint from his master.

'He's quite his old self!' Arik-Buka called out to Kublai, when he was again seated in the saddle. Then he reigned Fabo up beside Bosa and joyfully slapped Kublai on the shoulder. And you too, he was about to say. But when he saw how Kublai's teeth glistened as he laughed and how his eyes radiated nothing but good humour, he refrained from questioning him. I can see he's all right, he thought, and slowed down. Without even a sign from Arik-Buka, Kublai, too, slowed down and fell into step with him. They wanted to save up the horses for the *kulang* hunting.

There were not many lizards to be seen when they reached the panther ground, and they noticed few trails that excited them. In fact, they saw nothing much but birds. Flocks of them whizzed out of the bushes, and now and then the boys saw buzzards circling above them. Many of them flew so low that an arrow could easily have hit them. No Mongol kills a bird, however. According to them birds belong more to heaven than to earth.

The deeper the princes penetrated into the panther ground, the more hilly did the country become. From a dome-shaped hill-top they saw a dark-green strip of ground through which stretched a sparkling ribbon. It was the River Tundarik, which flows into the Koko-Nor, a lake with a wide belt of reeds around it. There were reeds by the banks of the river too, but the water could be reached at some points.

'We must go over to the river,' said Arik-Buka, 'because the wild animals go there to drink. And there, if we're lucky . . .'

Kublai nodded eagerly. Yes, they would surely come upon a snow panther there—there was no better place in which to lie in wait.

Broad stretches of sand lay between luscious patches of green. Kublai and Arik-Buka saw a herd of antelope flitting across a light-coloured stretch of ground. Because of the great distance they could not make out whether they were Karasulta or Gurush antelope. But in any case they were not out for antelope; and no horse could overtake the Gurush antelope.

It was nearing midday. There was such a flood of light from the sky now that the landscape was bathed in it and appeared to be floating. The herd of antelope seemed to disappear into thin air. And suddenly the princes perceived a large lake right in front of them, a considerable distance above the horizon. They were quite certain that no lake could be there, because the Tundarik flowed to the left, and the Koko-Nor, which was the only lake for far and wide, was also a long way off to the left.

'This landscape seems to tell lies,' said Kublai.

'And the hunters who told us about the panther ground seem to have done so too . . . Or perhaps your horse has already stumbled over a procession of lizards?'

'And there's not the least trace of any animals worth bothering about. Nothing but feathered creatures!'

'The day didn't begin very well either.'

'Don't say that,' said Kublai; 'we had undeserved good luck with Fabo.'

Just at that moment Kublai noticed a distant cloud of dust which was quickly coming nearer.

'Look at that!' he cried, pointing to the right.

'Horsemen!' said Arik-Buka at once.

'A whole crowd of them.'

'And they're coming straight towards us.'

'I wonder if they've seen us?'

'Could they, with all that dust?'

'There was no dust until they started to gallop.'

The princes thought no more of what they had said about the

peace of the Steppe as they were leaving the Dsaimans; they pulled their quivers round in front of them with the arrows ready to seize, and took up their bows. They did not dream of fleeing.

The cloud grew bigger as it came nearer; the princes recognized the outlines of horses. The clatter of hooves became more and more distinct.

'Now, this is something unusual,' said Arik-Buka, without looking at Kublai.

'Something which neither of us expected.'

'That's always the most exciting.'

'Perhaps robbers,' said Kublai. His mouth was dry.

'They can't be anything else.'

But they were no robbers. This was seen when the cloud wheeled round and vanished at the edge of a grassy plateau. From the cloud of dust a galloping herd of animals, somewhat smaller than horses, detached itself. The princes distinguished dark-brown backs and white flanks.

'*Kulangs*,' cried Arik-Buka hoarsely. '*Yabonah!*'

At the fastest gallop of which tiger horses are capable the princes advanced nearer and nearer to the herd of steppe asses. The *kulang* stallion, which smelled danger and had directed the sudden wheel round, must have been a cunning fellow. That was apparent from the fact that he was leading a considerable herd. But his manner of retreating was a master stroke. He turned back forthwith to the strip of sand; the whirling cloud which rose from it hid the herd from the pursuers. The nearer the princes came, the more dust they had to swallow. The herd of *kulangs* galloped on between the dune-like hills; the wall of dust remained stationary in the hollow. But the pursuers were lucky. The light-coloured stretch came to an end; the strip of sand proved to be a blind-alley. The cloud of dust now remained behind the herd, and in a few minutes was behind the tiger horses too. The hooves no longer plunged into crunching sand; the sound of the hoof-beats became muffled. Now the princes could see the *kulangs* so near that they were able to count the mares and foals; there were about thirty mothers, with perhaps ten foals. The lead stallion was galloping far ahead, and somewhat to the side raced two strong animals which very soon proved to be stallions too.

For now the lead stallion suddenly wheeled round. The herd stopped short and remained at a standstill. The foals pressed into the centre, and the mares pushed together, flank to flank, around them, forming a wall, their heads over the foals' necks, their hind legs free to kick out. And around this fortification, which could strike out from all sides, the three stallions stormed ceaselessly in a circle. Any enemy who tried to get in to the foals would have been thrown down by the stallions, and the hooves of the mares would have finished him off. Neither a wolf nor a tiger could have got through the roundabout. The princes gazed fascinated at the strange spectacle. The tiger horses danced under them, for the ground was trembling from the hoof-beats of the *kulang* stallions. All three stallions were strong and beautiful, their necks arched powerfully above their broad, light-coloured breasts; the short manes stood upright, bristling threateningly. The stallions flung out their gleaming hooves, their brown heads plunging up and down. Foam showered from their white nostrils.

The lead stallion was more magnificent than either of the others.

That one and no other! thought Arik-Buka.

That one and no other! thought Kublai.

They both stood up in their stirrups and laid an arrow on the bow.

'The next time!' cried Arik-Buka, as the stallion passed by.

'Now!' cried Kublai when the stallion reappeared.

With Arik-Buka's arrow in his neck the stallion suddenly reared upright. Kublai's arrow glided right behind the ribs deep into the body. The animal collapsed. The stallion behind him broke out and wheeled round; the other stallion followed his lead, and the mares and foals raced after them. The princes were about to leap from their saddles and give a finishing stab to the fatally wounded stallion, but the tiger horses were carried off with the fleeing *kulangs*.

It was immediately noticeable that the stallion which was now leading had not yet had experience. He fled at random and failed to see a broad stretch of sand which lay to the left. He left it to his hooves to seek a way of escape, and soon he had to give up.

The second roundabout had not the frenzied tempo of the first one. Nevertheless, it made the earth tremble and the tiger horses dance. This time too the princes fired their arrows as they had planned to do, chiefly because they wanted to release the animals for a new flight. For the most exciting thing was the hurried breaking up and forming of the roundabout. At the third roundabout they did not shoot again. The *kulangs* were so exhausted that the mares were trembling, and the stallion, and two mares which were circling in place of the two stallions that had dropped out, often fell into a trot.

'Now the panther can get them,' said Arik-Buka.

And Kublai said: 'They are finished. Come back to the stallion!'

As far as they were concerned, there had been only one stallion. On the way to it they wanted to give the finishing thrust to the second stallion, but they wished to drink the blood only from the veins of the first one.

The second stallion had already bled to death. An arrow had torn the artery in the neck.

The lead stallion was still alive. He began to beat with his hooves when the princes tried to approach him. The great brown eyes rolled in their sockets. An arrow seemed to have struck the windpipe, for there was a rattling in his throat and blood was oozing from his nostrils.

'He still wants to fight,' said Arik-Buka admiringly. 'The other stallion was nothing compared with this one.' And he said: 'It's not possible to get near him with a dagger.'

But Kublai had already pulled out his *purbu*. His glance had strayed from the stallion's eyes to his ears. Inside they were of a wonderful pure whiteness, like Bosa's . . . and the white nostrils, too, reminded Kublai of his horse. Before Arik-Buka could hold him back he made a rush at the stallion and gave it a thrust in the heart.

Kublai got a few kicks: one just grazed his face.

'Are you crazy?' cried Arik-Buka, pulling him away.

The animal now lay motionless. Flanks and breast, fetlocks and nostrils, and all the white parts were sprinkled with blood. Only the snowy white auricles were untouched by it.

Kublai looked at his hands.

'We must go over to the river at once,' he said.

'Why?' asked Arik-Buka, surprised.

'To wash,' said Kublai.

'To wash?' asked Arik-Buka. 'Since when does a spot of blood worry you? It can be taken off this way too.'

He began to wipe his hands in tufts of grass. Kublai's strange behaviour occupied his mind so much that he forgot to drink from the *kulang* stallion's blood.

'We can ride over there if you like,' he agreed reluctantly. 'We've had the roundabout. Now the panther ground has nothing to give us but the panther.'

Again and again Arik-Buka observed his brother askance as they rode over to the river.

How will it all end with him, he thought, if he takes every trifle so much to heart! That matter of Haltsundoriki has already worried him far too long—and now even the death of a steppe ass worries him . . . I must keep an eye on him.

CHAPTER NINE

The Ambush

THE Tundarik was the western boundary of the panther ground. One of the four troops of horsemen had taken up its position on top of a low hill not three hundred paces from the part of the river-bank towards which the two princes were riding. The three horsemen had cut peep-holes in the thick saxaul shrubs and had a good view over the section in their charge. Their horses were grazing behind the hill; their forelegs were hobbled and they were tied to the bushes with *arkans* as well. The three horsemen had watched the first roundabout without stirring from where they were. Now, as the princes arrived at the river-bank, one of the three men went down to the horses, took off their spancels, rolled up the *arkans*, and fastened them to the saddles. He remained with the horses, holding them by the reins. The horses stood head to head, so that the horsemen could quickly mount at any moment and ride off. The two horsemen up on the hill-top watched through their peep-hole as the princes came along to the part of the river-bank which was free from reeds, dismounted, and let their horses free. The horses cautiously pawed along the edge of the river-bank and stretched out their necks to drink. The watchers saw how warily the tiger horses put down their hooves. This did not surprise them, for a Mongol horse comes only near enough to a river or lake to be able to dip its mouth in the surface of the water; Mongols themselves do just the same.

For this reason, what the two watchers saw now was almost incomprehensible to them. One of the princes bent down and, when he had drunk, began to wash his hands thoroughly. Then he stepped back and undressed. Now he plunged naked into the water—the horsemen saw it splashing up. They looked at each other dumbfounded. A Mongol bathing! For them that was an even more unusual spectacle than a *kulang* roundabout. But the activity by the river-bank became still more surprising. The boy in the water seemed to be challenging the one by the river-bank. The watchers saw water being splashed up on the bank. The tiger horses went off to look for grass at a safe distance; but the prince remained where he was. Loud shouts were heard. The two seemed to be quarrelling.

And then the most unbelievable thing happened. The second prince also stripped and threw himself into the water, as if he wanted to prove that he, too, feared nothing, not even water. True, he did not frolic about; he simply threw himself on the other one, gave him a few cuffs, and immediately climbed up on the bank again.

At that moment the tiger horses threw up their heads in the air and began to gallop away from the river. The prince who was on the bank stared after them, and the other jumped out of the river. The two of them stood there naked in the sun, trying to make out what could have frightened the horses. But they could not see what the watchers had glimpsed from their hill. A light shadow had risen up from the reeds and glided noiselessly through the high grass along by the river bank up to the place where the two princes were standing unarmed.

'A snow panther,' whispered one of the horsemen, horrified. 'We must get them away from him alive!'

And they ran up to their horses. A few seconds later the race with death, in the form of a silently gliding white beast, had begun.

The princes hurriedly grasped their *purbus* when they saw the horsemen galloping headlong towards them. The snow panther behind them stopped short as soon as he sighted the horsemen. The scent of two naked people no longer attracted him strongly enough. He fled in great bounds.

The horsemen stopped abruptly a few paces in front of the princes. They stuck their arrows into the quivers. The princes toyed awkwardly with their daggers.

'Those wouldn't have been of much use,' said one of the horsemen, just for the sake of saying something.

'In the devil's name, where have you come from?' asked Arik-Buka, angrily. He brandished the *purbu*, which glistened in his hand.

'It was lucky we were not very far away.'

The horsemen nearly burst out laughing. Two Mongol princes who had just been bathing, with *purbus* in their wet hands—that was an unusual sight. But they remembered that it could easily have turned out differently.

'What do you want of us?' asked Kublai indignantly.

'We want to escort you.'

'Indeed?' said Arik-Buka. 'We'll just see!'

Kublai now noticed another group of horsemen. 'What do they want?' he asked.

'To catch your horses. Or perhaps you do not want to dress again, or ride on?'

The princes looked at each other, and they decided it would be better to dress first, and then continue the conversation.

'What are you still waiting for?' asked Arik-Buka when he was dressed. 'We will protest to the *Orluk* about this!'

One of the horsemen, an old warrior, said: 'Do you think, then, that it was our own idea to come to the panther ground?'

Now everything had come out. 'He assured us there would be no watchers after us,' said Arik-Buka furiously. 'He seems to think we're children!'

'He knows the panther ground,' said the old warrior. 'And when I think what you would look like now if we had not arrived at the right moment . . .!'

The princes looked at him baffled.

'You have spoilt the day for us,' said Arik-Buka.

'And the *kulang* roundabout—that was nothing, I suppose?'

'That was only half of it,' said Kublai.

'What else did you want to see?'

'A snow panther.'

The horsemen burst out laughing.

'Did you not see him, then?'

'A snow panther?' asked the princes indignantly. 'Where was he?'

'Not fifty paces from here,' said the old warrior. 'He looked just as if he was going to bathe with you. He was on his way down to you.'

The second group came galloping along.

'Wasn't he a splendid fellow?' they cried. 'We never saw one like him before!'

Arik-Buka and Kublai asked for two horses so that they could join in catching Bosa and Fabo. They could not bear to listen any longer to the talk about the snow panther.

F

'He was a magnificent specimen, wasn't he?' the horsemen of the other two groups replied. They had already caught the tiger horses, whose flight had given them the alert.

'For heaven's sake shut up!' cried Kublai angrily. The thought of having missed the prince of the Steppe by a hair's breadth preyed on him so much that he even forgot the *kulang* stallion for a moment.

The horsemen invited the princes to take a meal with them and share their camp-fire for the night.

'With spies—never!' said Arik-Buka. 'Continue to keep at the distance which the *Orluk* ordered you to keep!'

'As you wish,' said the grey-haired elder of the twelve.

The princes rode on a considerable distance farther that day. When they found the spot where they intended to camp for the night they were still far from being calmed down. Their thoughts had struck out in different directions during the ride. Kublai's had returned to the *kulang* stallion. Now that the hunting fever, which had attacked him during the *kulang* hunt and again at the watering-place, had abated, the panther seemed to him less important than the animal for whose death-agony he shared the guilt. If only I had known before that he had the same kind of ears, brooded Kublai.

Arik-Buka was so much occupied with his own anger that he could have sworn that Kublai, too, was infuriated at having missed the panther. Arik-Buka was enraged with everyone— with Kublai because he had bathed, with himself because he had bathed with him instead of remaining in the saddle and searching the reeds thoroughly; with the horsemen because they . . . and with Sorgan-Shira because he . . . How much longer was he going to treat them as children? How much longer was he going to interfere whenever they had anything serious on? They had been in a tight corner, true enough—they had had nothing but their bare skins; but after all their hands had been free, and they had had daggers in them . . . And while the snow panther was busy with one of them, the other would have had plenty of time to stab him in the heart . . .

CHAPTER TEN

The Greatest Son of the Steppe

'PLENTY of time, eh?' said Sorgan-Shira, when Arik-Buka paused for a moment, hungry from his story-telling, to help himself to a large lump of meat. The *Orluk* had listened to the prince's account without once interrupting him. He had already been given an account of the matter by the leader of the twelve horsemen, but he behaved as if he were hearing something quite new from Arik-Buka, who spent more time talking than eating during the evening meal.

'You think, then, that he wouldn't have done for you, but you for him?'

'There's no doubt about it at all,' said Arik-Buka. 'Just a snow panther like that . . .!'

'Hm,' said Sorgan-Shira, chewing vigorously. 'I certainly know you have a tough hide—but perhaps you over-estimate its toughness a little. Personally I would have preferred to have had something on me, if possible something untearable, if a panther came to visit me unannounced.'

'We had our *purbus* at hand.'

'A panther is no spectre.'

'We have practised the death-stab often enough! Besides, we were two against one.'

Arik-Buka gave Kublai a look which seemed to say that he, too, should speak up. But Kublai sat sunk in his own thoughts.

'Kublai came off with hardly a scratch from his fight with the stallion, though the stallion fought splendidly.'

'Hearing you talk like that,' interrupted Sorgan-Shira, 'makes people like us seem hesitant, if not actually timid.'

The princes pricked up their ears. Up to the present it had not been possible to gather from the *Orluk's* words what he was getting at. Arik-Buka said: 'And even if we had come off badly . . .'

'Go on!' said the *Orluk*.

'It would not have been as bad as———'

'As what?' asked the *Orluk*.

Arik-Buka bit his under-lip. He looked at Kublai to let him know that he should say what had to be said now. But Kublai was not disposed to speak.

'Well,' continued Sorgan-Shira, 'it is not even necessary for you to tell me. True, I no longer have my eyes, but I have still got my ears, and the old fox Sorgan-Shira hears right well what you two are thinking—he has been hearing it for some time past.

'He stands in your way—isn't that what you're thinking? It is only because he is there that you do not get what you have set your hearts on. He spoils your most beautiful hunting adventure for you, and what's more, he deceives you . . . No escort—and then—there they are at the most inopportune moment to do you out of your panther! And all that is nothing compared with the one most important thing: he stands between you and the South —the Gobi and all that lies behind it. He stands between you and Chin, the land of wonders, and the great battles. Isn't that it?'

Arik-Buka furtively eyed his face. Kublai, too, looked up.

'Go on eating!' the *Orluk* encouraged them. 'Indeed, I can well understand that you cannot go on being satisfied with the Five Mountains, or with the White Monkey, or even with *kulang* roundabouts. You are safer in the saddle than most horsemen who accompany the Khan on his expeditions and conquer kingdom after kingdom for him. If it were just a matter of your capability, you would have been ready long ago to strike out.'

The princes bent forward, for the last sentence had been spoken gently, and the last words had been almost whispered. These words had a second meaning—they also meant to strike with the sword.

'And when may we—strike out?' asked Arik-Buka excitedly. 'When may we go to him at last?'

'When he gives the order; not a day sooner,' said Sorgan-Shira harshly.

After the silence which followed Sorgan-Shira's declaration and which affected Kublai too, the latter asked hesitantly: 'And what if he has forgotten us?'

'He has not forgotten you,' replied Sorgan-Shira promptly.

'Has he not thousands of people to think of?' said Arik-Buka doubtfully.

'He forgets no one. Not he! But he thinks it's enough to have nine of the eleven princes fighting the enemy. That is why he keeps you here.'

Sorgan-Shira took hold of his tankard of rice beer and pushed it towards the princes. 'Drink this!' he said. 'It's the only thing from the South which you may sample—for the present.'

He shut his eyes more tightly and continued in a harsh voice: 'Perhaps you think I don't see exactly what you look like now, and that I'll continue to put up with those bitter funereal faces! Drink!' he thundered. 'The South won't run away from you!'

'And if they are finished with the Kingdom of Chin before we——?' objected Arik-Buka.

'There will still be the Kingdom of Sung and the West! In any case Genghis Khan has use only for cheerful fellows. Do you think it's easy for me to sit about here in the *Ordo*? But it does not occur to me to brood over that. He has given me the command, therefore it is good as it is. Pass me the Chinese swill!'

Sorgan-Shira took a mighty draught. Then he said: 'He is always right, no matter what he asks of us . . . since he is the Genghis Khan, the lord over all of us. You shall now learn how he came to be this. You have a right to know how he came to be the greatest Son of the Steppe, because you are of his blood. When I come to the end of my story it will no longer be so hard for you to remain where he wishes you to be.'

The *Orluk* ordered more tankards of beer for himself and the princes. Then he sent his servants out of the yurt. 'Drink!' he cried once more, as he raised his tankard. He was still drinking long after the princes had laid down their tankards. They remembered how they had felt the first time they had heard the Dsaimans' song of the Battle of the Green Reeds. They wanted to listen with clear heads to the story of the greatest Son of the Steppe. Sorgan-Shira wiped the froth from his beard and began:

'A son of the Steppe does not like to think back. Only in one matter does he try to remember everything exactly, namely, what concerns his ancestry. You know that at an early age Temuchin lost his father Yessugai, who was lord over many yurts. I shall tell later on how that happened. Yessugai's father was Katul, an important prince, and it is told of Katul's father, Kabul, that he had once had the daring to pull the beard of the Chin Emperor at a banquet; a very brave act indeed, for, after all, the Chin Emperor ruled over many millions, and Kabul-Khan over only a few thousand people, the tribe of Burtchigin-Kiut or cat-eyed Kiuts. From time immemorial Yessugai's ancestors had been chiefs of this tribe, which had got its name from its first ruler, a prince from Tibet, the land of mystery. That prince was Burt-Tshino—Grey Wolf, and the mother of his sons was Maral-Goa, Radiant Doe.

'Just as twelve months make a year, so do twelve years make a year of years. And each of these twelve years has a constantly recurring name. In the *Morin* year, the year of the horse, Yessugai marched against the Tartars and beat them. While he was on his campaign, his favourite wife Hoelun bore her first son. Yessugai came home to his *Ordo* a victor, and he gave the newborn child the name of the Tartar chief whom he had overthrown —Temuchin. For the boy was destined to be a warrior who would overthrow many chiefs in the course of his career. Hoelun told Yessugai that while the boy was being born a lark had hung in the air over the yurt ceaselessly singing the same word: "Genghis—Genghis—O, great one! O, great one!" And a stone in the middle of the yurt had split asunder, and a tortoise had appeared out of it. Yessugai questioned the *shamans* who declared that the newborn child would one day shatter the strongest walls and shake to their foundations kingdoms as firm as granite. And his rule would endure. This news delighted Yessugai even more than his own victory, and he began to teach Temuchin at an early age to be a horseman and warrior, and he did not conceal from him what had happened at his birth.

'When Temuchin was nine years old he had a strange dream. In this dream he saw a valley in which neither grass nor shrubs grew green; only large quantities of dry branches were lying about, and all round towered walls black as the bottom of a valley. There were two people in the valley, a man and a woman, and they had nothing to eat. They tried to escape from the bare valley, but the walls stood round them, unscalable as prison walls, reaching up to the sky. The man sat and stared in front of him. But the woman carried dry twigs and branches to the wall against which the man was leaning, and piled them up. "What silly thing are you doing there?" asked the man. The woman continued undeterred. She was going to pile up a mountain over which they would be able to climb out of the terrible valley. Her patience made the man angry.'

'But what she was doing was good, wasn't it?' interrupted Kublai.

'Yes, it was good,' said Sorgan-Shira, 'but what the man did was still better. When the pile of wood was even higher than ten yurts piled one on top of another the man jumped up, picked up one of the black stones which were lying about and hit the wall angrily with it. Sparks flew out, setting fire to the dry twigs and branches. The fire which blazed up from the pile of wood was so powerful that the wall began to melt, for it was made of iron. It flowed away in a red-hot glow. When it hardened again there was a gate in the prison and there was an iron roadway leading into freedom for the two. They went out into the world and said: "It will belong to us and to our children."

'The boy Temuchin at once told his father of the dream. And Yessugai again questioned the *shamans*, who interpreted the dream as meaning that Temuchin would prepare an iron road out into the world for the Mongol people.

' "But there were two people in the rocky valley," objected Yessugai, "not only a man—what does that mean?"

' "You must look for a bride for Temuchin," said the *shamans*. Temuchin had no desire to have a bride. But when he heard where his father was going to seek one, he was pleased and immediately wanted one.'

'And where was his father going?' asked Arik-Buka.

'To a chief who ruled over the Tsungirats and who was nicknamed Dai, the Wise Man,' replied the *Orluk*.

'And where did the Tsungirats have their pasture-lands?'

'In the South,' replied Sorgan-Shira hesitantly.

'But that is beyond the Gobi?'

'And why not?' said Sorgan-Shira. 'They just rode through the desert.'

'They?' said Arik-Buka, excited. 'Was Temuchin allowed to go too?'

'Well, yes, Yessugai took him with him.'

'But he was only nine,' said Arik-Buka sharply, 'and we——'

Sorgan-Shira signed so angrily to Arik-Buka to be silent that he stopped short in the middle of a sentence.

'I am astonished,' said the *Orluk*, 'that you would dream of interrupting the story of Temuchin in order to talk about yourselves.'

The princes looked at each other abashed, and Sorgan-Shira continued: 'And so they rode through the Gobi; they always found wells in time, and when the pasture-lands began again they were in the country of the Tsungirats, and they met the Dai. He had a daughter who was almost as old as Temuchin, and whose name was Burtai.

'The Dai received Yessugai and his son well. The night before he had dreamt that a white falcon had come from the north and had caught in its strong talons a young raven with blue-black glistening feathers. The Dai remembered the falcon the instant he caught sight of the fair face, rust-red hair and sparkling grey eyes of Temuchin. And his daughter Burtai had shimmering blue-black hair.

'The Dai kept Temuchin in his *Ordo*. The boy remained in the South four years. There he saw Chinese merchants for the first time. They came on camels from the Kingdom beyond the Great Wall, and Temuchin learned that there were huge cities and palaces and immeasurable riches in the southern country . . . that the Wall had no end and was so thick that six horsemen could ride along the top of it side by side . . . that it passed through valleys and up mountain-sides, and that a million men had perished in the building of it.

'The boy Temuchin thought: So the Chinese fear the People of the Steppe as much as that? Why trade with people who are so much afraid? Why not simply ride in with many horsemen, break down the walls and take what is waiting ready in the palaces . . .? Day after day he dreamed of the rich, vast cities. The merchants had told him that several times every month feasts were celebrated and the palaces shook with the sounds of merriment. Temuchin pressed his ear to the ground and stared southwards. None of the merry noises could be heard. The huge cities were too far away. But Temuchin heard the beat of horses' hooves, and they sounded muffled. They came from the north, and the boy Temuchin, goaded on by a dark foreboding, felt urged to ride in the direction of the hoof-beats. And when he came upon horsemen he found they were cat-eyed Kiuts who had come to look for him. Tartars had violated the holy laws of hospitality. Yessugai was dead. Tartars had entertained him with poisoned meat.

'The boy Temuchin rode through the Gobi for the second time. He rode more quickly than he had done the first time. He was four years older; and he was urged on, moreover, by the thought that he was now lord of the *Ordo* and his father's avenger.

'What happened after that you already know: how the kindred of Hoelun, the mother of the tribe, turned against her and her children; how Targutai maliciously made Temuchin a prisoner; how Temuchin fled in the *kang* and how Sorgan-Shira fed the fire in his yurt with that *kang*.'

The *Orluk* paused and turned towards Kublai. Kublai thought: Now he'll remind me of Bektar and of how Temuchin climbed into the gorge with Kassar.

'It was a miserable *Ordo*,' continued Sorgan-Shira. 'Temuchin had only nine horses at his disposal. All splendour had disappeared when the father died. But worse was to come. One day Belgutai had ridden off to take some goats and sheep to another pasture, and Temuchin and Kassar were on Burkan-Kaldun, the inhospitable mountain, hunting *argali*—wild sheep.

Horsemen suddenly fell upon Temuchin's eight horses, which were out on the pastures, and made off with them. A Mongol without a horse is a beggar, and anyone who arrives at another yurt on foot is an object of mockery.

'Temuchin ran from gorge to gorge looking for Belgutai. As soon as he found him he took the horse from him and galloped after the thieves. But their horses were even faster than Temuchin's, and the eight stolen horses had been rested. After a whole day's ride Temuchin saw nothing of them but the tracks of their hooves. But these tracks told him enough—they led to Targutai's *Ordo*.

'By the evening Temuchin's horse was so exhausted that it could only stumble along. Temuchin was just looking out for a place to rest when he caught sight of horses in the distance, and immediately rode up to them. There was a young Mongol with them, and as soon as he saw Temuchin he came towards him. Temuchin was astonished at this. But his astonishment was boundless when the young fellow, who was scarcely older than himself, told him that his name was Boghurtchi and that he knew already that he was speaking to Temuchin.

' "How do you know that?"

' "You are looking for your horses, aren't you?"

' "You know that too? What else do you know?"

' "One thing more. That is, that you have shaken off the *kang*. The news has gone round because no one but you has ever succeeded in doing such a thing. There are many who admire you, Temuchin."

' "I? I have nothing but this horse, and it's breaking down."

' "You will soon have your eight horses again."

' "Are you a prophet?"

' "No, but I would very much like to ride with you. I have the greatest wish to do so."

' "You would like to be put in the *kang*, would you? Targutai is quick to do that."

' "Targutai is a boaster, and besides, my father too has an account to settle with him. The Taichutes are altogether a bragging lot, and it seems to me that they are apt to take others for fools. Otherwise they wouldn't have let out to me that it was

your horses they had when they passed through here an hour ago."

' "Only an hour ago?"

' "We could overtake them. But it would be better," said Boghurtchi, winking, "if we only set out at twilight. Then we shall arrive on the pastures at night when the Taichutes will be celebrating their great victory over you, if I'm not mistaken."

'Temuchin thought this a splendid suggestion. He was hungry; Boghurtchi gave him food, and he ate like a wolf. Afterwards he slept for an hour while Boghurtchi watched; then they took the best horses and rode off without driving them too hard. When they reached the Taichute pastures, Temuchin crept forward alone. By gently calling them he collected his horses together, and got away with them unnoticed. On the journey back Temuchin and Boghurtchi let the horses take their time. They were certain that the Taichutes would need at least a day to sleep off their drunkenness. They were mistaken. At dawn the horses were missed and nine Taichutes set out in pursuit with their *arkans*. It was towards midday when Temuchin caught sight of the pursuers behind them. One of them was far ahead of the others.

' "He is already loosening his *arkan*!" cried Boghurtchi. "We must ride faster."

' "No, slower!" cried Temuchin. "He is in a hurry to meet his death. Lay ready an arrow!"

'And they let the one pursuer come still closer. Only at the moment that he began to swing his *arkan* did they shoot. The other pursuers stopped beside the one who was hit.

' "Do you see," said Temuchin, "in this way we'll pick them off. If there are too many at once, then one after another. And not a breath too soon or too late. If you shoot at the right moment, your arrow will hit the mark."

' "I would like to be with you always!" said Boghurtchi. "I will ask my father about it."

' "You may certainly come with me," said Temuchin, "but don't forget—my hands are empty."

' "It's only with empty hands that a man can take a lot," said Boghurtchi.

'In this way Temuchin got his first follower. Boghurtchi saw to it that other young Mongols, who wanted to ride with a daring leader, got to hear of Temuchin's deeds. More and more horsemen and horses joined Temuchin's *Ordo*.

'When Temuchin was seventeen years of age he said: "It is now time for me to fetch Burtai; she has waited long enough."

'With a few horsemen this autocratic, penniless young man set off to cross the Gobi Desert for the third time, and the Dai received him as if he were a prince. He had heard of his misfortune, and also of how he had shaken it off. He gave Temuchin a present of a black sable fur cloak such as only rulers wear, and he gave him his daughter Burtai. Temuchin was destined to have neither for long.'

'Was it Targutai again?' asked Arik-Buka.

'There were other envious persons besides him in the neighbourhood of the Burkan-Kaldun,' said the *Orluk*, 'and now there was reason for envying Temuchin. He had a beautiful young wife and a wonderful sable cloak. And the Dai had given his son-in-law some camels loaded with valuable goods. The news of this had gone round. Temuchin was no longer a penniless fellow—and as yet he had not many warriors about him ... One night the earth trembled around Temuchin's *Ordo*, and this time so many horsemen were there that Temuchin ...'

The *Orluk* stopped speaking. The princes did not dare to ask questions.

'He fled,' said Sorgan-Shira at last. 'He wanted to save his life at any cost. He left Burtai to her fate and threw the black sable cloak around him. He became part of the night and hid under its dark shade. That is the truth. Even Temuchin was afraid once in his life. But that is only one half of the truth. The other half is that Temuchin cast off the most terrible *kang* in which a man can find himself—ignominy. When Temuchin crept back to his camp he found everything had been trampled and laid waste, carried off or burnt. A few of his scattered people came back—his brothers Kassar and Belgutai, also Boghurtchi and —Sorgan-Shira. Yes, I went straight up to Temuchin as if he had called me. He had given me courage the time he was in the *kang* and I had been afraid. Now I gave to him and to the few who remained to him what a warrior horseman needs more than anything else except courage—horses.

'The tracks of the robbers led towards the north. The Merkits, a powerful tribe, lived there.

'Temuchin decided to ride to the west, to the Keraits. The chief of that tribe had been Yessugai's *anda*; it was only from him that the son could hope for help.

'First he climbed the Burkan-Kaldun. On the summit he laid aside his sable cloak, knelt down, touched his forehead to the stony ground and laid his belt over his bare neck. And in this posture he begged *Menke Kuku Tengri*, the Eternal Blue Heaven, for forgiveness for his weakness, and gave thanks for his escape from danger. Then he rode off to the Keraits with his little band. He gave his sable cloak, the only thing he possessed, to his father's *anda*. The chief of the Keraits accepted the princely gift and in exchange gave what was expected of him—horsemen. He gave permission to anyone in his *Ordo* who wished to do so to join Temuchin. Ten months later Temuchin invaded the Merkits' *Ordo* at the head of Kerait horsemen, who had been carefully trained for the attack, and put the robbers to flight.

'He found Burtai in the chief's yurt. She held a son only a few days old in her arms. Temuchin called this son Juchi, which means "guest". But now he had Burtai again, and his victory enticed young warriors to his camp. And those who came were the best, for Temuchin did not recruit them with presents. The splendour of his deeds alone attracted them. He demanded more from his followers than other chiefs did. His penetrating eyes very soon saw what was in each man, and he treated each one according to his worth. Soon it was considered an honour to belong to Temuchin's *Ordo*. After a short time he raised the most efficient to the position of leaders. He made Belgutai and Kassar, Boghurtchi and Muchli, Chelme, Altan, Kuchar, Daratai and myself commanders.'

The *Orluk* took a draught from his tankard and laughed. 'There was no lying about and no boredom in Temuchin's *Ordo*. The young chief divided the horsemen into *yaguns*; each ten hundred formed a *guran*. At that time Temuchin invented the sports which you two often exercise yourselves in. The steppe around Temuchin's *Ordo* was seldom quiet. Day after day it was trampled by thousands of hooves—a better recruiting ground for young Mongols could hardly be imagined. They came riding in from every side.

'When Temuchin had thirteen *guran*, thirteen thousand horsemen, he thought it was time to pay Targutai a visit. He wanted to show gratitude for the *kang*. Gratitude is one of Temuchin's strong points. With unfailing certainty he gives thanks for everything done for him, and does not remain in anyone's debt either for good or evil deeds. No one can accuse him of being slow to repay what he owes.

'Temuchin thoroughly beat Targutai, who had assumed the airs of lord of the Steppe. After the battle the Taichutes had no leaders left. They had been treated by Temuchin as rebels.

'During the battle Temuchin had been hit in the neck by an arrow. When the victors were on their way home a Taichute came riding along and asked to be brought before Temuchin.

' "It was I who fired the arrow," he said. "You can now take my eyes and my hands. Then you will be without them too. If, on the other hand, you allow me to keep my eyes and my hands, my eyes will slip into the arrows which fly for you, and my hands will hew a way for you through the brushwood of your enemies."

' "What is your name?" Temuchin asked the young Taichute.

' "Chirgatai."

' "In future you shall be called Chepe—Arrow. And you shall fly for me."

'Temuchin made Chepe leader of nine horsemen. At the end of six months he was leader of a hundred, and today he is one of the nine *Orluks*, and there is only one other man who can manage an army of horsemen better than he—the Khan himself.'

'A Taichute like you——' said Arik-Buka thoughtfully. 'The Taichutes cannot have been bad people.'

'Temuchin never asked where a man came from,' said the *Orluk*. 'He made Mongols of Taichutes just as he made Mongols of Kiuts. He eliminated the differences. He knew men only as being either for or against him. Those who rode with him were good horsemen, and beneath Temuchin's shadow Chepe became the greatest of all horsemen—Genghis Khan's arrow.'

I shall ride with him one day, thought Arik-Buka.

'After the victory over Targutai,' continued the *Orluk*, 'the most famous of all *shamans* came to Temuchin. His name was Goktchu and, it was said, he could ride into the Eternal Blue Heaven at any time he liked on his grey horse. Temuchin received him kindly, and at the victory feast Goktchu, sitting at the fire of camel dung, prophesied that Temuchin was destined to be lord over all the peoples of the Steppe. Now, what he said we "old ones" already knew without having first had to pay a visit to the Eternal Blue Heaven on our horses. But the prophecy made an impression on the "new ones". And the news spread so far that even the Chin Emperor Tshang-tschu heard it. He sent a messenger to Temuchin inquiring whether he would be willing to take part in a punitive expedition against the robber Tartars. Temuchin agreed at once. Now he would be able to take revenge on those who had entertained his father with poisoned meat . . . and for the first time he would get to know the warriors of Chin, and not only the Chinamen who came with silk and porcelain.

'They fought bravely, those Chinese warriors, but it was Temuchin's horsemen who made the victory decisive. The Chin Emperor got word of this, and he made Temuchin his general and gave him the title of *Chao-kuri*—Subduer of Rebels. Temuchin brought home great treasures, for the Tartars had immense hoards of plunder. The most beautiful of these treasures was a silver cradle with a coverlet embroidered in gold. You, my two wolves, have lain in it, for Temuchin gave it to your mother when his youngest son Tuli made her his wife.'

The princes knew the silver cradle in their mother's yurt, but up to now they had regarded it only as lumber, as they regarded everything which was not of definite use to a horseman.

'*Chao-kuri*—a nice title!' said Arik-Buka.

'Yes, indeed,' agreed Sorgan-Shira, laughing. 'When Temuchin was merry with drink he always used to boast about it. And his faithful followers always laughed at the joke. For the title showed how unsuspecting was the Emperor of the South. But his neighbours in the north formed a more correct estimate of the descendant of Grey Wolf and Radiant Doe. They observed with growing anxiety that the yurts of Temuchin's *Ordo* were becoming richer and richer and that the *gurans* were becoming *tumans*, divisions of ten thousand men. There were ambitious sons of chiefs among the other tribes of the Steppe, who observed with envy how Temuchin's power was increasing. Chamuga and Tuchta-Beg rode eagerly from tribe to tribe. "He will crush us all under his foot one day; he who was once stuck in a *kang* like a common thief now wants to make himself a khan! A hireling of the Chinese, that's what he is! *Chao-kuri, Chao-kuri* . . ."

'The year in which the envious were murmuring in this way around their *argal* fires was the *Kaka* year, the year of the hen. And the conspirators assembled at the River Argun and slaughtered a white stallion, a white steer, a white ram and a white dog, and felled nine trees. And they pushed them all into the river and spoke these words: "Thus may it happen to us if we do not ride united to battle against the upstart Temuchin!"

'They were quite sure of themselves. But Temuchin's ears also heard the oath, and they had earlier heard the plotting too, for Temuchin had spies everywhere. And when the enemies invaded Temuchin's territory they rode into a trap and were killed. Temuchin made an order prohibiting anyone from plundering before the end of the battle. When the enemy fled Altan, Kuchar and Daratai did not pursue them but made for the booty which lay on the battlefield ... Now, in the year of the hen they thought they might do this in safety. But Temuchin showed them that he was a true khan and not only a *Chao-kuri*. He hunted away the eager plunderers as if they were a flock of hens, and divided the booty among those who had remained in their saddles as long as an enemy still had a horse under him.

'The jealous tribesmen who had fled did not know where to turn. There was only one chief in the Steppe with whom they could find refuge, for he had perhaps even more power than Temuchin. That was the khan of the Kerait tribe. But had he not helped Temuchin when the latter was a penniless fellow who had shown himself a coward, deserting his wife in the time of danger? The khan of the Keraits would certainly not be easy to win over.

'But he had a son Sengun whom Chamuga and Tuchta-Beg knew to be jealous of Temuchin. So Chamuga and Tuchta-Beg went off to Sengun and swore to make him khan over all the tribes of the Steppe if he would lead them against Temuchin. Temuchin heard of this plotting, and tried by a clever stroke to thwart their designs. He sent messengers to the khan of the Keraits asking for the hand of his daughter for his eldest son, Juchi.

' "There, you see," said Sengun to his father, "he has an eye on your heritage. He wants to have it without striking a blow."

'The khan of the Keraits hesitated for a moment. Then he said: "You are right. Temuchin has lost all moderation. He once came to me as a beggar. I think it is best if we invite him here and entertain him in such a way that after the meal he will never need another one. Why have a war first? That wolf with the burning fur drags too many Keraits from their horses. Enough horsemen have bitten the grass of the steppe on his account."

'But it came to a fight all the same. For Temuchin found it strange that all his enemies as well as himself were to take part in the betrothal celebrations. So he preferred to await the father and brother of the bride and all the guests in his own *Ordo*. And they came. They came quicker than Temuchin had expected, and he

G

saved himself only by a ruse. He behaved as if he had not noticed how near the enemy were already. When night fell the camp fires were lighted as usual in Temuchin's *Ordo*. Sengun waited until midnight, then he broke into the *Ordo* with the Keraits. He met with no resistance whatever. Temuchin had departed with his own people under cover of darkness and had left only the fires behind. The following morning he went into battle with his well-prepared *tumans*. His four sons, Juchi, Jagatai, Ogotai and Tuli your father, who was about your age then, fought for the first time in that battle. It was the most frightful battle that had ever been fought in the Steppe. Temuchin lost more than half his warriors. He had to abandon all the pasture-lands and was driven right up to the Manchurian frontier by Sengun. Only in the marshes around Lake Baldchun did the tracks of his horses disappear. During this flight more and more of his followers fell away. Temuchin's hair turned white. And he said to the faithful followers who remained with him: "The burning wolf has turned into a snow panther—wait until the winter comes!"

'When it became impossible to hold out any longer in the marshes Temuchin sent his brother Kassar to Sengun's camp. Kassar, half starved and looking like a ghost, arrived there with a few companions. They begged for a bit of meat and to be allowed to warm their frozen fingers at the fire. They were the only ones left of the Kiut tribe, they said. All the others, including Temuchin, had been swallowed up in the marshes.

'Sengun put the brother of his redoubtable enemy in the stocks and ordered a feast to be prepared which was to last for thirty-six days. It lasted only eight days, for on the night of the ninth day the 'snow panther' broke into Sengun's camp and wrought such havoc that the power of the Keraits was broken for ever and Temuchin straight away became the strongest man in the Steppe.

'He raised to the rank of *ter-khan* all those who had drunk the waters of the marshes with him. They had the right to enter his yurt freely at any time and to commit without incurring punishment nine crimes for which others would have had to pay the death penalty.

'The winter had begun. Temuchin reminded his trusted

friends that the winter was the best time for snow panthers. Now Temuchin himself or his messengers approached all the tribes of the Steppe who up to now had kept at a distance from Temuchin's *Ordo* or had even shown enmity towards him. They were well received everywhere. News of Temuchin's victory over the Keraits had gone out in advance. The chiefs came to meet them with presents. It was not necessary for the snow panther to colour the snow with blood. The sons of the Steppe had recognized who was the greatest one in their midst.

'Temuchin summoned the chiefs of all the tribes to his *Ordo*. And he said to them: "In future no son of the Steppe shall bite another. Whoever offends against this command shall meet with my anger. And it shall no longer be the anger of Temuchin. From now on I am Genghis Khan—Lord of all. I, who even yesterday was nobody, shall raise you Mongols above all peoples. And the Steppe, my mother, I shall make the centre of the world."

'It was in the year of *Bars*, the year of the panther, that the son of Yessugai made himself lord of all. In the following years one *tuman* after another was formed and schooled by the *Orluks*. Genghis Khan sent spies into all the neighbouring countries. He made high-roads, and at the *urtons* or rest houses horses stood ready with legs and necks bandaged to enable them to stand the frantic rides. Genghis Khan was informed of everything that happened in the surrounding countries, and he decided to make the Kingdom of the South the first country to be subjected to the Steppe.

'Genghis Khan wanted to throw his whole strength undivided into the scales. He left only half a *tuman* behind in the Steppe with his *Ordo*. More than that is not necessary, thought Genghis Khan. There is no one who could be a danger behind my back; no one who is mighty except myself. Or is there, perchance, someone who has power besides myself?

'There was, and that was Goktchu, the confidant of heaven. Had he not power over hearts and souls? Had not this pious man tried to sow discord even between Genghis Khan and his brother Kassar, and had he not declared before everyone that he stood higher than the sons of the Khan? He was ruler of souls, whilst Genghis Khan was ruler of bodies . . .

'Genghis Khan consulted his *Orluks*.

' "He'll declare next that the soul is more important than the body," said Boghurtchi.

' "He has done so already," said Genghis Khan angrily.

'Then Chepe, speaking for all the *Orluks*, said: "If he has done that it is better that he should ride his grey horse into the Eternal Blue Heaven and never come back."

' "And who will speak, then, with the Eternal Blue Heaven when that is necessary?" asked the Khan.

'Chepe said: "You spoke to him when you were held in the *kang*, and he heard you. You spoke to him on the summit of the Burkan-Kaldun, when you laid the belt upon your neck, and he heard you. You spoke to him when we were in the marshes, and had become like ghosts, and he heard you. *You* are the soul of the Mongols. Shall there be one who is lord over the soul of the Mongols?"

'Genghis Khan saw that there was none among his *Orluks* who thought otherwise than he did himself. Then he sent for Goktchu. The confidant of heaven entered Genghis Khan's yurt without misgiving. He was accustomed to going in and out there. But when he saw the faces of the *Orluks* he knew that there was some great misfortune in store for him.

' "You have observed my *Orluks* well," began Genghis Khan.

' "Yes, they look different from usual," agreed Goktchu.

' "No wonder," said Genghis Khan, "for they have hidden their souls."

' "I do not understand you," said Goktchu. "From whom should they hide their souls?"

' "From you, O confidant of heaven! They are afraid that you could take it into your head to order their souls about."

'Goktchu cast down his eyes, abashed.

' "You alone are the confidant of heaven, is that not so?"

' "Yes, O Khan," said Goktchu.

' "But here on earth it is I alone who have command, is that not so?"

' "It is so," said Goktchu.

' "Then I order you to ride into the Eternal Blue Heaven

immediately, and not to return before you receive a further order from me."

'Goktchu turned pale.

' "My place is near you," he said. "The Eternal Blue Heaven has placed me by your side."

' "Do you not believe that he hears you better when you are somewhat nearer to him, and a little farther away from the Steppe? In the Steppe there is no longer a place for one who sows discord."

'Goktchu fell upon his knees.

' "Help him into the saddle," cried Genghis Khan.

'And as usual when Genghis Khan commanded, the *Orluks* acted instantly. They told their horsemen that henceforth Goktchu would look down upon them from the Eternal Blue Heaven, and that in the Steppe only one was to rule—Genghis Khan.

'And Genghis Khan ordered the horsemen to conquer the earth and to begin with the South. He placed himself at their head and led them through the Gobi Desert into the "kingdom of the nine hundred and ninety-nine thousand wonders"——But of this, my two wolves, those who come back will be better able to tell you. I will only tell you that beyond the Gobi and beyond the Great Wall the riders of the Steppe made a discovery which will cheer you. They discovered that the world is very big and does not surrender itself easily, even to warrior horsemen. For they have been riding southwards for many years already and have only now conquered the Kingdom of Chin, which is but one half of China. So do not worry; you will not arrive too late.'

Sorgan-Shira emptied his tankard. 'Enough for today. You know now that there is only one in the Steppe who has any say— since Goktchu rode away on his invisible grey horse. Now go to bed and dream of the panther ground, or of the Gobi . . . You may dream of whatever you like!'

The *Orluk* stood up with an effort and went out into the night. When he had left the yurt the princes noticed that they were dead tired. They attributed it to the ride . . . the Festival of the White Monkey . . . the hunt. . . . But it was not any of these, for such things had never yet affected them. Usually they dreamed of adventures, but this was a night without dreams. What paralysed them was the discovery that the snow panther's paw lay on them. And not only from today. Ever since they had ridden in a *yagun* the panther's paw had held them—and they had not known it . . .

CHAPTER ELEVEN

Crazy Camels

THE following day was a 'ninth day' for the *yagun* to which Kublai and Arik-Buka belonged. On such days the horses had a holiday; they were not taken in from the pastures, and there was no riding practice. The riders had a long sleep; they could do or not do whatever they liked.

Arik-Buka woke earlier than Kublai. His first glance sought Sorgan-Shira's couch. The *Orluk* was no longer in the yurt . . . Arik-Buka was annoyed with himself for having slept so late. He had a lot of questions for that blind old man who behaved as if he knew exactly from which angle a thing should be considered, and how it should be looked at to be seen properly.

Arik-Buka kept on tormenting himself: Why did I not see who was holding Kublai and me in the *Ordo?* It was all quite obvious. Why was I so blind? Simply because I saw the matter as I wished to see it—I saw everything only through my own eyes. The *Orluk*, on the other hand, no longer has his own eyes— he sees through the eyes of Genghis Khan . . . So now our eyes are opened, thought Arik-Buka bitterly. Alas for our hopes of the Gobi, and the South, and the big battles. There's nothing for it but to obey. There's no going against Genghis Khan. Any rebellion against his orders is senseless. But I don't want to go against him. I will ride for him and help to lessen the number of his enemies. I will ride like Chepe. Like Chepe I will be an arrow which flies for him. Does he think me too weak to be his arrow? Perhaps Sorgan-Shira has not kept him properly informed about us because he's afraid something could happen to us? Or

perhaps because life would be too dull in his yurt without us . . .
It's enough to drive anyone crazy! Now I'm back again where I
began—with that blind old man who lays blunted arrows on our
bowstrings. If he were in the yurt now probably I wouldn't ask
him at all because I know already what his answer to every
question would be—he has been our teacher too long for us not
to know. I would like to ask someone else—Chepe! But I would
like still better to go riding with him without any questioning; to
begin life anew at his side . . . far away from the wooden swords
and blunted arrows and wooden walls, and all that silly playing
about . . .

Arik-Buka looked at Kublai. He noticed a soft expression on
his face. Arik-Buka had never before thought of observing his
brother asleep. Now he looked at him intently.

But why is he still sleeping on? He used to wake up when I
woke up; mount his horse when I mounted mine; speed his
arrow at exactly the same moment that I sped mine, and always at the same target. And if we spoke but little with each other
that was only because words were not needed, as our thoughts
were the same. It is only since he killed Haltsundoriki that
Kublai is different. Those infernal wooden walls and wooden
daggers! Of course it was a pity about the good fellow—but why
should Kublai begin to look different on account of him? Why
should he get such a turn at seeing a wounded animal dying . . .
and ride over to the river only to wash the blood from his
hands?

Arik-Buka was so angry that he gave Kublai a push. Kublai
jumped up, dazed with sleep.

'What's the matter?' he asked.

'Don't you need a bath to waken you up completely?'

'A bath? But we have only just bathed.'

'Only just?'

'What really made you wake me?'

'You've never slept so late yet.'

'But we have our "Ninth" today,' said Kublai, lying down
again.

'We used to have more than ever to do on those days.'

'But if I'm not in the humour for anything today?'

'I have never known you to be like that. That is something else new.'

'Something else? What was there new?'

'All that washing business . . . Do you think it would have occurred to me to bathe at the Tundarik? I had wiped my hands in the grass, as I always do. But you . . . You no longer even look as you used to look, and all because . . .'

'Because what?' Kublai sat up again. Arik-Buka caught him by the shoulder.

'Can you not just forget him?' he pleaded.

Kublai cast down his eyes. He tried to picture Haltsundoriki's face, but noticed with horror that he could no longer recollect it completely. Some of the features had faded.

'I'm already beginning to forget him,' he said, more to himself than to Arik-Buka.

'I always thought well of him, you know that,' said Arik-Buka vehemently. 'But if he begins to push himself in between us—you *must* forget him!'

The tone of voice reminded Kublai of another time: 'I command you——' Sorgan-Shira had said to him at their talk that night in the yurt. Kublai shook his head.

'Why should I forget him? Since it happened I have only wanted to go to the South on his account.'

'What do you mean by "on his account"?'

'What was done to him there made it possible for all this to happen. If a Chinaman's club had not split his skull my blow would not have been fatal. They wanted to kill him, so they are more guilty than I am.'

'You have no guilt at all; don't persuade yourself of such nonsense!'

'I want to wipe it out by settling accounts with his enemies.'

'That is not at all necessary. Besides, there's nothing doing for us in the South. But we'll certainly be there when the war goes to the West.'

'What should I do in the West?'

'What should you do there?' Arik-Buka looked at Kublai astonished. 'The same as we would have done in the South, of course—ride, kill, conquer! What else would we do?'

'I have no account to settle with the West.'

'Account?' said Arik-Buka impatiently. 'That, too, is something new about you, that you keep worrying quite unnecessarily about all kinds of things. When I think of the *kulang* stallion . . .! How could you have been so silly?'

'What do you understand about it?' said Kublai angrily. 'There are many things you don't understand at all. Or perhaps you noticed, too, that the stallion and our horses had the same . . .'

'Why don't you go on?'

'Leave me alone now!' said Kublai. He regretted having begun the sentence. He never wanted to say anything to Arik-Buka about the pure white of the shell of the ears. After all, he would only laugh at it.

'Anyhow, we made ourselves ridiculous at Tundarik just because you wanted to bathe, and only on account of the bit of blood on your hands!'

'Now you are back where you began,' said Kublai.

'You would drive anyone crazy,' said Arik-Buka enraged, as he stood up. He thought: Never before have we spoken so much with each other. That's new too. He is no longer the same person. I must see about knocking this nonsense out of his head and getting him on to more sensible ideas.

While he was slipping into his leather jerkin he thought of Buriboko, the crazy camel stallion. All camel stallions went crazy in the middle of May—but Buriboko was crazy for several weeks longer than the others every year, and during this time all kinds of fun could be had with him. The camel driver who had charge of Buriboko led other stallions near him when there was an audience, and this made him break into a fury. It was exciting to see how he would rush at his supposed rivals; but it always ended well because the other stallions' 'time of anger' was over and they thought of nothing but saving themselves by flight. Buriboko quickly got tired of this each time, and he would walk proudly back. And he was just as funny a sight in his triumph as in his senseless rage.

'We could go out to the camel pastures. What do you think? Buriboko is in his funny mood now,' suggested Arik-Buka.

'That's a good idea,' said Kublai at once. He was always ready for fun. 'It would be a pity to miss it this year.'

At the end of May there were many funny things to be seen on the camel pastures. The hair had been shorn off the camels and they were just beginning to grow a mouse-coloured coat. They would give sudden jumps to try to shake off the crows and magpies which settled on their humps and were picking about on them. And when they caught sight of one of these tormentors on the ground they spat out angrily and aimed so surely and strongly that before it could fly away the bird fell over with a smelly slime all over its feathers.

The camels looked pitiable in their nakedness. They had gone through exciting weeks, and many of the mares had foals by their sides. The princes passed by a foal which was only one day old and still quite naked. It was not yet able to stand up properly and was lying against its mother's udder. Somewhat older foals were moving about. The sun played on the pale, downy coats which covered them lightly. The foals always pressed close to the mares.

The princes easily found Buriboko, the 'wrestler'. The herdsman beckoned from a distance when he saw them coming, for he guessed at once what they wanted. He looked upon the visit as a great honour and got ready at once to stage a performance which would make the princes' visit worth while. Putting both hands to his mouth he signalled with a few yodels to the herdsman on the neighbouring pasture, and when the man led over a *burun,* as camel stallions are called by the Mongols, the herdsman immediately went over to Buriboko, loosed the *arkan* with which the stallion was tethered to a post, and held him by a short lead. Buriboko was a huge animal with a squat body, a powerful head and broad feet. True, the two humps, which were far apart, hung loosely to the side; the animal's fat reserves were exhausted, for the hungry time was not long over. But even in this state Buriboko was a sight to inspire respect. His four high pillars of legs, his tower of a neck arched outwards and his tall, steep hind-quarters made a dangerous sight. A red band on his head increased the war-like impression. When the neighbour approached with his stallion, Buriboko began to pull at his lead, the *burunduk.*

The lead rope, which was drawn through the nasal cartilage, was fastened to a block, and this made it possible for the herdsman to keep Buriboko tractable. Besides, Buriboko obeyed his herdsman at once as every *burun* does, and he alone could bring him to reason when he raged. The other stallion was trembling, yet the herdsman drove him nearer. Buriboko began to drum on the ground with his forefeet. A mighty bubble sprang from his mouth and disappeared again when he drew in his breath. He roared angrily; his veins swelled. The herdsman let him free and he rushed at once at his rival. The other camel spun round once and tossed sand and pebbles against Buriboko's breast and legs. Buriboko soon seemed to tire of this. He suddenly stood still with his forelegs spread out, and spat into the air. Everything about him betrayed his contempt for the coward. He set down each hoof as if he were imprinting his seal on the steppe.

Kublai and Arik-Buka were full of praise for this *burun*, and as soon as the herdsman had Buriboko again on the lead he proudly gave a shrill call in another direction. The stallion which arrived now had a more determined gait than the first one; this could be seen from far away.

'Except that his "time" is past,' said the herdsman, 'I'd say he'd compete well with Buriboko.'

But when the *burun* came nearer the herdsman said: 'No, I wouldn't like to advise him to; he is much weaker—but a beautiful animal.'

But now the most unexpected thing happened. The other stallion tore himself free from his driver, and Buriboko did the same. The *buruns* rushed furiously at each other, and neither of them thought of leaving the field to the other.

'Confound it, that one has it still!' cried Buriboko's driver. With the princes, he ran after the stallion. The princes reached the fighting animals before the driver.

The *buruns* fought bitterly. They uttered wild cries and tried to trample each other down. When one of them received a blow and fell, raging anger brought him quickly to his feet again. When the stamping around did not bring about a decision the *buruns* began to bite. Buriboko was the first to succeed in catching his opponent by the throat. A shred of skin was torn away and at one stroke the beautiful animal was mutilated.

'Separate them!' cried Kublai.

'Let them alone!' cried Arik-Buka. 'That's something to see at last!'

'It will cost him his life!' cried the drivers.

'I'll answer for the damage!' cried Arik-Buka.

Meanwhile Buriboko had given his rival two more wounds, and now he tried to trample him down with his forefeet. The other *burun* did not yield, but only held his own with difficulty. There were long gaping tears in his almost hairless skin.

'A battle at last!' cried Arik-Buka. 'And what a battle! Let no one touch them!'

Kublai now rushed up to Buriboko, but while he was still trying to grab the dancing lead rope, Arik-Buka dragged him back and pulled him clear of the camel's hooves. Then he cried: 'Leave them alone, you—weakling!'

Kublai was dumbfounded for a moment. He had thought that his brother had interfered through care for him. But Arik-Buka cried: 'I suppose you're taking pity again!' He stood there with narrowed eyes, holding his balled fists right under his chin. Then Kublai made a jump and hit him in the face. There were no further blows. They had immediately come to grips, and each was trying to throw over the other. But they were equal in strength, and when Arik-Buka fell back over a stone, Kublai fell with him. They rolled on the ground, the face first of one and then the other sweeping the steppe, but they only let go when both were out of breath. When they stood up again and stared at each other they were hardly recognizable, because the shingle had scratched their faces thoroughly. They stood scowling as if they wanted to attack each other again. Their fingers were spread out like claws, and trembled. Each saw only the other's eyes, nothing else.

Suddenly shrill laughter was heard. The boys looked over and saw the two camel-drivers, who were standing aside, at a safe distance, laughing uproariously despite their difficulty in holding the stallions. Their laughter seemed to mollify the *buruns*' anger, especially as the drivers gave a sharp tug to the lead ropes again and again.

'I thought you wanted to watch them!' said Buriboko's driver with another burst of laughter.

'And now they're watching you!' roared the other driver.

'It's crazy! Quite crazy!'

Kublai was infected by the camel-drivers' wild laughter. 'We were fine camels, weren't we!' he said.

Now he could not understand how he could have let himself be so carried away. Arik-Buka did not laugh. He knew exactly why he had pulled Kublai back. It was not on account of the camels' hooves! He had wanted to force Kublai to remain hard and look on at a battle right to the end. Well, Kublai had remained hard, but he had preferred to fight himself than to look on. It was all crazy!

'How could you do such a thing as to interfere?' he asked, still very angry.

'It wasn't a good fight.'

'But there were shreds of skin flying about!'

'Buriboko was much the stronger. It would have been murder. Besides, the other wasn't your stallion.'

'I would have paid for it; it would have been worth the fun.'

'You play the prince a bit too much, I think. You know the *Orluk's* ideas about that.'

'Well, we can ask him his opinion about this whole affair. He's not the sort of man to be upset about a spot of blood.' Arik-Buka said this though Sorgan-Shira did not meet with his approval in every respect. But he could be counted on for one thing—he was hard and had never yet shown the slightest weakness.

I will never permit Kublai to become weak! thought Arik-Buka. I hate everything that is weak . . . And I do not want to hate him. Arik-Buka was determined to fight for Kublai. In this fight he welcomed any ally.

CHAPTER TWELVE

Spirits of the Gobi

THE *Orluk* was in his yurt, but he was not available to the princes; he was only at home to the man who was with him. Sorgan-Shira's servants were standing in a cordon round the yurt, and the man whom Kublai and Arik-Buka went up to explained that the instructions in this respect applied to them also, but that they were to remain within reach.

Kublai and Arik-Buka looked at each other significantly. Only very rarely were they not allowed to enter the *Orluk's* yurt. When this did happen it was always because a courier of Genghis Khan was there. Kublai looked at the servant inquiringly, pointed to the yurt, and then over his shoulder in the direction of the South. The man nodded.

'Has he been there for long?'

Again the man nodded. Then the princes turned away and sat down in the grass on an open spot which could be seen from the yurt. They had been sitting there for quite a while when Arik-Buka said: 'We certainly can't talk about that with the *Orluk* now.'

'No,' said Kublai.

'He's sure to have something more important to talk to us about.'

'I hope so.'

'Besides, it's not his business, but our own. Our quarrel concerns nobody but ourselves.'

Kublai made no answer to this.

'I'm very anxious that we two get this straight between us,' urged Arik-Buka.

'The scuffle?—Oh, that was really nothing,' said Kublai, and he thought of the wounded camel.

'But the other things . . . don't you want to talk about them?'

'No,' said Kublai.

'I want to know once and for all what's the matter with you!' Arik-Buka burst out violently.

'I don't know that myself,' said Kublai, after a pause.

Arik-Buka was about to begin again. The reproaches which were on the tip of his tongue could be seen in his face. At this moment one of the men came over from the *Orluk's* yurt. The princes stood up at once and went to meet him.

When they entered the yurt they tried to hide their excitement as well as they could. They saw an exhausted-looking man sitting there. The *Orluk* was standing, and it could be seen that he was greatly agitated. He pointed to the courier and said that his name was Tosh-To and that he had arrived an hour ago on a camel accompanied by some horsemen, with a command from Genghis Khan.

'Sit down!' said the *Orluk*. He himself did not sit down.

'Genghis Khan is on the way here. The Kingdom of Chin has been conquered. The conquerors are already approaching the southern edge of the Gobi.'

The princes were so surprised by this news that they were unable to utter a word. They stared at the *Orluk*. His face was little in keeping with this news. He was as gloomy as if he had heard that Genghis Khan's army had been forced to retreat.

'It's the most important news we have had for years,' he said, 'and it has reached us too late.'

The princes looked at Tosh-To.

'It wasn't my fault,' said the courier. 'There were other couriers on the road before me.'

'And did they not arrive?' asked Arik-Buka eagerly.

'Not one of them,' said the *Orluk*. And in great excitement he went on: 'That is the Gobi; it alone can take the liberty of holding up the couriers of Genghis Khan.' Then he added in a more gentle voice: 'Tosh-To has told me that the leader of the couriers was a man who had been honoured with this order for his bravery in the battles in the South.'

'Can nothing be done to save them?' asked Kublai.

The *Orluk* made a movement which betrayed his perplexity. Arik-Buka watched him distrustfully.

'What if all the *yaguns* ride forth . . . if five thousand go on the search . . .? After all, the couriers cannot have gone so far off the courier-route!'

The *Orluk* appeared not to hear Arik-Buka's passionate suggestion at all.

'It has so many faces,' he said half aloud, as if he were talking to himself, 'so many more faces than the Steppe . . . And it's full of life, even when it sleeps . . . swarms of larks over the black stony soil, and *cholo-choro*, the birds which flash over the sand like streaks of lightning . . . floods of light—— It dreams only bright dreams—— But when the desert wakes up it is full of death and gloom. The sand which had been under the camel's hooves before is now on top of the riders, making the animals stagger, and the riders cling to them . . .' Sorgan-Shira's thoughts seemed to be far, far away as he asked: 'Where can they have fallen upon you, where . . .? The Khan will ask about you, he will grieve for you.'

How he talks! thought Arik-Buka, and his distrust increased. He talks almost like a woman—certainly not like a warrior. Kublai listened too. I've never known him to be like that, he thought. I didn't know he could be——

He's incapable of making up his mind, Arik-Buka decided grimly, and aloud he asked: 'What's the man's name, then?'

The *Orluk* evaded an answer. 'How many were there, Tosh-To?' he asked.

'Ten, as always,' said Tosh-To.

He keeps the name secret, thought Arik-Buka. Perhaps he is jealous of the man and won't do anything for him.

Arik-Buka returned to the charge. 'Five thousand riders—if five thousand feelers pushed out into the desert—it would be a grand manœuvre,' he said.

The *Orluk* signed to him to be silent. 'The courier route leads through the most dangerous parts of the Gobi. More than ten riders together have never been put on that trail. And Tosh-To has brought an order which will set everyone in the *Ordo* busy.

A yurt high enough to touch the clouds is to be erected for the victory celebrations. And it is to be big enough to hold all those who have distinguished themselves.'

'So it's to be a festival yurt!' said Arik-Buka, with bitterness. Then, giving free vent to his indignation, he continued: 'Since when has a yurt become more important than a brave man? If he knew . . . If he were here . . . I have never heard that the Khan ever left anyone in the lurch who was in danger!'

If he doesn't silence me now, thought Arik-Buka, he's really an 'old man'.

Kublai, too, was expecting a severe reprimand. But instead the *Orluk* groped uncertainly for his chair, and let himself sink into it.

'It was a wonder that we got through,' said Tosh-To. 'There must have been frightful sandstorms before, because all the direction posts were buried.'

'The darkness of the Gobi,' said Sorgan-Shira dismally. 'I know it. But it did not get the better of us that time. It took us by surprise near an oasis. We reached it and were saved. Only when daylight came again was our terrible situation apparent. The desert had changed. There were no longer any tracks. We relied on our camels, but the sandstorm had confused them. Perhaps the nearest water-hole which we tried to reach first was silted up. We could not find what we were looking for. Our camels, those roaming fountains, preserved us for a few days from dying of thirst. But once we had lost them the Gobi began to carry on its pitiless game with us. Suddenly someone would jump up out of a sleep of exhaustion and shake his companions awake. And when they would look at him inquiringly he would point in a certain direction and whisper: "Don't you hear, they're coming!"

'We heard nothing, and told him so.

' "Nothing? Just listen—horses! They're coming with horses to fetch us!"

'We listened and heard no sound of horses' hooves. But I heard Zun, my old comrade, calling me, and although I knew he had remained behind in the *Ordo*, I distinctly heard his voice calling: "We're coming! We're coming!" I could have sworn I heard him call my name. And another time someone jumped up and shouted out: "They're beating the drums!" He heard the

drums being beaten and mussel-horns being blown so shrilly
that he covered his ears . . . We others heard nothing. But we
knew: they were the spirits of the Gobi. They took one after
the other in hand and tortured him until he lost his reason. That
was the second, the invisible darkness of the desert which tried to
shroud our minds in darkness. The spirits of the Gobi took their
time. Again and again I saw Zun coming to me, but he never
took the final step which separated him from us. And it was
terrible to hear how he laughed! For how can a man laugh when
he sees ghosts? We were ghosts, and no longer recognized one
another. There were deep hollows in our cheeks, and two flames
burned and danced beneath our foreheads. The spirits of the
Gobi had kindled them and were trying now to blow out the
flames . . . They did not succeed with us; for Zun really came.
He had been sent after us by the Khan, together with a caravan-
leader, in the nick of time. The caravan-leader had scented the
storm days beforehand.'

'And if the riders set off at once, all the five thousand—five
thousand Zuns?' asked Arik-Buka hoarsely.

'The Gobi has already had too much time now,' said the
Orluk. 'It is too late.'

Arik-Buka felt a repugnance towards Sorgan-Shira rising up
in him. 'Too late?' he cried. 'That's a word you forbade us to
use. Now you use it yourself! You don't want to do anything
for the man—I can see that. You have something against him.
Otherwise how could you, having once been saved from the Gobi
yourself, leave others to their fate there?'

Sorgan-Shira put his hand in front of his face. At this Tosh-
To jumped up and went over to Arik-Buka.

'You have a dirty tongue!' he said indignantly. 'You don't see
anything at all!'

Arik-Buka was pale with anger. 'Why, then, does he not name
the man whom the Khan honoured?' he asked.

'Because it's his son,' said Tosh-To. 'It's best for you to leave
the *Orluk* alone now.'

That night the princes slept beside their horses. When day
dawned Kublai woke feeling chilly. He stood up cautiously in

order not to waken Arik-Buka. As he moved about he quickly became warm. The sun rose; the dew began to sparkle. Larks soared up into the sky. Everything pointed to a beautiful day.

Later Kublai noticed that Arik-Buka was sitting up, and he went over to him.

'Why didn't you waken me?' asked Arik-Buka.

'I thought you needed a sleep.'

'Rubbish! You know I don't like getting up later than you.'

'You were tossing about a long time before you went to sleep.'

'Because I was raging.'

'With yourself?' asked Kublai hesitantly.

'Why with myself?' retorted Arik-Buka.

'Don't you feel sorry?'

'Now you want to act the teacher with me!'

'I think you should apologize to the *Orluk*.'

'It wouldn't have come to that if he hadn't left me in the dark.'

'That's just what I find wonderful about him, that he really didn't want to say it at all.'

'Those are matters of sentiment,' said Arik-Buka. 'They make everything difficult.'

'Many a thing isn't easy.' Kublai took Arik-Buka by the arm. 'Won't we go to him now? I imagine he's expecting us.'

'You worry too much,' said Arik-Buka, 'and that's what makes me wild more than anything else. You are too weak. And now the *Orluk* too—didn't he always preach that a horseman should never look back; that he should never permit a dead person to have a hold on him? And now, there he is himself—mourning. We have nothing more to learn from him. He has given us a bad example.'

'He was his only son. I understand him,' said Kublai quietly.

'Did you not see him, then? He wept! Am I to learn that from him? Chepe would never have done that!' Arik-Buka looked across the Steppe towards the South. 'He'll soon come,' he whispered, 'at the head of the vanguard. And the Steppe will tremble under his *tumans*. And one day we will ride with him! Do you hear that, Kublai? We two will ride with Chepe!'

CHAPTER THIRTEEN

Prince Arrow

ON the day that the yurt for the reception of Genghis Khan was finished a courier who did not wait, as other couriers did, until the old *Orluk* had him admitted, arrived at the *Ordo*. He leaped from his horse, and before the fellow to whom he threw the reins had realized who the tall man in unadorned riding-jerkin was, the latter had already entered the yurt, cast a hurried glance at the princes and greeted Sorgan-Shira boisterously.

'Chepe! You here already?' cried the *Orluk*, stretching out both arms. 'But why should I be surprised? You always come before you're expected.'

'At least my enemies say so,' replied Chepe, laughing.

'And when is *he* coming? The yurt is ready for his reception.'

'I've seen it,' said Chepe. 'It's wonderful, a white mountain in the Steppe—only it's in the wrong place.'

Sorgan-Shira raised his face inquiringly.

'It's too far to the east,' said Chepe. 'Since Genghis Khan conquered the Kingdom of Chin and crossed the Gobi Desert, he's been thinking only of the West. From here it's too far to Bokhara and Samarkand.'

'And where does he wish to have his *Ordo*?'

'By the Dsungarian Gate,' said Chepe. 'That is the gateway to the countries of the Shah and the Caliph.'

'It's a ride of at least fifteen days from here,' said Sorgan-Shira.

'The army has a good thirty days' ride still before it. How long do you need to transfer the victory yurt?'

'We have become experienced yurt-builders meantime,' said Sorgan-Shira wryly.

Chepe turned to the princes. A smile made the strong curves of his cheek-bones seem more prominent. Black fire gleamed from the oblique slits beneath the broad brow.

'I also have a command for you two. You are to accompany me.'

'Kublai and Arik-Buka?' asked Sorgan-Shira, surprised.

'The Khan thinks that it's time for you,' said Chepe. 'Actually, I was not quite clear about your names, because whenever there was mention of you he always called you "the inseparables".'

Arik-Buka threw Kublai an ardent glance.

Now everything is all right, he thought. The ally whom I need has come. Genghis Khan has sent him. Arik-Buka's eyes turned again to Chepe.

Kublai, too, looked at the broad face, which shone like steel. But his thoughts were with Sorgan-Shira.

Now he has no one left, thought Kublai, and he noticed with emotion that he had begun to love that blind old man.

CHAPTER FOURTEEN

Cage People

In the evening the two *Orluks* sat by the yurt fire with Kublai and Arik-Buka. Rice beer was brought for the two princes as well.

'You owe us stay-at-homes of the *Ordo* a good supply of stories,' said Sorgan-Shira to Chepe, as they began the first tankard.

'We've the whole night for it,' replied Chepe, with a laugh. 'But you two—wouldn't you rather creep into your sleeping places? We'll be riding off at break of day.'

The princes, enlivened by the rice beer, protested loudly. How could they find any rest in their beds while Chepe was telling of the Kingdom of Chin, and Sorgan-Shira was banishing all thoughts of sleep from the yurt with his thunderous laughter?

Kublai was intensely interested. Arik-Buka noticed this with increasing satisfaction. Chepe will soon bring him to reason, he thought. Shadows cannot last in Chepe's neighbourhood; he's like the morning light, or the flash which comes from a dagger— or an arrow. No one has ever deserved his name so well as Chepe ...

'You've needed a long time in the South!' said Sorgan-Shira jokingly.

'You're right,' admitted Chepe. 'Nevertheless, we have only got the Kingdom of Chin and must leave the Kingdom of Sung until later on.'

'And what kind are the people of the South?'

'Quite different from here. They live in cages.'

'In cages?' asked the princes, surprised.

'Yes, in huge cages made of stone. They call them "towns" or "fortresses". In many of these gigantic cages millions of people are shut up. And inside these each family has, besides, its own individual cage. They call this a house. And inside a house it is not like a yurt, where everyone lives together. In the houses each person has his own cell. The people out in the country do not live as we do either. Instead of riding and hunting and keeping herds of cattle, they hit the ground with pointed instruments, incessantly soak it with water and force it to produce other things than grass. They no longer know that people should live on animals, and that the animals should live on what grows. Perhaps it's from eating so much rice that they get the strangest ideas. Instead of riding they have themselves carried in upholstered stands. On the whole they are very keen on upholstery and like everything soft. Their garments, too, are soft. Even their shoes are made of soft leather. But of course only one kind of Chinese are like that.'

'Are there several kinds, then?' asked Kublai.

'There are two kinds,' said Chepe, 'rich and poor. The one have almost everything and the other almost nothing—except hunger. When two of the poor kind meet, they greet each other with the words: *Che fen la moa*? Which means: Have you eaten rice? And the other thanks for the greeting and replies: *Che pao la*—I have eaten rice.'

'But if he hasn't eaten rice?' asked Arik-Buka.

'They always say *Che pao la*,' explained Chepe, 'and often they haven't eaten.'

'So they lie, then?'

'They don't call that lying. They say: One must keep face. They think a lot about keeping face. They never show what they really think. The poor clear the stones out of the way of the rich, and carry bowls behind them into which they can spit, though while they do so they would prefer to spit in the faces of the rich. But they do not dare to. When he is going away they take the old shoes off an official who may have plundered them, and put new shoes on him, so that he may have a lucky journey. And they lock up the old shoes in a wired box, so that they may not be troublesome to their blood-sucker. In reality they think: May he stumble to his death! When we came it became clear that the poor people think like that. They saw that there is only one kind of Mongol, and that with us no one has to ask the other: Have you eaten? And their hunger and their hatred of the rich became our constant allies. For the humbler kind of Chinese had no desire to fight us, since it was only the richer Chinese who had anything to lose. And the rich, too, had little desire to stick out their necks.'

'Hearing you speak,' said Sorgan-Shira, 'one wonders why you needed such a long time in the country of the cage-people.'

'There were so many of them,' said Chepe. 'And of course there were Chinese armies too, for the rich Chinese had bought soldiers, a whole lot of them, and as they never let the soldiers starve, they fought fairly well. For all that, we soon conquered them. Only the enormous cages, the fortresses, gave us a lot of trouble. At the very first fortress, which was called Wolohai, our siege failed. To be sure, we took it, the Khan took it alone. When he saw that the wall would be the death of his horsemen he sent an envoy to the commandant of the fortress threatening a long siege if he did not deliver to him within three days a thousand cats and ten thousand swallows. The commandant thought: What funny fellows these Mongols are! Well, if I can get rid of them at such a small price . . .

'For three days he had cats and swallows caught, delivered them punctually, and waited behind well-locked gates for the Mongols to depart. But when he had got all the cats and swallows Genghis Khan suddenly sent word to the commandant that he really did not know what to do with so many animals, and would prefer to send them all back. And he had little bunches of oakum wetted with naphtha tied to the cats and the swallows, and set them alight. The cats and the swallows flew back to the town into their hides . . . but bunches of oakum continue to burn under the roofs of houses . . . and they set fire to the roofs! It was a murderous joke! It soon became so hot within the walls that the gates flew open. So of course we took the town. But naturally no other commandant was taken in by such a nice little game. There was nothing for us to do but to become cats ourselves, and as there were many fortresses we had plenty of opportunity to practise. In spite of that we were never able to take the Emperor's City. Its walls were as high as ten horses one on top of the other, and there were trenches full of water wider than the Onon and Kerulen rivers; and water—you know water is even worse than a wall for horsemen!'

Chepe saw how eagerly Arik-Buka assented, and he said, looking grim: 'Besides, the Chinese don't seem to think water such a bad thing, for in their houses they have pools in long basins which they lie down in, and under which they have fire. They feed the fire with black stones which they steal from the devils who live under the earth.'

'Ugh, how horrible!' said Sorgan-Shira. The princes, too, shuddered with horror.

'Anyway, the water-ditches were frightful for us,' continued Chepe. 'We had the whole Kingdom of Chin, but the Emperor's Palace stood behind the walls and the water ditches, and it was the Palace we wanted; for the Emperor was no longer there. A fat eunuch named Hushahu had killed him, because he, too, wanted to be lord of the Palace—just as we did. And as the Emperor had never fought, it was easy for the fat eunuch to kill him. But the eunuch Hushahu did not have the palace for long. A Chinese general, who also wanted one day to be lord of the Palace, killed the eunuch. And so it went on, as there were many others in the Emperor's city who wanted to be lord of the Palace. We had only to wait outside.'

'Those town dwellers are a rabble stinking of treachery!' cried Arik-Buka.

'We treated them accordingly,' said Chepe. 'We drove them together in herds, and then we put them through a sieve.'

'What did you do with them?' asked Kublai.

'We divided up the Chinese anew,' explained Chepe. 'In one group we put the useful ones, and in another the useless.'

'And who belonged to the useless?'

'All those who had done nothing up till then except fill their stomachs and have their skins caressed with silk. The Khan decided that the useless ones should not deprive the useful ones of another bite.'

'Quite right,' said Arik-Buka.

'And what about the useful ones?' asked Kublai.

'You will meet numbers of them in the army—all kinds of artisans. Far too many,' continued Chepe vehemently. 'They cling to the army like leeches. There are also far too many cart-loads of treasures! What shall we do with them? Our women will get a passion for finery. All the gold, and the glitter of the precious stones will turn their heads—and even the horsemen's heads too! We are dragging too much away with us—far too much! Jesters and musicians give me pleasure, but if you knew all the things the people there imagine are useful! Our *tumans* have become slower. You needn't be afraid, Sorgan, that we'll arrive at the Dsungarian Gate before you. The worst thing about them is—but they're really not worth talking about at all!'

Chepe drank a whole tankard in one draught.

'What is the worst thing about them?' asked Sorgan-Shira.

'They are weak!' Chepe burst out.

'They can be trampled on all the easier for that,' said Arik-Buka.

'You're greatly mistaken,' said Chepe. 'Their weakness is their strength, a very cunning strength! You grasp and then have nothing in your hand. They are like water; that's the most dangerous thing about them. Don't forget this; in the long run water takes the sharp edges off the hardest stone. What's the good of "putting through a sieve" if too many trickle through? I often think the Khan shouldn't let one of them near him.'

'Does he tolerate some of them near him?' asked Sorgan-Shira.

Chepe looked before him grimly. 'He has a preference for one variety amongst the useful, and he even sieves out these for himself. He calls them scholars or wise men.'

'What kind of people are they?' asked Kublai.

'They are people who know nothing about either arrows or horses, and who claim that they know all possible kinds of things, such as what the stars are called and how they move about.'

'And does the Khan consider such people to be useful?' asked Arik-Buka.

'They are extremely clever with their tongues,' said Chepe, 'and they have talked him into many things. For instance, one of them named Tatatungo has persuaded the Khan that it is better to write out commands, and that a ruler needs to have a seal.'

'A seal—what is that?' asked Kublai.

Chepe gave the information with reluctance. 'It is a sign cut on a jade stone,' he said. 'The Khan chose a tortoise for his seal.'

'Very good,' said Sorgan-Shira.

'Why, a tortoise jumped out of the stone when the lark sang above Hoelun's yurt,' said Kublai.

'I have no objection to a tortoise either,' said Chepe, 'but only to the fact that it is Tatatungo who dips the seal in colour and with it stamps the order which he himself has written out for the Khan. Who is to know what he writes? The Khan trusts this man blindly.'

'So it has come to that!' said Sorgan-Shira, dismayed.

'I should never trust anyone with the name of Tatatungo!' said Arik-Buka. 'What horrible names—Hushahu, Tatatungo! And what on earth is the seal for? Is Genghis Khan's simple word not enough?'

'You think as I do,' said Chepe, 'and it's a good thing that all true Mongols think the same.'

'I had imagined the people of the South to be just like that,' said Arik-Buka; 'untruthful and weak. I hate them.'

'And what about you?' asked Chepe, turning to Kublai. 'You are so silent.'

'It's all so new to me,' said Kublai.

'And what have you to say about the towns?' insisted Chepe. 'It's important for me to know that.'

Kublai met Chepe's black eyes. He felt Arik-Buka observing him intently from the side, and he sensed how eagerly the old *Orluk* was waiting for his answer.

'I'm very anxious to see what the cage people look like,' said Kublai.

Arik-Buka cast an angry glance at him. 'They should be sieved, sieved until nothing is left of them!' he said.

'The Khan must know why he takes many of them into his service!' said Kublai.

'You are certainly defending them,' said Arik-Buka, getting ready to fall on Kublai.

'*Bolna!*' cried Chepe. 'Surely you're not going to quarrel about those cage people—you inseparables! Once Kublai sees them near—and that will be in a few days . . .'

There were still a few stars in the sky when Chepe and the princes mounted their horses. Chepe did not fail to notice that Sorgan-Shira's men were already dismantling the victory yurt.

'Unnecessary haste,' he said as he took leave of the old *Orluk*. 'When the *tumans* take up their position in the plain before the Dsungarian Gate, the white mountain will long since have been erected—and in the right place! And then! We'll turn it into a volcano with our noise and merrymaking.'

They left the *Ordo* at a quick trot and rode due south.

'When shall we be there?' asked Arik-Buka.

'In ten days,' answered Chepe.

'Not for ten days?'

'In ten days at the earliest. The *tumans* are long because we have so many of the "useful" hanging on behind them.'

'The devil take them!' said Arik-Buka.

Kublai was too tired to say anything. He blinked through half-closed eyes, and his gaze was fixed on one star which stood right to the south, a little above the horizon, and still shone brightly though dawn was beginning to break.

What name might it have? pondered Kublai. And he thought to himself dreamily: In the Khan's camp there are men who know this. Perhaps I shall one day ask one of them . . .

PART TWO

The Gentle Conqueror

CHAPTER ONE

The Man with the Beautiful Beard

THE ride took twelve days, and they had already given up hope of reaching their goal even by the twelfth day. Then, as darkness was falling, they saw a strange spectacle far ahead of them. A dragon appeared to rise up out of the ground, a monster with a thousand glistening scales.

'At last!' said Chepe.

'Are those the camp-fires?' asked Arik-Buka.

Chepe nodded. 'The camp will be sleeping by the time we arrive at it,' he said. 'Only the fires and the sentries will still be awake.'

Chepe was mistaken. The camp-fires went out one after another while the three horsemen were approaching. But still they heard noise going on in the camp. Everyone seemed to be up and doing.

'What does that mean?' asked Kublai.

'Who knows?' said Chepe. 'The Khan gets many ideas. Perhaps he's just now at the sieving again. He doesn't need much sleep.'

It was a cloudless night and the moon was full. It stood sharply outlined against the sky. The Steppe was bathed in silver light, and even the horsemen's yurts glistened.

Chepe and the princes rode up to the sentries, handed over their horses and mingled with the crowd. The *Orluk* was recognized at once, so in spite of the crush of people it was easy for him and the princes to push their way to the middle of the camp. The warriors had been drinking; they were grumbling noisily, and again and again Chepe and the princes heard them saying: 'It will be singed! The beautiful beard will be singed off!'

Chepe tried to obtain more detailed information, but he could get nothing out of the men.

The yurt in the centre of the camp towered over all the others. Beside it stood a gigantic mast from which was hanging a white standard, as big as a sail, with nine points. White horse-tails were fastened to the ends of each of these points. This was the *Tug*, the Khan's standard. The horse-tails were the insignia of the nine *Orluks*.

A wide space was left clear around the yurt with the *Tug*. The men who formed Genghis Khan's bodyguard, all of them well-grown men and all a foot taller than the other horsemen, stood around, forming a loose cordon. There was room enough between them—but no one pressed forward. The men of the bodyguard were not drunk—that could be seen at once by their sure, firm step.

A guard wanted to make way for the *Orluk* at once, but Chepe remained standing. What was to be seen on the open space astonished even him; and the princes were simply spellbound. The Khan's throne was in front of the entrance to the yurt. At each side of it there were seats, five on the right and four on the left. They were the *Orluks*' seats. Two of them were vacant; one had been reserved for Chepe and another for Sorgan-Shira. The Khan was sitting on his throne. Seven *Orluks* were sitting on the seats, and all were being looked after by servants who came running with tankards. All the *Orluks* were in the best of humour.

Chepe was thirsty after the ride, but he hesitated to take his seat. He did not think it wise to disturb the Khan just then. Obviously something special was going on.

The only fire to be seen in the camp was burning in a bowl placed right at the Khan's feet, and a servant was looking after it and keeping it blazing well. A few paces away stood a post to which a man dressed in silk was bound. The cloak which he wore shone in the moonlight more brightly than the leather jerkins of the *Orluks*. A band was wound round the man's forehead and fastened to the post, so that the head inclined backwards and the face was turned towards the moon. The man's beard, a long, black shining beard, stood forward in front of him. The beard, too, was tied up. A man was holding it by a silken cord, so that it could not fall on his breast. Another attendant was holding a large hour-glass.

'What is it all about?' asked Arik-Buka.

'I fancy it has something to do with the moon,' said Chepe.

'What is there unusual about the moon?'

'Sometimes when the sky is bright it disappears,' said Chepe. 'The night swallows it; you know that yourself; and that is a spectacle which the Khan loves. But he always wants to know in advance when this is going to happen.'

'And the man at the post?' asked Kublai. 'Why is he bound? And his beard—why, even the Khan hasn't such a long beard!'

'That is much to be regretted,' said Chepe. 'If he had, he probably wouldn't have so much time for long beards—and for people like that man there, who wear long beards.'

'But he doesn't seem to treat him with special favour,' said Arik-Buka.

'That has yet to be seen, if I am not mistaken . . . that is, if the man with the beard is not mistaken.'

At that moment the man who was holding the hour-glass made a sign to the Khan, who then raised his hand. Immediately there was a roll of drums, and then silence reigned over the wide square. The Khan spoke: 'The time is up, astrologer. The sand has run out,' he said.

'The sand was in too great a hurry, O Khan,' said the man at the post, in a firm voice.

'You are too sure of yourself.'

'The heavens do not err, O Khan.'

'But it seems to me that you do. I'm very sorry about your beautiful beard. I agreed that you could keep it if you proved that you understand the heavens. But you can see for yourself that what you foretold has not happened. The eclipse has not come to pass.'

'It will come as I have said, O Khan,' said the man tied to the post.

'The sand has run out, and my patience too!' Genghis Khan made a sign to the man who was guarding the fire, and the latter

lifted up the bowl and stood with it right beside the bound man.
Now the man's face could be seen more distinctly; it was the
fairest face in the whole camp. Kublai saw that it was different
from the faces of the horsemen. There was not the slightest trace
of either ferocity or fear in it.

'May I speak again, O Khan?' asked the man at the post.

'Speak! But if you speak foolish things I shall have your
mouth singed too.'

'That is all within your power, O Khan,' said the bound man.
'But you will offend heaven if you trust it less than the sand in an
hour-glass.'

They should singe his mouth! thought Arik-Buka. And
Chepe thought: None of them has taken such a liberty as that
till now. Kublai glanced over at the Khan. The Khan seemed to
be pondering the matter.

'May I speak again, O Khan?' asked the strange man once
more.

'Well, speak on! But it is the last time.'

'Wait for the space of a thousand heart-beats, O Khan! If
the moon has lost none of her fullness by then, cut off my head!'

'He knows how to bargain,' whispered Arik-Buka.

'Like all the people of the South,' hissed Chepe. 'But this one
here beats them all!'

'Loose him!' ordered the Khan. He turned his face towards the
moon, which was standing clear against the sky. And while the
man who had been holding the fire cut the ropes and the other one
freed the beard from its imprisonment, a round shadow began to
move over the face of the moon. Before the space of a thousand
heart-beats was up, anyone who looked at the moon could perceive it.

The Khan signed to the man in the silken coat to come up to
him.

'You have put the astrologers whom I have had up till now to
shame. And the *shamans* too. They said that no eclipse was to be
expected so soon. I need a man who is on good terms with the
heavens. I am told your name is Yeliu.'

'Yeliu Chutsai of the Liao family,' the stranger confirmed.

'That is a family which has had much to suffer from the Chin

Emperor,' said the Khan with emphasis, 'and so I have also avenged you.'

'I was in the service of the Emperor of Chin by my own free will, as my father was before me,' said Yeliu. 'I was a counsellor and minister of the Emperor. It would not be fitting for me to speak ill of him just because he has perished.'

A murmur passed through the line of horsemen at these words. But the Khan showed no sign of displeasure.

'It seems you are accustomed to say what you think. I like that. Come to the supper-table with me! I should like to learn more from you.'

The Khan looked up at the moon. 'The eclipse is moving forward quite distinctly. A good omen! You, my Mongols, shall move forward like that, and take one kingdom after another. Light the fires! And if you like, go on drinking. Your Khan has found someone who is on good terms with the heavens!'

At a sign from the Khan a seat was brought along for Yeliu.

'A fine reception!' said Arik-Buka. Chepe gripped the prince's arm. 'It's best for us not to go to the Khan until to-morrow,' he said. 'Or do you wish to sit beside this Yeliu?'

Chepe put up the princes in his yurt. He invited them to stay with him permanently, and the princes immediately agreed to do so. And although the noise continued in the lanes throughout the camp for a long time, the three quickly fell asleep. The twelve-day ride had taken it out of them.

As he dropped off to sleep Kublai saw Yeliu's face before him just as it had looked when the fire was blazing up right beside it.

I could ask him about the names of the stars, he thought.

CHAPTER TWO

The Ants that had gone Wild

THE camp was being broken up, but the Khan detained Chepe and the princes, who had presented themselves to him early in the morning, in his yurt. He pushed the best morsels of food over to them and questioned them ceaselessly. He was full of jokes, and his grey eyes shone when he laughed. He reproached the three for not having come to him during the night.

'There was so much going on,' said Chepe hesitantly; 'the new astrologer——'

'A man such as I have not met before amongst those of the South,' said the Khan so definitely that Chepe preferred not to touch on the subject again.

The Khan was just about to rise from the table when an officer of the life guard arrived and announced that a prisoner had been captured by the sentries who were roaming the countryside, just as he was about to creep into a hole in the ground.

Anyone who tried to flee condemned himself to death; everyone who had endured the 'sieving' process and been declared a useful person knew this. Up to now no one had dared to make off and seek a way back to freedom. The Steppe offered too few hiding-places—and the Gobi, that deadly barrier, stood between them and the South.

'I wish to see him,' ordered the Khan.

The man was dragged in by two life guards. His hands were tied together. His face was scratched. There were traces of blood in his beard.

'He refused to walk,' the Guards officer announced. 'We had to drag him.'

128

'Free him!' said the Khan. The horsemen freed him. The man fell forward and remained lying down with his face pressed to the ground.

'Is he too weak to stand up?' inquired the Khan.

'He doesn't want to stand up,' said the officer. Then he pushed the man with his foot. 'Look here, won't you speak to the Khan?' he said.

The man on the ground did not utter a word.

'Lift him up!' ordered the Khan. 'I want to see how he looks at me.'

The man was lifted up. He looked at the ground in front of him.

'I wish you to look at me!' said the Khan. 'Look at me, or you will lose your eyes!'

The man stood there, his face unmoved. He did not raise his eyes a hair's breadth.

'What's the man's name?'

'Tang Liweng,' said the officer. 'He's an expert on the old script. He belongs to the Liao clan.'

'Call Yeliu!' said the Khan at once.

Then the man said: 'I would prefer to look at you than at that one!' and he stared into the Khan's face.

'What does that mean?'

'That I despise him a hundred times more than I do you! You were born a devil, but he made himself a devil by entering your service!'

'Free him!' ordered the Khan.

Why doesn't he strike him down? thought Arik-Buka.

Tang Liweng was an old man, but he stood erect. Then he said: 'When you made him appear ridiculous bound to the post I was glad, and I hoped his beard would be burnt.'

An officer entered. 'Yeliu is outside the yurt,' he said.

'Send him in.'

Yeliu entered. Tang Liweng looked at him with hatred.

'He didn't want to look at you,' said the Khan to Yeliu. 'Do you know this man?'

'He is a great scholar,' said Yeliu.

'He is the greatest blockhead ever born,' said the Khan

furiously. 'He has abused you because you entered my service.'

'He was my pupil,' said Tang Liweng, 'but now I am ashamed that he was. We were related; now we are no longer so.'

Yeliu remained silent.

'Why did you want to flee?' the Khan asked Tang Liweng.

'I wanted to go to the country to which I belong.'

'And what did you want to do there?'

'To gnaw,' said Tang Liweng excitedly.

'What's that you wanted to do?'

Then Tang Liweng whispered: 'You turned us into ants to drag burdens for you. I wanted to go from one ant to another and remind them all that only one thing remained for us to do: to gnaw . . . to gnaw at your throne until it would collapse.'

'You have no doubt forgotten that I have broken your jaw-bones,' said the Khan mockingly.

'One can gnaw even with broken jaws—provided one isn't too half-hearted,' said Tang Liweng.

'What nonsense!' said the Khan. 'You do not understand how things are since I have been in power. Even if you had escaped and incited others against me, you would only have become their murderer. I would have had to crush the breakers of the new order which I have set up. You forget that I am everywhere—wherever my horsemen have marked the ground with the hooves of their horses. You have even forgotten the Gobi, great scholar! Or do you think the desert would have spared you?'

'You are the desert!' said Tang Liweng so violently that the scars on his face began to bleed.

Why does the Khan not strike him down? thought Arik-Buka again.

'And you are the darkness which makes the desert even more terrible,' said Tang Liweng, turning to Yeliu. 'Have you forgotten what he has done to your people—the people who speak your language and are of your mind? He trod them down until they mingled with the earth. He trampled down the towns be-cause he suspected that freedom dwelt in them. And he is only beginning. He aims at making these countries, these gardens of the earth, into Steppe. He intends to quench millions of lives.

And you, creature of fear, are walking in his shadow because you fear for your life!'

Yeliu remained silent. The Khan looked at him.

'Have you nothing to say to that?'

'No, O Khan!' said Yeliu, with an impassive face. The Khan observed him more sharply.

'Do you regret having entered my service?'

'No, O Khan,' answered Yeliu.

Thereupon Tang Liweng took two steps towards Yeliu and dealt him a blow in the face with his clenched fist. Yeliu staggered, but again stood firm when the men of the life guard pulled Tang Liweng back.

'Are you not going to hit back?' asked the Khan angrily.

'No, O Khan,' said Yeliu.

'Then beat him, you!' cried the Khan. 'And let all those whom we are feeding be present, although they have forfeited their lives, so that they see how we treat ants who emit poison instead of doing what they should do.'

Tang Liweng stood there just as if what the Khan was saying did not concern him at all. The Khan suddenly interrupted himself. Pointing to Yeliu, he said to Tang Liweng: 'You are a Liao, so is he. For his sake I shall give you an hour. If you make up your mind . . .'

'I do not want to die,' said Tang Liweng, 'and this alone would be death: to enter your service.'

'They will make short work of you.'

'You cannot kill me,' said Tang Liweng. 'You cannot kill what alone is important to me. You can destroy my body, but you cannot subjugate my mind. You cannot stamp out the spark of freedom which I am.'

'You talk insanely,' said the Khan. He turned to the officer. 'I have never seen a greater fool,' he said. 'Take him out! No one is to look on. He is to disappear and be forgotten for ever!'

The guard led Tang Liweng away.

'A madman, isn't he?' said the Khan, turning to Yeliu.

'No,' said Yeliu.

There was an eerie silence. Chepe and the princes looked at Yeliu spellbound.

'You do not consider that rebel to be mad, then?'

'He went *his* way,' said Yeliu quietly. 'He saw that way clearly before him.'

'You do not despise him, do you?' asked the Khan.

'Tang Liweng was a great man,' said Yeliu.

The Khan fixed Yeliu with cold eyes. 'And why, then, do you not do the same as he does?'

'His way is not mine,' said Yeliu. 'I am no rebel. My star has led me into your service. I knew for a long time past that that would happen. My father, who foretold to the Chin Emperor the exact day of his downfall, told me that I would end my life in the service of the lord of half the world.'

'I shall one day be lord of the whole world,' said the Khan angrily.

Yeliu shut his eyes. 'The heavens are not mistaken,' he said.

'Speak!' said the Khan. 'I want to know what the heavens know.'

Yeliu still kept his eyes shut. He looked as if he was being tortured by some vision. He began to speak in an altered voice: 'All will tremble before you, O Khan, and you will establish an enormous empire such as no one before you ever thought of, and your sons shall extend your power still farther. But it is only your grandson who shall inherit it fully.' Yeliu opened his eyes. He looked around as if searching for someone. Then he pointed to Kublai and said: 'It will be that one.'

Kublai saw the hand pointing to him, and his face began to burn.

'How do you know that?' asked the Khan, startled by the force of Yeliu's words. 'And why Kublai?'

'Feng Huang, the phoenix, ruler of all the three hundred and sixty-five feathered creatures, stepped through your yurt, O Khan. Without taking notice of the others, the bird walked up to Kublai, and with his beak he touched the spot on the breast beneath which the heart beats. Feng Huang has three voices. In the morning he calls: *Ho shi*—May things go well in the world! At midday: *Ki-tshang*—Turn at the right time! In the evening: *Shan dsai*—Now all is well! Up to the present the bird phoenix has been seen three times. Under the Yellow Emperors of olden times he lived at the southern gate of the Imperial Palace. When the Chao music originated under the Chun emperor, he came flying, and danced to the Emperor's songs. Now he has appeared for the third time. The Emperors of olden times had the power which is without blemish; Emperor Chun had the music, which directs men and animals and even the growth of plants, without force; and in Kublai, your grandson, wisdom shall dwell.'

Chepe and Arik-Buka looked at each other, dumbfounded. This man is more dangerous than Tang Liweng, they both thought, and Chepe cast an icy glance at Yeliu. Restraining himself with an effort, he said in a casual tone: 'Forgive me, O Khan, if I speak now! I have not seen in the yurt the bird of which the astrologer speaks. But perhaps that is because I am only one of your warriors—not a wise man.'

'I didn't notice any bird either,' said Arik-Buka contemptuously.

The Khan took no notice of these remarks. He seemed to have eyes only for Yeliu. Looking at him keenly, he said: 'One who is of my blood should attain to the knowledge which is yours. I wish you to become Kublai's teacher.' The Khan's voice became threatening. 'He shall learn to see what is hidden from me. He shall be able to read what Tatatungo writes out for me. And you shall remain near me always so that I may be able to see which way you lead him.'

Only then did the Khan turn to Chepe. 'And now we shall ride on!' he said.

CHAPTER THREE

The Star in the South

IN the days that followed the Khan allowed his army only brief rests. He seemed to have lost the wish to hold up his progress any longer with 'sieving'. Nevertheless, Chepe was deeply troubled. The astrologer, whom the Khan had appointed to be Kublai's teacher, seemed to him a weird person. The other *Orluks* thought as Chepe did. Arik-Buka, above all, looked upon Yeliu with the greatest distrust. He heard plenty of stories from Chepe and other warriors in which the Chinese and their kind played a pitiable role. He repeated all these to Kublai, always ending by speaking of the astrologer.

'I like these townspeople just as little as you do,' said Kublai. 'But what have you against Yeliu?'

'One can't see through him,' said Arik-Buka.

'I have found his candour astonishing,' said Kublai.

'He knows exactly how best to attain his end. He'd swindle the blue out of the sky! Or perhaps you believe that he really saw the bird which he raves about?'

'I did not see it,' said Kublai, and for the second time his face darkened and burned.

'But he wanted to catch you with that story, and he tried it on you because he noticed that you have weak spots—and that you are taken in by prophecies . . . Once he has got you, he'll also get the Khan. That's what he thinks.'

'The Khan is stronger than he is,' protested Kublai. 'And as for me, well, I'm his grandson just as you are.'

'I know that,' said Arik-Buka, irritated.

'The Khan has nine *Orluks* who are conquering the world for him. Why should he not have a wise man?'

Arik-Buka cut him short. 'But don't become one of those who gaze too much at the stars,' he said. 'Remember what we promised one another on the middle peak of the *Tobu dolo gam*. It would have been better had we sealed our promise with blood.'

'Why?' asked Kublai, moved. 'You are my brother. No one will ever be nearer to me than you.'

Arik-Buka pressed Kublai's arm. 'Never forget that we promised each other to trample on the snake which tries to touch either of us with its cleft tongue. Stick to Chepe as I do!'

'What are you thinking of?' asked Kublai, perplexed. 'How could I ever be anything but a warrior! I like Chepe very much.'

'That's not enough,' said Arik-Buka. 'You must become like him, hard and bright like the point of an arrow. I hate this stranger who is like—water. Believe me, he's against us warriors!'

'Who says that?' asked Kublai fiercely.

'Chepe does. He has an eye like no one else,' said Arik-Buka. 'Don't get too friendly with that man, Kublai! Try to learn as much as possible from him—but in the way one learns from an enemy! And as soon as he tries to say anything against the warriors—promise—you will come to me.'

'I promise you I will,' said Kublai.

It was the night in which Genghis Khan's army had set up camp for the last time before reaching the Dsungarian Gate. Orders had been given for everyone to be called at dawn, but Kublai woke up even earlier. He crept out of the yurt, in which Chepe and Arik-Buka were still sleeping. As he walked out of the door, despite the dim light he immediately saw Yeliu, who was occupied with measuring instruments in the middle of the open space. Kublai went up to him. Yeliu did not interrupt his work. He loosened the screws with his slender hands, moved the metal circles on which were signs, and observed individual stars once more.

When Yeliu turned his apparatus towards the south, Kublai perceived above the horizon the same star which he had seen when setting out from the *Ordo* with Chepe and Arik-Buka. Now the star was shining far more brilliantly.

Kublai grasped Yeliu by the arm and asked him: 'What's the name of that star?'

'That is the Dew Star,' said Yeliu. 'It appears in the fifth moon and is at its brightest on *Moun Tshun* day, the Festival of the Rice Shoots. That is today. Formerly the rice farmers used to walk in procession round their fields at this hour, praying.'

'Why do they no longer do so?'

'Because they're afraid,' said Yeliu.

Kublai pricked up his ears. He hesitated, but then he asked with severity: 'Of whom are they afraid?'

'The horsemen,' said Yeliu. 'The horsemen of the Steppe have burnt their huts and killed many of them.'

A feeling of defiance rose in Kublai. He thought of Halt-sundoriki. 'Why do you say things against the horsemen, knowing that I'm one of them?' he said.

'You asked, and I said what there is to say about it. I would give the Khan the same answer,' replied Yeliu. 'Or perhaps I should first twist and turn some truth before each ear until it suits that ear?'

Kublai tried to observe Yeliu's face closely through the twilight.

'You will one day be lord over the South, but then you will no longer think of revenge.'

Kublai suddenly remembered Arik-Buka's warning—'and that you are taken in by prophecies'—and he said: 'I did not see the bird.'

Yeliu looked at him and said: 'Feng Huang was in the yurt, and he pointed to your heart. Yet your heart is still blind.'

'I will never be anything else but a warrior!' protested Kublai.

'Your time will come only when the time of the warriors is nearing an end,' said Yeliu calmly. 'The rice farmers will not tremble before you.'

At that moment the drums sounded to waken up the camp.

Now I must go to Arik, thought Kublai. I promised him I would come if Yeliu spoke against the horsemen. And he *did* speak against them . . .

But Kublai did not go. Spellbound, he watched the hand of Yeliu, who was finishing his observations just as calmly as if he had not heard the drum-roll.

CHAPTER FOUR

A Volcano in the Steppe

A WHITE mountain gleamed in the plain in front of the Dsungarian Gate, and on bright moonlit nights it glittered with a spectral radiance. From a distance it looked as if the snow-covered summit of a volcano, over which the glow of fire played night after night, had been moved by magic into the middle of the Steppe. A rumbling noise was audible from a considerable distance, and anyone coming from the south at night could see through a crevice into the glowing interior of this strange mountain.

It was the victory yurt which was filled with the jubilant merrymaking of the returned conquerors.

The magician Sorgan-Shira, who had only had to give a sign for the artistic dome-like erection with its white felt-covered roof to be transferred from the banks of the Kerulen to the Dsungarian Gate, had carried out his instructions in time, despite the hurried march of the *tumans*. Now he was the only one missing from the yurt. For Sorgan-Shira was dead. He had been killed by a falling beam when he had been urging on the workmen with loud shouts in the almost completed yurt. The seat immediately beside the Khan's throne was empty. Yet the Khan had not ordered the usual mourning ceremonies. He did not wish to spoil the feast which he had promised his warriors—nine times nine days of drinking and hunting pleasures.

A fire was blazing in the middle of the yurt. Metallic ornamentation and gilded pillars stood out weirdly in the firelight. The horsemen and their women-folk were dancing and laughing

loudly and boisterously; the yurt was ceaselessly shaken with out-breaks of wild joy. Above them all, the Khan sat enthroned on a brocade-covered dais opposite the entrance in the middle of the north wall, the princes and *Orluks* on his right, Burtai and his concubines on his left.

Tankards of many kinds of drinks and valuable plates laden with choice foods stood ready on enormous tables. When Genghis Khan took hold of a tankard, one of the *Orluks* called out a loud 'Ha!' and the musicians beat their instruments for as long as the Khan was drinking. The tankards were filled from the branches of a tree which stood in the middle of the yurt beside the fire. The tree was gold and silver, and numerous tubes hidden in its trunk were fed from inexhaustible tanks. The fountain-tree had many branches, and a different drink flowed from each.

Besides the warriors whom the Khan had honoured by his invitation, and their women-folk, there were only musicians and jugglers to keep the Khan and his guests merry with their per-formances. There were magicians who made goblets and plates move through the air up to the Khan's table without a drop being spilt. The Khan rewarded such clever feats generously, but he dispensed the gifts as one throws scraps to a dog. The feast was for his horsemen, and whenever he bestowed his favour on one of them, all had to listen.

During the banquet the Khan received delegations from all the peoples whom he had conquered up to the present. The dele-gates had to take off their shoes before they entered the yurt. They were severely informed that they were not to dare to let their feet touch the threshold; and before they arrived at the entrance they had to pass through a whole lane of life guard men. These were holding torches and singed the clothing of the new arrivals in order 'to drive away all signs of treachery from the folds'. The delegates had to prostrate themselves before the Khan and touch the ground nine times with their foreheads.

It was a festival of the conquerors, and the vanquished were admitted only in order to impress upon the warriors that the Mongols had been raised up for all time above all peoples by *Menke Kuku Tengri*, the Eternal Blue Heaven, for whom a window had been left in the middle of the dome of the yurt, through which he could look down and keep his eye continually on the great Son of the Steppe.

Kublai and Arik-Buka had never felt themselves so unwanted as during this time, when it seemed as if the horsemen had forgotten their horses. The princes fetched their tiger horses from the pastures every day, and spent hours in the saddle roaming about the new surroundings of the *Ordo*. Chepe had little time for them; the *Orluks* had always to be near the Khan. And what about Yeliu? The Khan always wanted him near him in order to have his counsel at any time.

Kublai's thoughts continually revolved round this enigmatical man, whom he inwardly resisted and who nevertheless attracted him forcibly; who spoke against the warriors; who called Tang Liweng a great man, yet did the opposite of what Tang Liweng had done; and who did not hit back when struck. Was Yeliu a coward with no feelings of honour? Was Yeliu courageous only with words and incapable of any deed? Was this power which he radiated a dubious power? If so, why did the Khan, who had never been deceived in anyone before, listen to him and see in him 'a confidant of the heavens who does not err'? Yet it is on account of Yeliu that I deceive Arik, thought Kublai again and again.

As if he had guessed his thoughts, Arik-Buka said: 'I'm glad the astrologer has so little time for you.'

'No one has time for us,' said Kublai. 'Chepe hasn't either. It looks as if they were never going to ride again.'

'They have been years in the saddle; their horses need rest.'

'Every horseman has three or four horses and need not exact as much from any one horse as from himself.'

'They have been away from the Steppe for a long time. And they have much to tell about the South.'

'About the South, always the South,' said Kublai impatiently. 'There's never a word about the West.'

Arik-Buka pointed to the gaps in the mountain-chain behind which lay the West. 'We are much nearer to the West here than at the Kerulen,' he said. 'One day we shall ride through the Dsungarian Gate.'

'But when?'

Arik-Buka looked at Kublai surprised. 'But you have no account to settle with the West?' he said.

Kublai, confused, looked at his horse's mane. 'From what I could worm out of Chepe,' continued Arik-Buka, 'the South is by no means firmly in our hands yet, at least not all the South. True, the Kingdom of Chin no longer exists, but there's still the Kingdom of Sung. Perhaps there will still be a ride to the South some day.'

'It's all the same to me where we ride to,' Kublai burst out, 'if we only come up against enemies! The more enemies, the better; the better the enemies, the more I'll like it! I'm very much looking forward to a campaign in which blows will be hard on both sides.'

'What do you look forward to in it?' Arik-Buka asked, surprised at the vehemence of his tone.

'I don't know,' replied Kublai, as he set Bosa galloping so hard that it was difficult for Fabo to keep up with him. Kublai knew very well what he expected from a campaign in the West. There he could prove that he was a warrior like Chepe and Arik-Buka. During the ride there and during all the battles everything would be clear and definite, and he would be at his brother's side as formerly, and not standing between Yeliu and Arik.

I love Arik, thought Kublai. But have I not already begun to love this strange man whom Arik hates? Does he not already mean more to me than my own father, who hardly bothers about us at all? Yes, is he not almost as much to me as the Khan?

Kublai noticed with alarm that he was thinking of the ride to the West as a way of escape. He longed for the war because he hoped it would spare him from making a decision which had faced him since Yeliu had come into his life.

CHAPTER FIVE

A Man with a Letter on his Head

WHEN the Khan received ambassadors from abroad all the princes had to be present. Kublai and Arik-Buka found these receptions, which were always carried out in the same form, very tedious. All the ambassadors prostrated themselves before the throne, made hollows in the ground with their knees and their foreheads, presented gifts and stammered lies, saying that they deemed it a favour to be ruled by the kindest of all conquerors; praying that Heaven might grant the ruler many more victories, and so on.

They all say the same, thought Kublai; the conquered do not say what they think. They are changed people. They have lost face. There is nothing worse than to be vanquished.

The ambassadors of the subject peoples came in magnificent clothes, thus lying even before they opened their mouths. For the peoples in whose name they appeared before the Khan had been poor since the *tumans* had laid waste their fields and razed their towns to the ground.

On the thirty-fourth day of the festivities a dishevelled-looking man whom the sentries had captured among the hills round the Dsungarian Gate was brought to the commandant of the life guards. At first glance the commandant took him to be a 'useful person' who had succeeded in living in hiding for a long time. Yet the horsemen who had brought him had declared that he had beckoned to them from far off, having made himself conspicuous, and when he recognized them for Mongols had looked pleased and asked them in broken Mongolian to be brought to the Khan

143

of all Khans. For he was an ambassador, he said, and had an important message to deliver. Even now there was not a trace of fear to be seen in the man. He seemed glad to have arrived at the *Ordo*.

'You an ambassador?' asked the commandant of the life guards, eying the man's ragged clothing. 'Is the master who sent you a penniless beggar, that he lets you go in rags?'

'Oh, no,' said the man; and a roguish smile could be seen under the beard and the crust of dirt which covered his face. In an almost incomprehensible Mongolian, but with extreme energy, he demanded to be conducted to the Khan, and concluded with the statement: 'The Caliph of Bagdad has sent me.'

Thereupon the commandant of the life guard had the man searched for arms, as was done with all strangers, and he himself went to announce this ambassador who had come like a beggar.

'From the Caliph?' asked the Khan, astonished. The Kingdom of the Caliph was the most remote part of the Western world of which the Khan knew.

When Genghis Khan had ascertained that Yeliu was acquainted with the language and writing used in the Kingdom of the Caliph, he gave orders for the peculiar ambassador to be brought in.

All the princes had assembled. Kublai was in great excitement, and whispered to Arik-Buka: 'The West is announcing itself. It is coming to meet us!'

The horsemen noticed with astonishment the cool way in which the ambassador approached the Khan's throne. This man, who had neither splendid attire nor a suite of servants to prove that he was the plenipotentiary of a sovereign, did not throw himself on the ground, but showed his respect merely by making a deep bow. After the Khan had addressed him he tried to deliver his message in Mongolian, but he so distorted the Mongolian words that in spite of his dignified voice and bearing the horsemen burst out in loud laughter. All the *Orluks* and princes laughed. Only the Khan and Yeliu kept a straight face.

'Tell him to speak in his own language,' ordered the Khan.

Meantime the ambassador had looked around him with an offended expression and asked Yeliu if his Mongolian was really so laughable.

'The Khan has never yet heard the language which the Caliph speaks,' said Yeliu, politely bowing.

'Ask him for his message!' ordered the Khan.

The Caliph's ambassador seemed not yet to have recovered from the laughter of the bystanders, and to have little desire to open his mouth again. He pointed to his head. The Khan was unpleasantly surprised at this strange behaviour. He looked inquiringly at Yeliu, and the latter said: 'If the Khan understands you rightly, you have the message in your head, have you not?'

The ambassador nodded.

'And so you intend to give your message verbally?'

The ambassador denied this energetically. Then the same mischievous smile which he had shown to the commandant of the life guards crossed his face, and he said: 'I have the message in my head, yet I have to deliver it in writing, as is customary between great rulers. But my journey was long and full of dangers, and my message is of great importance. The kingdom which lies between your kingdom and that of my master is ruled by Mohammed the Shah, who is an enemy of the Caliph. The message had to be made inaccessible to the Shah's spies. Therefore the Caliph in his wisdom used the skin which covers my head as his writing tablet, and he took a red hot style as pen. First of all he had my head shaved, then he wrote upon it, and then he waited patiently until my hair grew again.'

The mischievous smile remained on the ambassador's face while Yeliu translated; and he enjoyed the murmur of admiration which ran through the yurt.

'So there remains nothing for me to do but have your head shorn for the second time,' said the Khan, and Yeliu translated.

'Your wisdom far surpasses that of the Caliph,' said the ambassador.

A barber was called, and he shaved the ambassador's head. Now written characters could be seen distinctly on the scalp. The ambassador bowed his shorn head before the Khan, and at a sign from the latter Yeliu bent over the strange letter.

Breathless silence reigned in the yurt while Yeliu was reading. When he had read to the end, Yeliu said to the Khan in a voice so low that none of the bystanders could hear him: 'The Caliph offers to make an alliance with you. He proposes that you invade the Shah's country—from the east, and he will do the same from the west. He is prepared to go to war, and share the Shah's kingdom with you.'

Despite eager attention, Kublai had not found it possible to read more than one word from Yeliu's lips. But that one word was the word he had secretly hoped for. It was—'war!' Therefore Kublai was intensely surprised when, after some reflection, the Khan ordered: 'Read aloud what the Caliph has to say to me, so that all may hear it!'

The ambassador, too, was astonished when Yeliu repeated in a loud voice what he had told the Khan. And he cast down his eyes dumbfounded when Yeliu translated to him at the Khan's command: 'Tell the Caliph that I am not in a position to accept this offer. I am not at war with the Shah. I intend to live at peace with him and to exchange the goods of my kingdom for the goods of his kingdom, as I wish to do also with the Caliph and with every other ruler of the West.'

The horsemen held their breath when they heard the Khan speaking like this, and while Yeliu translated their faces became blank. Kublai pressed the tips of his fingers into his palms until they hurt. He looked from Yeliu to the Khan, then to Arik-Buka . . . Chepe alone returned his glance. It was only a fleeting flicker of the black fire beneath the broad forehead, but it sufficed to show Kublai that Chepe was pleased with the Khan's answer.

CHAPTER SIX

Thousand-Moon-Bear

KUBLAI and Arik-Buka were invited by Mangu and Hulagu, their two elder brothers, to stalk a bear with them the next day. Mangu had discovered the tracks in a ravine. They led to a cave.

On the journey to the ravine Kublai said to Mangu: 'It will surely be some time before the Caliph's ambassador sets off on his return journey.'

'I don't think so,' said Mangu.

'Mustn't he have his hair grown first?'

'The Khan will have it grown in a few hours, as soon as the courtesy period is over,' said Mangu; and in his eyes was the same haughty gleam which Kublai had seen in Chepe's eyes when Yeliu had finished translating the Khan's reply to the Caliph's ambassador.

'Can that be done so quickly—making hair grow?'

'Amongst the "useful" there are some who are often really efficient,' said Mangu. 'Chinese barbers can do real wonders. They transform bald heads so cleverly that no one would doubt the genuineness of the hair. The burnt-in letter is better hidden under a well-fitting wig than under hair which is suspiciously thin.'

'*Bolna!*' cried Kublai. This means: 'Very good!'

'Chepe put the plan into the Khan's mind. And the Khan considered it the best way to get rid of one who was waiting for hair to grow.'

'Then will the Khan get rid of the ambassador quickly?'

Arik-Buka joined in. 'Do you think he wants to feed a spy for long in the *Ordo*?'

'A spy? But he's an ambassador!'

'A rejected ambassador,' said Hulagu.

'But the Khan isn't at war with the Caliph!'

'Not yet,' said Mangu.

'Nor even with the Shah!'

Mangu looked at Kublai with pity.

'He even declared that he wished to live at peace with him!' said Kublai.

'It seems to me,' said Mangu derisively, 'that you don't listen with the ears of a warrior when the Khan says something.'

'You think too much of your ears!' said Kublai, offended.

Hulagu laughed. 'Don't take it badly, Kublai,' he said. 'But all the horsemen understand the Khan's answer to the Caliph to be: "We don't need you; we can do it alone".'

'Above all, it means: I won't share with you!' said Mangu.

'And perhaps the Khan has certain hopes with regard to the wig; it's always removable, and therefore it could happen that the Shah's spies would still get a sight of the letter, and that's very important for the Khan!'

Kublai looked at Arik-Buka, who nodded and said: 'Did you not notice, then, how all the horsemen suddenly put on a false expression of face?'

'Yes, I noticed it,' said Kublai, embarrassed. 'But, then, the Khan himself had a frank expression.'

'That is *his* way of dissembling,' said Hulagu.

'And Yeliu spoke in a tone of voice which dispelled any doubt as to the credibility of his words.'

'Yeliu can do that all right,' said Mangu. 'And he did it so excellently that I would advise everybody to be on his guard against him. It seems he can use words to more effect than anyone.'

Kublai looked in front of him, annoyed. Arik-Buka rode up to him and slapped him on the shoulder. 'We shall not have to wait much longer, Kublai,' he said. 'Soon you'll have enemies enough before you.'

'For the present we have to be satisfied with a bear,' said Mangu. 'It's not far to the gorge now.'

They saw fresh tracks which led to the cave. At an appropriate distance they dismounted and tied their horses to a tree. Mangu examined the ground. 'He's at home,' he said.

A cleft, no wider than a man's shoulders, formed the entrance to the cave. The princes now exchanged only a few whispered words.

'I will tickle him out,' said Mangu. 'As soon as he turns on me, I will clear out of the cave. Then he's yours.'

He drew his *purbu* and was about to disappear into the cave when Kublai suddenly said aloud: 'That bear must be an unusual fellow!'

The three others turned round indignantly, and Mangu hissed at Kublai: 'Not so loud, please! The bear——'

'It's not a bear,' said Kublai, who was eagerly examining the tracks. Mangu, Hulagu and Arik-Buka looked at each other and shook their heads. Arik-Buka said: 'And what is it, then?'

'I don't know yet,' said Kublai.

'Perhaps there's a new kind of cave animal here at the Dsungarian Gate,' said Mangu from above.

'There's certainly something not quite right with your eyes,' jibed Hulagu, examining the tracks more closely. 'If these aren't the tracks of bears! Here's the left hind-paw mark quite distinctly—and there's the right one!'

'And what about a front paw?' asked Kublai.

Now all four searched very zealously.

'It's strange,' said Mangu. 'There's not a track of a front paw.'

'It seems to be a bear which always walks upright,' said Kublai.

'Perhaps a dancing bear which has escaped,' scoffed Mangu. 'It's a puzzling business!'

Mangu, Hulagu and Arik-Buka became eagerly intent upon the tracks again.

'Meantime I'll visit the two-legged bear,' said Kublai.

'*Yirr, yirr!*' a voice called at that moment from the entrance to the cave. *Yirr, yirr!* in the Mongol language means: Come on in!

The princes jumped up as if a ghost had addressed them. But

there at the entrance to the cave stood a bear which could speak. He had not a bear's voice, but had said the words '*Yirr, Yirr!*' in a high-pitched tone. The princes stared at the bear which was not a bear, for it was a man covered up to his neck in a bear's skin. He was a huge man, for the bear's skin fitted him, and he must have been a very old man because he had white hair which hung down to his shoulders, and a long white beard with a greenish gleam in it.

'I haven't much to offer you,' said the strange cave-bear, 'but come in!'

Without further ceremony he started to creep back into the cave in advance of the princes; and his appearance and whole demeanour were so impressive that the princes followed him. In the beginning the cleft in the rock was narrow, but then it became higher and more spacious, and at the end of the passage there was more room than in a yurt. A low, flat stone in the middle served as a table. The bear-man sat down at it and invited his guests to be seated too. Then he put his hand behind him and took grass-seeds and roots and a few honey-combs out of a niche in the rock and laid them all on the table.

'An old bear no longer brings much home,' he said, with a smile. 'Eat!'

There was not much to eat; the princes awkwardly nibbled a few seeds or a root. At last Mangu plucked up courage and said: 'We will come back again and bring you something more suitable to a bear. A *karasulta* antelope will do you a long time.'

The bear-man shook his head. 'A bear who gathers seeds and roots doesn't touch game,' he said.

'How long have you been a bear, then?' asked Kublai, who was less embarrassed than the others at the strange apparition.

'Since a thousand moons ago,' said the bear-man dreamily. 'I haven't counted them.'

'We should like to call you by your name. Won't you tell us your name?'

'I have forgotten it,' said the bear with the greenish shimmering beard.

'Have you any objection if we call you "Thousand-Moon-Bear"?'

'I think that's a good name,' said the ancient man.

'If you're so prone to forgetting,' said Arik-Buka, amused, 'I suppose you've also forgotten how you came here?'

'I have not forgotten that,' said Thousand-Moon-Bear. The paws moved, and two huge hands appeared out of two slits.

'For many years these did only what they wanted to,' said Thousand-Moon-Bear. 'It's only since I started gathering with them that I'm master over my hands.'

'And what did you do with them in the past?'

'What do the hands of a robber do?' asked Thousand-Moon-Bear.

As the princes looked at him in astonishment, he continued: 'I was Robber Nameless, of whom songs have been sung. I crept away from those songs.'

'You could be taken for a monk from Tibet,' said Mangu, who found Thousand-Moon-Bear's talk uncomfortable. 'You only lack the string of beads for drawling prayers on.'

'Gathering grasses is a good practice instead of that,' said Thousand-Moon-Bear, and he smiled again. 'But now I will tell you about Robber Nameless, who knew the Desert as none other, and about the promise which the Desert made him. It promised him that it would never show him anything but a friendly face, and at most would only play a little joke on him now and then. By a little joke the Desert meant sandstorms in summer and blizzards in winter. The Desert kept its word and let Robber Nameless survive all the blizzards. And it had put on its friendly face when Robber Nameless carried out a robbery which proved to be his last one. He fell upon a caravan though it was swarming with horsemen. As long as he had a weapon he fought a good fight. And when he had to flee it was a great flight. The pursuers did not hold out. But then everything great came to an end. His horse, the best a man had ever ridden, stumbled into a *tabargan* and lay there with its foreleg broken. Robber Nameless remembered the last well he had met. The next one would be a good ten days distant on foot. So he opened a vein in his horse and drank. Then he stood up. He did not take the water-bag from his saddle. He had drunk the last drop in it as soon as he had caught sight of the caravan. When the horse was dead

Robber Nameless looked at the Desert. It had a friendly face and said: "There will be no sandstorm." It said "sandstorm", for it was summer . . . and the sun was long in the sky. On the third day Robber Nameless suddenly found a man beside him who was not staggering but was walking erect and still had enough strength to support Robber Nameless. And this man said: "Don't worry—I'm your *anda*."

'Robber Nameless had been a solitary all his life, and he shook his head.

' "Everyone has his *anda*," the unknown man said to him, "but many only recognize him late."

'Robber Nameless cast a furtive glance at the man who alleged he was his *anda*. "You are a complete stranger to me," he protested, "at the very most your voice . . ."

' "You see," said the *anda*, "at least there's something you remember."

' "But why are you here at all?" asked Robber Nameless.

' "I'd like very much to be present," said the *anda*, and he winked significantly.

' "At what?"

' "When you begin to live."

'Thereupon Robber Nameless became angry, although he was almost without strength. "You see how things are with me," he said. "I can scarcely stand on my legs and I have blood in my mouth. Leave me alone! I have always been alone!"

'The *anda* smiled. "You were never alone," he said. "I was always with you."

'Robber Nameless pricked up his ears. Now he recognized the voice correctly, and he knew by it that the other was not lying. "You really believe I shall not go under?" he asked expectantly. "That there's still a way out?"

' "So you don't want to die?" asked the *anda*.

' "It is still too soon," admitted Robber Nameless.

' "Do you not think that those people whom Robber Nameless struck with his sword also——"

' "Until now I never had time to consider that," interjected Robber Nameless. "My hands were always quicker than I was."

' "How often were your hands quicker than you were?"

' "I never had time to count. My hands were often simply insatiable. I had to do what they wanted."

' "How much longer will you let yourself be ruled by your hands?"

'Robber Nameless had to sit down because he was too weak.

' "Oh, my voracious hands," he groaned. "They have brought death to so many people!" He beat his forehead on the sand. The *anda* bent over him and whispered: "And if someone should come tomorrow and say: 'Drink!' "

'Robber Nameless jumped up. "Give me—give me a drink!" he cried greedily. The *anda* calmed him. "Tomorrow . . . tomorrow . . .!" he said.

' "I do not want to die," whispered Robber Nameless, "and never again shall anyone die through me . . ." His head fell upon his hand, and after a while he noticed that his hand was wet, and when he licked it, it was bitter salt . . .

'The next morning a caravan picked him up, and as he had no weapons, no one thought he was a robber.

'The leader of the caravan took him with him. At the edge of the desert the man who had been Robber Nameless recovered. He parted from the caravan.

'Hitherto I have lived like a blood-thirsty animal, he thought. And he decided that he would go about in the skin of such an animal for the rest of his life, so that he would always be reminded of this. He wandered about until he came upon hunters who had just killed a bear. And with the gold which he found in his pocket he bought the skin of the bear, cured it and then went on searching until he found this cave. And since then he has been here and has got the name of Thousand-Moon-Bear from you.'

'And the *anda*?' asked Kublai.

The three other princes thought this question silly, but Thousand-Moon-Bear said with delight: 'He comes often. Oh, he's a clever one.'

'I think it's time for us to go,' said Mangu, morosely.

'A bad host,' said Hulagu, when they had mounted their horses again, 'and a bad story.'

'It makes one think,' said Kublai.

'It's a bad story just for that reason,' said Mangu.

L

'He calls that living!' said Arik-Buka. 'Grass seeds, roots . . . and he has hands with which he could throw over a horse or strangle a tiger!'

'We must see that we ferret out something sensible, a wolf at least,' said Mangu. '*Yabonah!*'

'*Yabonah!*' chimed in Hulagu and Arik-Buka, as they galloped off. Kublai's horse joined in their gallop. But they only came upon a herd of Gurush antelope, which scampered off before the riders. Mangu, Hulagu and Arik-Buka were in bad humour when the hunt was over. On the ride home they made Kublai the target for their sneers.

'Thousand-Moon-Bear seems to have made an impression on you.'

'One doesn't meet a person like that every day,' said Kublai.

'I do not think that the Khan would consider a man like that to be useful?'

'Well, he doesn't take anything from anyone,' said Kublai.

'I consider him dangerous,' said Mangu.

'But he isn't that any longer,' objected Arik-Buka.

'You misunderstand me,' said Mangu. 'He is dangerous in a special way. Just imagine, if it suddenly occurred to everyone to live as this man does, the Khan would have no more warriors. The grass-seed man gives infernally bad example. He does with his hands just what pleases him.'

'A few such people—what harm can they do?' said Kublai.

'A warrior horseman thinks otherwise!' said Mangu sharply. 'One who has been born a man of the Steppe has no right to creep into a cave. He cheats the Khan of . . . just think of those enormous hands!'

'And of that white beard!' said Kublai ironically.

'You can use words nearly as well as the astrologer,' said Mangu, irritated. 'You're an apt pupil!'

'Why are you all against him?' asked Kublai.

Mangu looked severely at Kublai. 'If someone killed all your relatives and bound you to a post to be mocked at by everyone, would you enter the service of that man as soon as you had been freed from the post?'

Kublai could not endure Mangu's glance for long. Mangu

laughed contemptuously. 'When he was fixed ready to have his beard singed off, I thought it very funny,' he said.

'And I was pleased when it didn't come to that,' replied Kublai.

'It would have been better if it had come to that than that he should swathe you in his beautiful beard!'

'Or in his beautiful words,' added Hulagu. And when Kublai ceased to answer back, Mangu added: 'A man who can't even use a bow and arrow—how can he be a fit teacher for a Son of the Steppe?'

They have nothing but contempt for him, thought Kublai, and they make me feel it . . . Lost in his thoughts, he rode on, and all the way home his thoughts revolved round the man whom all his brothers were against. And Chepe too, and all the horsemen.

CHAPTER SEVEN

The Victory Yurt

THE Khan alone seemed to have nothing against Yeliu. He sent for him every day and questioned him about countries and people, even about those which his spies had already reported on.

'The day will come when he will trust Beautiful Beard more than his warriors!' whispered the princes. 'And it's bad enough that Kublai is his pupil!' Particularly Juchi and Jagatai, the Khan's eldest sons, expressed themselves unfavourably about Yeliu whenever the conversation turned on him. 'If a man has never hit the mark with an arrow, how can he do so with his thoughts? Cage-people have only crooked thoughts. That is because towns have so many nooks and corners!' they said.

One day the father Tuli spoke to his son Kublai about the astrologer. Kublai was all the more surprised at this, as Tuli had hardly bothered about him or Arik-Buka up till then; in fact, just as little as he bothered about Mangu and Hulagu. Tuli regarded his sons as sons of Genghis Khan; he did not claim them for himself. The Khan had entrusted Tuli with the supreme command of the whole army. He could not have found anyone more suitable. Tuli's bravery and judgement in battle were proverbial amongst the Mongols. He had often proved that he was willing to risk his life for the least of his warriors.

'How is your tongue?' Tuli asked Kublai derisively.

Kublai did not take the sarcasm seriously.

'Let's hope it won't be so overpowered as to make you mix up Mongolian words with other words, as happens with your teacher every day!'

'Yeliu is no Mongol, and it's asking too much to expect him to become one,' said Kublai.

'I've heard that you're practising writing a great deal too,' continued Tuli. 'What will the arrows which are waiting for your hand to speed them say to that?'

'That will be seen—and I hope soon!' said Kublai.

'We'll hear about it—by and by,' said Tuli.

Since the day Yeliu read the message from the Caliph on the head of the ambassador, he had been instructing Kublai in the beautiful yurt which had been erected for him by order of the Khan. 'You will be undisturbed there,' the Khan had said ... Why should I worry about the jibes of the others? thought Kublai. They scent treachery and malice in everything; even Thousand-Moon-Bear appears dangerous to them ... One evening Kublai told Yeliu about the strange hermit.

'They say he gives a bad example,' he said.

'I understand their saying that.'

'They even say that he's dangerous.'

Yeliu smiled. 'He makes people think, and that is not harmless,' he said.

'Above all they say that such a person cannot be reckoned as among the useful.'

'They are right,' said Yeliu. 'But whether he is considered useful or not is not what decides the worth of a man.'

'In what does the worth of a man consist?' asked Kublai.

'In how far he gets on his way,' said Yeliu. 'Thousand-Moon-Bear, it seems to me, has got pretty far. He has even become another person, and few attain to that. He sets a good example.'

'But if no one sees it, is not his life devoid of meaning?'

'There is no life devoid of meaning,' said Yeliu.

'But Thousand-Moon-Bear does nothing which is of benefit to anyone but himself,' objected Kublai.

'He does not think one evil thought,' said Yeliu.

'Is that something, then?' asked Kublai, in the tone of voice in which his brothers usually questioned him. At this Yeliu looked at him attentively. 'They try to perplex you, don't they?' he said.

'They all distrust you,' said Kublai, taken by surprise. 'They have no respect for the thoughts which you think.'

Yeliu smiled again. 'That is not surprising. My thoughts are different from theirs,' he said.

'They say your thoughts are crooked.'

'My thoughts very often take roundabout routes.'

'And they say: "How can a man who has never hit the mark with an arrow, do so with his thoughts?"' Kublai looked at Yeliu earnestly. 'I do not think as they do,' he said vehemently, 'but I would prefer it if my teacher could also hit the mark with an arrow, and not only with his thoughts.' He hesitated a little. 'I could easily instruct you in shooting with a bow and arrow.'

'I can do so a little,' said Yeliu, smiling.

'You can use a bow and arrow?' asked Kublai excitedly. 'Can you hit a man from a hundred paces?'

'I have never yet aimed at a man,' said Yeliu.

'Or a horse, or a tiger?'

'I have never aimed at a tiger either.'

'What have you aimed your arrow at?'

'At a smaller target,' said Yeliu. 'If you like I can show it to you some time. The victory yurt would be a good place for that.'

It was late in the night and the camp was sleeping when Yeliu and Kublai went over from Yeliu's yurt to the victory yurt. It stood empty, for the great festival had come to an end a week before. Kublai had his bow and quiver full of arrows with him.

'I need only two arrows,' said Yeliu when they entered the yurt and Kublai offered him the bow and the full quiver.

It was a bright, clear night, and only the light of the stars fell through the round opening in the dome. The gilded pillars cast a pale radiance.

The pillars would be a good target, thought Kublai, but only for someone who could really shoot an arrow.

Yeliu took the bow and laid an arrow on the string.

'And what will you aim at?' whispered Kublai.

'This arrow shall be my mark,' said Yeliu. 'And now please have patience for a moment.'

Yeliu bent his bow, the arrow sped off and hit the most distant pillar. It was the pillar immediately behind the Khan's throne.

He has hit it, thought Kublai joyfully. I heard it strike. And he was about to fetch the arrow, but Yeliu held him back. 'The arrow shall be my target,' he repeated. 'The second arrow shall join the first.'

'But the arrow can't be seen,' said Kublai. 'How can you aim at it?'

'I beg you to have a little patience,' said Yeliu gently.

Kublai thought of the target behind which Sorgan-Shira had stood directing his arrow by calling out. But no one was standing behind the Khan's throne. The pillar was silent, and not the slightest trace of the arrow was to be seen. Kublai listened as the second arrow whizzed off, and he heard the sound of splintering.

'Now you may go,' said Yeliu. 'It's the breadth of a hand above the upper edge of the throne.'

Kublai could see the arrow only when he almost knocked his face against it. A shudder passed through him, for it looked as if three arrows were stuck in the wooden pillar. But when he touched them he noticed that the outer ones were the halves of one arrow. He immediately broke off the split arrow from the post.

'None of us can do that,' said Kublai, when he came back to Yeliu.

'Put the split arrow into your quiver!' said Yeliu. 'Perhaps one day you will find yourself in circumstances when it will be good to be reminded of this hour.'

None of those who speak against him can split an arrow in the dark! thought Kublai. 'I will make them shut up!' he said angrily.

Yeliu made a gesture of protest. 'The Khan knows what I am capable of,' he said quietly, 'and now you have seen it.' He turned towards the exit. 'It's best if no one hears about this arrow shooting,' he said.

'No one shall hear about it,' promised Kublai, although he did not understand why he should not hit back.

When they had left the victory yurt Yeliu said: 'Now go to Chepe's yurt! Before the moon is full you will be riding off with him.'

'How do you know that?' asked Kublai, stopping.

'There are signs,' said Yeliu.

'And you wish me to ride with Chepe?' Kublai pointed to the silver band on his wrist. 'I killed the man who gave me this band. I did not wish to kill him; nevertheless, he still haunts me. Will many others keep haunting me?'

'One day you will preserve more lives than the Khan and his horsemen destroy,' said Yeliu. 'You will one day protect the gardens. It is a good thing if you first see for yourself how quickly gardens can become deserts. You cannot learn that in my yurt. You must be there when they ride forth and invade the Garden of Allah.'

'Arik will be there. He will leave nothing undone to prejudice me against you. He hates you as no other hates you.'

'As long as you love him you will be stronger than he is,' said Yeliu.

'Your words are not always easy to understand,' said Kublai.

'You must have a little patience with me. Once you get as far as splitting arrows . . .' Yeliu did not finish the sentence.

They walked across the open space. It could be seen from the stars that morning was not far off. When they had parted Kublai approached the yurt silently in order not to waken Chepe and Arik-Buka. Then he heard the two talking in a whisper to each other.

Chepe said: 'You should go to sleep, Arik!'

'I cannot sleep when Kublai is not here! In the past we always went to sleep together and wakened together. That damned astrologer! He's bringing us farther and farther apart.'

'As soon as we ride off, he's finished with,' Chepe consoled him. 'War will make a man of Kublai—up till now he's been a boy.'

Kublai started. He listened as Chepe continued: 'At present he listens with wonder to what another with a skilful tongue says to him. In battle he'll get narrow eyes which let in nothing that could confuse him . . . panther's eyes!'

'I doubt if that will ever happen!'

'Why? He has the making of a warrior in him.'

'He hasn't only the making of a warrior in him,' said Arik-Buka. 'There's something in him which incites me against him.'

'There will be an end of that once the red intoxication of battle gets him,' said Chepe, trying to console Arik-Buka.

'He falls for everything he hears from the astrologer. That foreigner is ruining him. A horse which is spoilt with rice and bread forgets how to scrape grass from under the snow. Then it can't last out. I'm against all who are soft. Must I be against Kublai?'

'In war he'll learn very quickly what is important and whom he can rely upon.'

'How I hate him, that renegade!' said Arik-Buka violently. 'Today he serves one, tomorrow another! And why? Because he wants to rule from behind.'

'You're right,' said Chepe. 'But we'll keep a watch out and see that that moon-darkener does not cloud the Khan's vision.'

'Above all, we must tear Kublai away from the claws of that traitor—before he himself becomes a traitor.'

'We shall soon be riding,' said Chepe, 'then he will no longer be in danger. Now go to sleep!'

'I will have to kill him,' said Arik-Buka gloomily.

These last words gave Kublai such a shock that he stood motionless for quite a while. Then he felt for the split arrow as if for something to hold on to. His hand jerked back as soon as he touched it.

He is bringing us farther and farther apart . . . Arik is right, thought Kublai; and Arik loves me so much that he would sooner kill me than let me become a traitor. I will never part from Arik, I will ride and ride and get narrow eyes like a panther—like Arik and Chepe.

He stood motionless outside the yurt for a long time, and when he crept into his sleeping place at last, he was shivering.

CHAPTER EIGHT

A Singed Beard

A FEW days later a group of horsemen arrived from the West. It was a delegation of Mongols whom the Khan had sent to the Shah after the fall of the Imperial City. Their leader was named Undur, and he was a general known to every warrior. The Khan received him at once, and having heard his report, ordered all the royal princes and *Orluks*, and the leaders of every *tuman* and of every division of a thousand men, to come to the victory yurt. By nightfall they were to appear under arms—as a warrior mounts his horse when he is not expecting to return home: that was how the order was worded.

The centre of the yurt was in darkness, for the great fire of peace had not been lighted. Torch-bearers stood near the wall of the yurt. From the torches a dim light fell on the faces and the iron helmets. As the Khan entered the warriors stood motionless. The Khan mounted the dais and sat on the throne. He looked down at the warriors for a long time. Then he began: 'I note indeed that your ears are open. So nothing that Undur, my ambassador to Mohammed, has to say to you will escape you. Keep your eyes open too, so that it does not happen with you as it happened with me.' The Khan's voice trembled. 'I no longer recognized my ambassador. Let Undur come in!'

As Undur walked up to the throne every neck was craned to watch him.

'Throw the lights on Undur's face!' ordered the Khan.

Then everyone saw it. Instead of the beard which had adorned

Undur's chin, the lower half of his face was covered with the scars of burns.

'Now report what you have already told me!' ordered the Khan.

Undur spoke: 'I did not get as far as the Shah. He, too, has his kingdom secured with fortresses just as the Emperor of Chin had his. As I had not come as a warrior but as an ambassador, I had myself announced to the commandant of the first fortress which we came to. It was the fortress of Otrar. And through the interpreter I said that I was an ambassador of the Khan. "You are a spy", said the commandant roughly, "a dirty barbarian of the Steppe!" I let it be said to him that the haughty dragon would have reason to repent. Then he singed my beard off and said that it was his duty to keep the stink of the Steppe far from the gardens of the West.'

An angry growl ran through the yurt.

'Now, my stinking Sons of the Steppe,' said the Khan, 'I think we have heard enough.'

The growl became louder.

'And our horses have been feeling bored long enough.' The Khan stood up. He was trembling with rage as he cried: 'What is done to one of you, is done to me. What one of the Shah's men makes bold to do, is done by Mohammed. We will turn our attention to him. That man is called the Shadow of Allah. We will free Allah of his shadow, even before the moon is full.'

The Khan's words were drowned in a wild outburst of shouts which shook the yurt.

'Quench the torches!' cried the Khan. And when the yurt was enveloped in darkness, he cried: 'Lift up your eyes to *Menke Kuku Tengri*! I will speak with Heaven! Call that he may hear me!'

'*Tengri! Tengri!*' cried the warriors.

'Hear, O Eternal Blue Heaven!' cried the Khan. 'When we marched forth to take revenge for all the outrages which the South had inflicted upon the Steppe, I prayed you to give us all the good spirits to accompany us. You did so, and we thank you for it!'

'*Tengri! Tengri!*' cried the warriors.

'Clearly, the malice of the West is still greater,' continued the Khan, raising his voice. 'So, Eternal Blue Heaven, who has destined us to be victorious, let not only the good spirits accompany us to the West; let the wicked ones, too, be in our service there! Make us Sons of the Steppe your scourge by which you will scatter the rich and subdue the arrogant!'

'*Tengri! Tengri!*' cried the warriors. And as they looked up at the sky through the round dome window of the yurt, they imagined they saw the stars swaying. But the stars were peacefully following their courses. It was the victory yurt which was swaying, shaken by the wild cries.

CHAPTER NINE

Horses' Boots

WHEN the *tumans* were ready to march the summer sky suddenly darkened. Cold flakes whirled down from the black clouds,
and everything was shrouded in white—the iron helmets, and the
saddles, and the hand grenades which had been taken apart and
packed on to yaks and camels. *Kohinar Salkin*, the icy north wind,
made a devilish music at the same time.

The Khan noticed the faces of the warriors becoming gloomy.
His own expression darkened. He called the princes and *Orluks*
into his yurt. He sent for Yeliu too, and when they were all
assembled, the Khan said: 'I have never started anything contrary to the direction of Heaven.' He looked around him inquiringly.

Juchi, the eldest prince, raised his voice: 'Heaven is certainly
against our riding forth—but perhaps one should not take Heaven
too seriously.' Saying this, he looked askance at Yeliu.

'Juchi has spoken for us all,' confirmed Chepe.

'Heaven has humours too,' said Tuli.

'And what have you to say?' asked the Khan, turning to Yeliu.

'He who calls upon Heaven should listen to Heaven,' said
Yeliu firmly. The *Orluks* murmured, and Jagatai said: 'Perhaps
he's afraid that his yurt is not lined warmly enough. What about
leaving him at home with the women?'

'You have spoken loudly,' said the Khan reprovingly, 'but
not as my son. Yeliu, who understands the language of the
heavens, shall interpret the sign.'

'I already know what his interpretation will be,' said Tuli

violently. 'Riding to war is a matter for warriors, not for wise men!'

The Khan silenced Tuli with a glance. 'What does heaven wish to say to me?' he asked Yeliu.

'The winter king has invaded the realm of the summer king, when he was not expected,' declared Yeliu. 'The North will overpower the West.'

The princes and *Orluks* looked at each other astonished. Jagatai burst out: 'You are for riding forth—you?'

'Heaven is for it,' said Yeliu. 'My thoughts are of no importance at all.'

During the uncertain silence which followed the Khan announced: 'In future Yeliu shall have first voice in the Council.'

Then he gave his army leaders orders for the start. He dismissed them all except Chepe.

'You have heard that we will pay the Shah our visit from the north,' said the Khan to his youngest *Orluk*.

'Yes,' said Chepe. 'Over the Hungry Steppe and the Forty Rivers.'

'Don't worry,' said the Khan. 'We have bridges with us in our baggage train, and as for the Hungry Steppe, I have heard that it does not equal the Gobi.'

'I mentioned the difficulties,' said Chepe, with a merry face, 'because I'm not interested in very comfortable journeys.'

'I am glad to hear you speak like that,' said the Khan.

Chepe pricked up his ears. But he did not show his excitement and said quietly: 'It's said that the northern route is the only one for horses and riders. There is no choice.'

'Perhaps there is a second route, even if Yeliu knows nothing about it.'

'Possibly,' said Chepe casually. 'All the routes have not yet been found.'

'It would be well worth while,' said the Khan, 'to have a second route from which some "stinking Sons of the Steppe" might emerge unexpectedly behind the Shah's back. It would cause great confusion. If there was one single *tuman* which would suddenly appear like ghosts in the south . . .'

'It is not numbers which matter,' said Chepe, when the Khan did not continue.

'You know what lies to the south from here?' asked the Khan significantly.

'The Roof of the World,' said Chepe, without hesitation. 'But there are said to be two passes over it.'

'Yeliu says that a herd of white-nosed horses tramples to death anyone who attempts to cross them.'

'Yeliu is a great man for fine words,' said Chepe. 'He probably means the snow which rolls down from the mountain-tops and in doing so makes a faint thundering sound, as happens in all mountain regions.'

'That is exactly what he means,' said the Khan. 'And blizzards too.'

'And when we have the Roof of the World behind us, what comes then?' asked Chepe.

'The Garden of Allah,' said Genghis Khan, looking buoyantly happy.

'I have a great wish to get into that garden through a door which has not yet been discovered,' said Chepe. Then he suddenly stopped short.

'You are thinking of your *tuman*?'

'I am not troubled about my *tuman*,' said Chepe. 'It consists of devils who would shrink from no hell. But I am thinking of two young warriors who have their first campaign before them. I promised to secure permission for them to ride with me.'

At this the Khan laughed. 'Do you think that I fetched Kublai and Arik-Buka only that they might sleep with you in your yurt?' he said.

The Khan noticed that Chepe still remained standing there, looking thoughtful. 'Or do you doubt whether the neighing of the white-nosed horses would be suitable for their ears?' he asked.

'For Arik it is all right, I know that.'

'And what about Kublai?'

'He hears with other ears,' said Chepe, and a shadow passed over his face. 'And I don't know what he would think of a route which in his teacher's opinion does not exist.'

'There's nothing more simple than to ask him,' the Khan decided, 'and it's best to do so in Yeliu's presence.'

The Khan sent for the two. When Yeliu and Kublai arrived the Khan was in the act of sewing together a strip of the hide of a yak, to make a wide tube.

'Come here, Kublai!' said the Khan. 'Here's something to learn which will be useful to you in the near future.'

'What is it meant to be?' asked Kublai.

'A horse's boot,' explained the Khan. 'I have invented a boot into which a horse can stick its leg.'

'What does a horse need boots for?' asked Kublai, surprised.

'For a route which does not exist,' said the Khan, giving Yeliu a wink. 'I imagine that such boots are just the right thing with which to trample the herd of white-nosed horses. What do you think of them, Astrologer?'

Yeliu answered without hesitation: 'Since I have been in your vicinity, I have seen that you make many things possible which formerly no one considered possible.'

How well he knows how to chime in with the Khan! thought Chepe contemptuously.

The Khan continued eagerly sewing his horse-boot. 'And what do you think of this business, Kublai?' he asked.

'I wouldn't for anything miss the fun of seeing horses in boots.'

'You'll miss a lot of your lessons,' said the Khan good-humouredly.

'Perhaps I can learn something on the way. I don't know many words of the Shah's language yet.'

'In the kingdom of the beard-burner,' said Chepe mockingly, 'you will at last be able to speak the language which you have practised in Sorgan-Shira's school and which I hope you have not forgotten in the astrologer's yurt.'

'You'll just see,' said Kublai, with shining eyes.

'I see that you two pull well together,' said the Khan, laughing. 'But if you prefer to march with me . . . and with Yeliu?'

'I have made my choice,' said Kublai firmly.

'Against Yeliu?' asked the Khan, surprised at the brusqueness of his tone.

M

'I've decided to ride with Chepe,' said Kublai. 'Arik and I have had that in mind a long time.'

'Where shall we report to you again?' asked Chepe, his face beaming with happiness.

'Before Samarkand,' said the Khan, as sure of himself as if he had already won the victory. 'The beard-burner lives in Samarkand.'

CHAPTER TEN

The Herd of White-nosed Horses

THE nearer Chepe's *tuman* came to the chain of mountains in the south, the higher rose the peaks. In the mountain valleys to right and left the walls stood almost perpendicular.

Chepe had ten thousand horsemen with him, and there was a second horse for every man. A long procession of specially strong yaks dragged the fodder which was to save the horses from starvation on the Roof of the World. The horsemen were to live on the yaks which were freed of their burdens or were unable to go on . . . That had been arranged. Yaks would not be needed in the Garden of Allah—if only they succeeded in getting the horses across, that would suffice.

The way up to the Kisil Art Pass had been reconnoitred. Below the snow-line the mountain tribes had marked it out in a strange manner with low fences made from the horns of the native mountain sheep which were straight as rods. These fences had been set up against wolves. But wolves could not get at the *tuman* anyway—either at the horses with their hooves hard as iron or at the yaks with their heavy hair coats which hung down to the ground. Chepe kept watching out for the herd of white-nosed horses. 'They seem to be asleep,' he said to the princes, pointing to the motionless mass of white which towered up at each side. 'We will not waken them.' And he ordered the boots which the Khan had invented to be put on the horses, though the horses were still stamping along cheerfully and not sinking much above the fetlocks in the snow. But Chepe had noticed slight traces of blood; the snow had formed a hard crust which rasped and chafed the fetlocks.

'They're a good thing!' said Kublai approvingly, as he tied the thongs above Bosa's hooves.

'Yes, very good,' agreed Chepe. 'But it will come down on ourselves first.' He looked ahead to where the great mass of seemingly endless white lay waiting for them and said casually: 'The splendid thing is that you two are here—you inseparables! You needn't worry because you missed the Gobi. The Gobi is merely a playground compared with the Roof of the World.'

'Up to now it has been just fun,' said Kublai.

Chepe pointed to the red rim around the hoof-prints and said seriously: 'Now it's really beginning!'

The herd of white-nosed horses did not move. They seemed to be benumbed in their sleep. The panting of the horses, which sank to their knees in the snow at every step, did not disturb them; neither did the bellowing of the yaks which were being killed with dagger thrusts as they became useless. The baggage caravan was dwindling. But the horses, covered with the shaggy hides of the slaughtered yaks, continued to struggle on. Chepe ordered longer and longer periods of rest for the *tuman*. He gave himself hardly any rest.

'What lungs he must have!' said Kublai to Arik-Buka, as they watched Chepe tramping from one *arban* to another during a rest period.

'One can learn a lot from him,' said Arik-Buka. He was as exhausted as Kublai and pressed up against him until he felt warmth and stopped shivering.

No snow-flakes were falling from the sky, yet the snow became deeper from day to day. The snow-boots were no longer of any use.

The herd of white-nosed horses did not move. But they were not dead; their breath cut into the lungs of the horses and the horsemen. A whiff from their icy nostrils paralysed every living thing. The veins of many of the horses burst as they strove against the terrible wall of snow. Every day the track up to the Pass was more deeply snowed up. The horses of the vanguard had to be changed every thirty paces. The *tuman* pushed forward at about thirty paces an hour. There was not a horseman in his saddle, and many of the men no longer held reins in their hands.

Chepe was the first to lose his horse. He had yet to learn how long a horse can keep in a track when the snow reaches up to its breast and the boots let in the snow at every step. Kublai and Arik-Buka walked side by side and drew Bosa and Fabo behind them. Up till then Chepe had spared the tiger horses. But now, when the summit of the Pass gleamed in front of them, he beckoned the princes forward.

What he meant to say was visible in Chepe's benumbed face: There are no longer any distinctions between princes and commoners, or between the royal tiger horses and other horses.

Chepe pointed to the Pass. Behind that Pass the way goes downhill, the benumbed hand was saying. Behind that Pass begins the hope that there is still another colour in the world besides this pitiless, sinister white. The Garden of Allah, the benumbed hand tried to say. And the fur-covered head, with which Chepe indicated the mountain-tops to right and left, seemed to utter by its jerks: There they are up there . . . but they shall not get us . . . they won't if they continue to sleep . . .

Chepe's eyes searched back along the track, moving from one dark spot to another—horses and riders. Then he grasped the princes by the shoulders and whispered: 'Nine thousand . . . suffocated by the icy breath of the mountains! But if only one hundred come through——' He pressed Kublai and Arik-Buka close to him: 'Don't listen to death around us! Listen to my heart! It is beating: Genghis Khan . . . Genghis Khan . . . If only a hundred hearts survive and beat his name . . . You are there, come on!'

Kublai and Arik-Buka let go their reins. They needed both hands for keeping in the track. Bosa and Fabo had laid their nostrils on their shoulders. The princes did not hear their own panting. The breathing of the horses was stronger in their ears. Kublai was the first to notice that his shoulder was red with blood. It was red ice which was glistening there on his shoulder. Each time Bosa's nostrils rubbed against his shoulder, the red extended a further finger's breadth. Kublai turned round startled when he saw that the ice on Bosa's nostrils was red and that it increased with every pant. As if he had only been waiting for Kublai to look at him once more, the horse suddenly fell down. Kublai poked Arik-

Buka with both fists. Arik's shoulder was red too. The princes leaned their backs against the snow. Chepe pushed himself between the two princes. 'Go on!' he panted.

Kublai stared down at his horse, whose eyes were bigger than ever before.

'Go on!' panted Chepe.

Kublai seized the reins and tried to speak to Bosa, but there was only a bitter taste in his mouth, and not a single word. Chepe saw that Kublai's eyes were filling with ice. He pulled out his sword and before Kublai could move he stabbed the vein in the horse's throat. The blood spurted up on to Kublai's breast.

'Drink!' croaked Chepe. 'Drink your horse's blood! Then your Bosa will be with you still on the other side.' Kublai now pressed his mouth to the wound, and Chepe held him by the shoulders while he drank. When Kublai raised his face he saw the shells of Bosa's ears closing. Now there was no longer any white thing around Kublai that was not full of horror.

'Forward!' panted Chepe. He walked the track between the princes. The Pass gleamed in front of them. Kublai heard his heart giving huge beats: Genghis Khan ... Genghis Khan ... Or was it Arik's heart, or Chepe's, the strong heart of Chepe, that great warrior who was tender even when he was killing?

A-rik ... Chepe ... Genghis Khan ... Kublai's heart beat the names frantically one after the other, as if he feared that the name of the most glorious of all horses might escape his lips. Suddenly Kublai saw the light on the snow beginning to flicker; there were red flames jumping about on the Pass. Then the red flames were displaced by dark flames; they came towards Kublai and spread out in front of him—a black carpet. Kublai felt his face sinking down in the black carpet which was incredibly soft. And now his heart was beating only one name: Bo-sa ... Bo-sa ...

'Where am I?' asked Kublai.

'In the Garden of Allah,' said a man with Chepe's voice. But he looked unfamiliar. Kublai stared at him, puzzled.

'Do you not recognize me?'

'You speak like Chepe,' said Kublai uncertainly, trying to sit up.

'I am Chepe.'

'But you look quite different.'

'We have all altered a little—all who came through,' said Chepe. Gently but firmly he pressed Kublai back on the skin on which he was lying.

'Where is Arik?' asked Kublai, full of anxiety.

'There beside you,' said Chepe gently. 'He's asleep; don't wake him up!'

Kublai turned his head and looked into a face which bore the marks of frightful hardships.

'Is that Arik?'

'Be quiet,' said Chepe gently. 'None of us looks the same as he used to. That was just our luck.'

Kublai did not understand what Chepe meant. He asked: 'How many came through?'

'Enough to frighten the Shah,' said Chepe. 'Now sleep! They are all sleeping.'

'And what about you?'

'Someone must keep watch.' Chepe tried to force a smile on to his distorted face. 'At least with half an eye,' he added.

'How did I get here where there's no snow?' asked Kublai. 'What happened to me?'

'You half a handful,' said Chepe tenderly; 'of course, I mean in weight, nothing more. They all pushed each other to carry you on a bit.'

'No more snow!' stammered Kublai. 'And as soon as I shut my eyes there's nothing but snow ...' He blinked. 'Green, warm green ... and no more snow. Or is there snow? What is that whiteness over there?'

Then Chepe bent down close to Kublai's face and whispered: 'Horses, Kublai, a herd of white-nosed horses! Those horses are all white. And they did not make off when we arrived. We have horses again, Kublai, horses with white nostrils and white ear-shells—and they waited for us.'

Now Kublai was all of a sudden strong enough to push Chepe aside and sit up. He saw the white horses grazing. But he did not see any herdsmen. Nowhere was a human being to be seen.

'Where are the men who own those horses?'

Chepe made a careless gesture of the hand. 'Gone away!' he said.

'And they didn't kill us first?'

'Can people slay ghosts?' asked Chepe, and he sounded almost pleased. 'They didn't believe we were human beings because we came down from the Roof of the World. No human being had ever come down from there before.' Chepe pointed over to where the white mountain peaks were glistening. 'They fled as soon as they saw us appearing. But we'll overtake them. As soon as we've slept enough we will mount the white chargers. And we will ride until the red lust of battle takes hold of us.'

Kublai perceived that Chepe was trembling with eagerness to fight. His eyes were fixed on the herd of white-nosed horses, each one standing out so magnificently against the green background, like a dream from the Eternal Blue Heaven.

'On them we will accomplish three hundred times more against the Shah than if we came from the north with twenty *tumans*,' whispered Chepe. 'We come from the south . . . How will the Shah understand that when he hears it?'

Kublai felt Chepe's excitement taking possession of his own heart.

CHAPTER ELEVEN

The Shadow of Allah

THE Shah Mohammed was waiting in Samarkand, the strongest of his fortresses, for the 'stinking Sons of the Steppe'. He was not in the least worried. Had he not many fortresses to protect his kingdom from the People of the Steppe? And had not Allah himself placed mountains, broad rivers and deserts between him and them? If a few hordes really did succeed in getting through, they would come up against the Shah's warriors, both Persians and Turks, who wore shirts of mail and carried steel shields. They were standing ready for them on the northern frontiers. The chief of the yurt dwellers could only come from the north, through the Hungry Steppe. The Shah felt quite sure of himself —his well-equipped army would finish off Temuchin's starved horsemen in a few days. They could only come from the north . . .

A courier came rushing up to the Shah: 'Mongols from the south-east!' he cried.

The Shah laughed. 'The Pamir and the Tien Shan Mountains, which none can climb, guard the south-east!'

'They have crossed the Pamirs and laid waste the Ferghana Valley. The gold smithies and glass-works of your Serene Highness are no more.'

'They will break their heads against Khajent, my mightiest fortress in the east!'

'Khajent has fallen.'

'And what of Timur Melik the commandant, one of my bravest generals?'

'He fled.'

The Shah began slashing the courier's face with a whip as he shouted: 'Thus will I take from him his face, with which he swore me fidelity!' Then the Shah whipped the courier on the back, crying: 'And thus will I cut the chain-mail from his back, so that he may fear ever again to flee, because of arrows!' After which he cried: 'Report how it happened!'

'Timur Melik fought in the city until the city was devoured by flames. Then he fought on the island in the river, until the island sank.'

'The island sank?'

'Yes, that happened because the Mongols filled up the river. They forced all those whom they did not kill to throw stones into the river. And the river rose and flooded the island, and the Mongols swarmed over the dams. Then

Timur Melik and the few who were not yet slain got into war sloops and broke through the chain with which the Mongols had barricaded the river. Timur Melik killed more than thirty Mongols with his own hand, but they grew no fewer.' Trembling, the courier continued: 'They are fighting their way ahead like spirits . . . And they must have wings which cannot be seen, for they have come over the Pamirs.'

'Get out of my sight!' roared the Shah. 'You stink of cowardice!'

Khajent taken! That was Juchi and his five *tumans*.

Another courier came rushing up to the Shah: 'Mongols in the north-east!'

'They will have a hard nut to crack at the fortress of Otrar!'

'Otrar has fallen to them.'

The Shah trembled with rage. 'And the commandant of Otrar—has he fled too?'

'He fought with arrows as long as he had arrows. Then he fought with his sword, until the sword broke. Then he fought with bricks which he tore from the walls of the tower in which he had entrenched himself. And after the Mongols had undermined the tower he fought with his nails and his teeth. The Mongols have rewarded him with gold and silver.'

'Rewarded him for what?' asked the Shah, dumbfounded.

'For helping them to pull down the walls; for they forced the survivors to do this. Of the walls of Otrar not a stone remains upon a stone. Their ordinary helpers the Mongols paid with steel —they cut off their heads. They paid the commandant with nobler metal; but first they held it over a fire until it was melted, then they poured it into his eyes and ears.'

'Go!' cried the Shah, 'and never offend my ears again! If you do, I will reward you with gold and silver!'

Otrar destroyed! That was Jagatai and Ogotai and their ten *tumans*.

A new courier appeared: 'Mongols in the west!'

'What a fantastic tale!' cried the Shah. 'You are inventing fables, you cowardly wretch! In the west are seven rivers which no army can cross.'

'They came on rafts light as air, made of the skins of their beasts sewn together. They crossed the rivers clinging to the manes of their horses. And they rode over bridges which their magicians took from the backs of frightful beasts whose hides hang down to the ground.'

The courier was referring to yaks, and by magicians he meant the Chinese engineers who travelled with the armies of Genghis Khan. For it was Genghis Khan himself who had crossed the Sandy Desert of Kisil-Kum in forced rides and gained the upper reaches of the Amu-Daria River with ten *tumans*. He was now moving forward from the west against Bokhara and Samarkand. But the Shah still hesitated. Bokhara was a fortress which was believed to be impregnable. The Khan from the Steppe would meet his match there. But if Bokhara fell the south would lie open . . . In the south was the gateway to the other provinces of the kingdom.

Now a courier arrived from the south: 'Mongols on the upper course of the Amu-Daria River!'

'In the south?' asked the Shah, dismayed. 'Mongols in the south?'

'Mongols or spirits, who can say which? On their white horses they ride down everything in their path. They come murdering, robbing and burning, and then disappear.'

'In the south? Have they come up out of Hell?'

'They have come down from the Roof of the World,' replied the courier, 'yet they are devils. They have come out of the ice under the heavens, but wherever they turn they leave fire and ashes in their wake. They spare neither the man who fights nor him who flees.'

That was Chepe with the herd of white-nosed horses . . .

The Shah dismissed the courier hurriedly. When he was alone the sweat broke out in big drops on his forehead. Mongols in the south . . . Mongols in the south! . . . If he hesitated any longer there would be no way of escape left to him. Overcome with panic, the Shah had the swiftest racers in his stables—white horses from the royal stud on the upper Amu-Daria—saddled for himself and his life guards. He did not even wait for night to fall.

'Hold Samarkand until I bring relief!' he cried to his generals, who watched him in dismay. Then he galloped away.

The herd of white-nosed horses was grazing by the bank of a little river—half-way to Samarkand. The horses had been galloping hard and needed a rest. Their riders lay round about, fast asleep. Chepe had not posted any sentries. The terror which the sight of the white-nosed horses inspired wherever they halted created a zone of safety around them which none dared to penetrate.

Arik-Buka was sleeping deeply and dreamlessly, like a beast of prey which has been pursuing its booty for days on end and has at last killed it and satiated itself. Kublai was still galloping onwards in his dreams. He was sitting on a white horse, but it did not feel warm under him like Bosa, but cold as ice, and strange. And it did not obey Kublai; it just tore along because the horses to left and right of it were tearing along. It was a silent, frenzied gallop; the horses' hooves flew high as a man over the ground. And again there were fleeing people in his path. Kublai tried to draw up his white horse to jump high over them, but his hand seemed as if paralysed. It was frozen hard to the white mane. And the white horses were striking the people down with deadly kicks on their heads, and the people were sinking down without even looking round.

Man against man, man against man, whispered Kublai in the rhythm of the ceaseless hoof-beats, only to make a sound in the frightful silence in which there was no rest and nothing to hold to. The white horses kept tearing on over burnt-out, black space, and it smelt of ashes.

'Man against man . . . Man against man . . .' cried Kublai, as they overtook fleeing men once more. He called out to them to turn round and fight. He tried to get out of the saddle because the fugitives had no horses; but he could not free himself. He was frozen firmly to the horse. And the hooves of his horse were striking human heads again—exactly on the spot where Kublai had hit Haltsundoriki with the hilt of his dagger. Then Kublai turned round with such a violent jerk that his back hurt, and looked back at the men he had ridden over. And he saw them silently rising from the gound. Swift as spirits they ran after the horses, and behaved just as if they were the pursuers. They came nearer and nearer, and when they were near enough Kublai discovered that they all had the same faces. 'Haltsundoriki!' shouted Kublai—and he found himself looking into Chepe's face.

'A bad dream?' asked Chepe.

Kublai turned on his side and groaned. Chepe drew a stone from under Kublai's back.

'No wonder!' he said, gently. 'Now sleep on!'

'I must ask you something,' whispered Kublai. And when Chepe looked at him intently, he asked: 'Will it always go on like this?'

'What do you mean?' asked Chepe, surprised.

'This hunting down?'

'But that's what we're here in the west for! And it's going on splendidly!'

'This slaughtering from behind . . . without fighting?'

'I, too, would prefer it to be different,' said Chepe evasively.

'Look at the white horses—they look like ghosts—there's no longer any magnificence about them!' stammered Kublai.

'It's not a question of what they look like,' whispered Chepe. 'The Khan will stroke each one of them, and he knows why.' As Kublai looked at Chepe perplexed, the *Orluk* continued in a whisper: 'You understand too little of war yet. In it there is no choice for the individual. There is only one law—victory. Whatever contributes to it is good. It's a good thing if the horses suddenly have red wings, for it makes the enemy lose their heads without our first having to cut them off. It's a good thing if as many enemies as possible stumble to their death in fleeing.'

'I imagined war as something quite different,' said Kublai tonelessly. 'Man against man! What we're doing is simply atrocious.'

Chepe did not become impatient. He saw how Kublai was suffering. 'Each one thinks of it in a different way,' he said, gently. 'Formerly, and sometimes even yet, it's the same—man against man. But now that we're engaged in conquering the world, there is no time left to behave in a noble manner. Do not forget that the Khan also invoked the help of the wicked spirits. The Eternal Blue Heaven has sent them, and has never left us in the lurch for a single hour. The hour of horrors is passing like the sand in the hour-glass—and we are holding the hour-glass in our hands. We have spread more terror than ten *tumans* from the north. That is what matters, and nothing else.'

Chepe stopped suddenly. He pressed his ear to the ground. The thunder of distant hoof-beats made him jump up. His eyes flashed. 'Now it comes: man against man!' he cried.

The *Orluk* wakened his horsemen with a sharp call: '*Yabonah!*' The horsemen jumped up and ran to their horses. Kublai and Arik-Buka reined their white horses close up to Chepe's white horse and looked at him inquiringly. Chepe said nothing and pointed to the cloud of dust in the distance, which was coming towards them.

'Enemies in front of us at last!' cried Kublai.

'Don't rejoice too soon!' said Chepe, without taking his eyes off the cloud of dust. 'They're coming for sure! They're making straight for us! All on white horses! Perhaps it's the Shah!'

'Look!' cried Chepe. 'Now they have seen us! They're fleeing! That can't be the Shah!'

The cloud made a swift wheel round. For a moment the watchers could see the shimmering expanse of white horses, just the same as the horses they themselves were riding . . . The herd of white-nosed chargers began the pursuit, but for the first time they did not overtake the fugitives. They were too tired out. The distance between pursuers and pursued increased. After half an hour Chepe gave up.

'They must be marvellous horses,' said Arik-Buka, 'even better than ours.'

'Who knows who it is that's fleeing!' cried Kublai disconsolately.

'He's a Persian in any case—and no Persian is worth harrying a horse to death for,' said Chepe ill-humouredly.

'They came from the direction of Samarkand,' said Kublai thoughtfully.

'Exactly,' said Chepe. 'We will go there now.'

Arik-Buka noticed how Kublai's eyes brightened up.

I wonder who he is thinking of, the Khan or Yeliu?

Then Kublai said: 'The battle for which I've been waiting will be for the house of the Shah! It will be man against man!'

Arik-Buka would have liked more than anything to embrace Kublai at that moment. But Chepe shouted: 'Come on! Otherwise we'll arrive too late when the Khan starts the head fox!'

'You have come just at the right moment!' the Khan called out to Chepe and the two princes as they came to his yurt to report. 'Tomorrow we'll rout out the beard-burner. His lair is already burning at every corner.'

Light from fires blazed in through the entrance to the yurt. Many houses in Samarkand were in flames. The Khan was in the best of humour.

'As long as this campaign lasts the Eternal Blue Heaven shall not have to complain of boredom. We owe him that much, he is obviously on our side. Otrar—laid waste. Khajent—laid waste. Bokhara—laid waste. But all that is nothing compared with what you have accomplished—you, my spirits from the Roof of the World!' The Khan took Kublai by the shoulders and looked at him closely. 'Your faces have become thin,' he said.

'Only a hungry dog is any good for hunting,' said Chepe, laughing.

'I'm glad the perpetual hunting-down from behind is at an end,' said Kublai.

'Tomorrow morning you will see enough Persians in front of you,' said the Khan consolingly. 'And you three shall set a torch to the face of the beard-burner, you, Arik and Chepe.'

'Only once,' interjected Arik-Buka, 'people from the west were riding towards us. They evidently came from Samarkand.'

The Khan pricked up his ears.

'They were in a great hurry,' added Chepe.

'To meet you?' asked the Khan.

'To get out of our way.'

'Did you not say they were riding towards you?' persisted the Khan.

'Yes, they were, but as soon as they saw the troop of white-nosed chargers they doubled round. They were the only ones who escaped us.'

'Had they such speedy horses, then?' asked the Khan, in the greatest excitement.

'The strange thing is,' said Chepe hesitantly, puzzled by the Khan's demeanour, 'that the horses were white like ours.'

A tense silence followed. Chepe and the two princes looked round the yurt, and only now did they notice that besides the Khan's sons, Yeliu was also present. The Khan said: 'For the first time *Menke Kuku Tengri* has played a trick on us. The Shah has escaped.'

'Can that have been the beard-burner?' asked Chepe, dumbfounded.

'None other,' confirmed the Khan.

'How can one know that?' said Chepe, on the defensive.

Then the Khan pointed to Yeliu. 'He has found out many things. And when we heard of you and your horsemen, he learned from prisoners that the troop of white-nosed chargers could only be those white horses which the Shah reserved for himself and his life guards.'

Yeliu said quietly: 'No one has ever before dared to take horses from those studs—no one except yourselves.'

'And that it should be you, of all men, who let the Shah get away in a cloud of dust!' concluded the Khan. His voice was full of anger and scorn.

'The Shah seems to attach importance to having horses which no other horses can overtake,' said Chepe scornfully. He looked at Yeliu with as much animosity as if Yeliu had helped the Shah to flee.

'Tomorrow we shall knock at an empty house,' said the Khan.

'I will overtake him,' cried Chepe, in a rage.

'There's nothing else for you to do,' said the Khan. 'And if he creeps into the ground, you will be after him like a dog. If he hides in the sky, you will overtake him like an eagle; and if he becomes like a fish, you will harry him like a fish of prey until he is your booty. Tomorrow Samarkand shall fall. The walls of a fortress are only worth the courage of the men who defend it. Three hundred charges of naphtha are ready, and over seven hundred cannon. As soon as we have made sufficient breaches in the walls, we shall ride into Samarkand.'

N

'Ride?' asked Chepe, greatly astonished. 'And what about the moats?'

'There will be no moats in front of the breaches. They will be filled in beforehand.'

'I understand,' said Chepe, 'the first "wave" of attackers will remain in the ditches as always . . . But surely not so many of our people as to fill up the moats?'

'Not our people,' said the Khan. 'That's a thing of the past. In future not a single Mongol shall be in the first "wave". We will drive the others against the walls and see to it that they don't flow back.'

'Whom shall we drive?' asked Chepe.

'For what purpose, do you think, did we conquer Otrar, Khajent and Bokhara and spare the young men?'

Now Chepe understood what the Khan was going to fill the moats with, and the Khan appeared greater than ever in his eyes.

CHAPTER TWELVE

White Flags

F o r three hours the naphtha-filled cannon spat fire against the fortress and the siege-engines hammered the walls with missiles, as had been arranged. But no breaches were made; the walls of Samarkand were too strong. Wave after wave of prisoners was driven forward, and the moats were filled up in many places. But the walls remained standing behind the ditches as they filled. They yielded no more than did the iron gates. The Khan was beside himself. He sent a twelfth, a thirteenth, a fourteenth wave against the walls. And now it was the Sons of the Steppe who were sinking into the trenches struck by the arrows of the defenders. The Khan called the *Orluks* and princes into his yurt. As soon as they were assembled he shouted indignantly at Yeliu: 'Are we to break our heads against the Shah's empty house?'

'I have advised against the fighting,' said Yeliu.

'You have asserted that the people of Samarkand are not devoted to the Shah. Why, then, do they sacrifice themselves for him?'

'They are not fighting for the Shah,' said Yeliu.

'You have asserted that in the eyes of the Persians the Shah is an upstart, being the grandson of a slave!'

'To them he is an oppressor who has garrisoned the citadels with Turks, to safeguard the town,' insisted Yeliu.

'Why then do they fight so well?'

'They are not fighting for the ruler who has left them in the lurch in their hour of danger. I have cross-examined hundreds of

prisoners. They are fighting through despair. They are fighting for their lives.'

'I will exterminate them to the last cat!' raged the Khan.

'They know that,' said Yeliu. 'They have heard what happened in Bokhara. That strengthens their resistance tenfold.'

The Khan walked up to Yeliu in a threatening manner. 'Perhaps you think I should spare them?' he said.

'It would be better,' said Yeliu, without moving back one step.

A wild tumult broke out. 'How much longer is that one to be allowed to have his say!' cried Tuli. The Khan silenced the uproar. He asked Yeliu: 'How shall I become ruler of the West, if the fortresses defy me?'

'They will open of themselves,' asserted Yeliu.

The *Orluks* and the princes broke into wild laughter.

'Explain yourself!' commanded the Khan.

'One should not talk with the walls but with the men.'

At this Jagatai said scornfully: 'Must we sit down with Persians, and caress their ears with words?'

'Cannon are too loud,' said Yeliu. 'They hinder the enemy from thinking.'

The *Orluks* roared and slapped their thighs. But the Khan became thoughtful and looked at Yeliu keenly. 'I don't like driving my Mongols to their death. Will you speak with the people behind the walls?'

'Yes, in this same hour,' said Yeliu willingly. 'But I know a better ambassador, whose voice has more weight than mine.'

'Whom do you mean?' asked the Khan.

'One of your own blood,' said Yeliu; 'Kublai.'

At this Chepe interjected: 'No doubt you're afraid to go too near the walls?'

'It cannot be done without my going too,' said Yeliu, smiling. 'I hardly think Kublai knows enough Persian yet to be able to do it alone. But if we both try, taking white flags with us to show our readiness to negotiate——'

'I have never heard more contemptible advice,' said Tuli.

The Khan looked at his sons and at the *Orluks*. In the faces of all of them he read contempt for his counsellor. Something in his own breast, too, revolted against Yeliu's suggestion. But his reason told him: He is right. What we have been doing up to now is madness. We are too few to do away with so many. He turned to Yeliu. 'It will be difficult for us,' he said, 'to win my *Orluks* over to the new kind of warfare which you advocate. How will you convince them?'

'It is a matter of simple calculation,' said Yeliu. 'Twenty-five *tumans* on our side. Three hundred fortresses on the other side. Up to the present each fortress has cost at least half a *tuman*.'

When the Khan looked round him now he saw perplexed faces. Turning to Kublai he asked: 'Now, how much Persian do you know?'

'If Yeliu helps me with it . . .' said Kublai. He stopped short, for he felt a hand firmly grasping his arm. Turning, he looked into Arik-Buka's face.

'If you do that,' said Arik-Buka, 'with that turncoat who wants to make others traitors too . . .!'

Kublai freed himself from Arik-Buka's grasp and looked at the Khan. The Khan said bluntly: 'So far Yeliu has given me nothing but useful advice, Arik. If he opens the gates of Samarkand, I shall make him my Chancellor.'

Three hours later Yeliu and Kublai rode up to the principal gate of Samarkand. Large white flags were carried in front of them.

Chepe sat in his yurt staring into the fire. Arik-Buka lay face downwards on the couch, digging his teeth into the hand with which he had tried to hold back Kublai.

'Let your hand alone!' said Chepe.

'I want to bite it away!'

'It's not its fault.'

'Since it's not strong enough to hold him, what good is it any more?'

'It can still hold a dagger,' protested Chepe. 'Think of the traitor!'

'Traitor!' laughed Arik-Buka bitterly. 'He is Chancellor! The Khan's Chancellor! Imagine a man of the South being Chancellor! People of the West will be having a say in our affairs next! We have come to a sorry pass!'

'One day he will be no more.'

Arik-Buka jumped up and looked at Chepe inquiringly.

'Or should we quietly look on and see the Khan falling under the spell of that man?' asked Chepe angrily.

'But if it succeeds—this stratagem with the white flags? If they open the gates which we could not burst open with all who have fallen? What if *he* is the victor of Samarkand?'

'He will be both—victor and Chancellor,' declared Chepe.

Arik-Buka stared at Chepe, horrified. 'You think that he will carry it through, that he will conquer without *tumans*? Is there any sense, then, in going against him?'

'It is then indeed that there will be sense in it,' said Chepe. 'For he wants to entice us on to victories which will destroy us, the victors.'

'I don't understand you,' said Arik-Buka.

Chepe now gave free expression to his thoughts. 'There is only one sure victory: the extermination of the enemy,' he said. 'Conquered people who are allowed to live forget sooner or later that it was the conqueror who spared them. We must conquer Yeliu; he is the most dangerous enemy, because he permits too many enemies to live.'

'Kublai will stand in our way,' said Arik-Buka gloomily. 'We carried him out of the ice, and now he rides with that one behind white flags!' Arik-Buka began trying to bite his hand again. Chepe seized the hand and said: 'Leave it alone! You'll still need it. You must hold Kublai and keep him from falling to that man!'

'He has become a traitor,' said Arik-Buka, pale with anger.

Chepe shook his head. 'Kublai will not stand on the wrong side when our hour comes.'

'When will that be?' asked Arik-Buka, perplexed.

'When the seeds sown by the traitor shoot up,' said Chepe.

'You're speaking in riddles today,' said Arik-Buka.

Then Chepe drew him closer to him and said: 'Tomorrow we set out on our ride of pursuit, on which we are going to hunt down and kill the Shadow of Allah. Subotai, one of the Khan's four "dogs", will be with us. And now listen! The Khan does not wish to touch one hair of the head of anyone except the Shah —the astrologer has brought him to this already! Subotai thinks as I do about it. We are not going to die of boredom when there's nothing left to hunt down. Meantime you shall keep an eye on the shadow which has attached itself to the Khan. Yeliu must know that he is not left unobserved for a single day.' Chepe said this firmly, and in doing so nipped in the bud any hope Arik-Buka had had of riding with them.

Before dawn the following morning Chepe and Subotai set out on their pursuit with one *tuman*. The horsemen, who had been picked for the expedition,

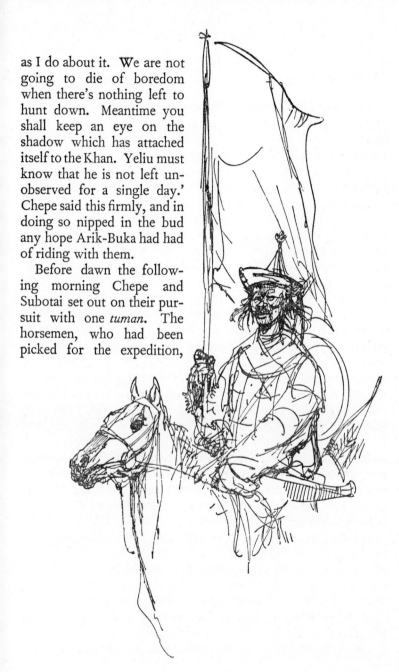

had been allowed to choose the best of the army's horses during the previous days.

After Samarkand had been handed over to Genghis Khan with all formality Yeliu, now confirmed in his position of Chancellor, deliberated day after day with the spiritual and secular dignitaries of Samarkand as to what could be done to save the other cities of the country also from being destroyed. The *imams*, *mullahs* and *cadis* were willing, as ambassadors of their new lords, to make arrangements for the voluntary submission of the remaining provinces. Despite the opposition of the *Orluks*, Yeliu succeeded in getting the Khan to allow the Mongols escorting the negotiators not to carry arms but to take with them white flags with Persian inscriptions. This was done, and every day representatives arrived from towns and provinces which were more willing to accept the fate of Samarkand than that of Bokhara.

Yeliu had advised the Khan to station few *arbans* in the citadels of the town and to instruct the strictly chosen soldiers not to offend the orthodox by entering the mosques and praying-towers without authority. Kublai, who had been present at all the conferences, had lost every hope of ever putting his foot inside a mosque or being allowed to climb up a minaret. Then, about three weeks after Chepe and Subotai had ridden off, Yeliu himself made the suggestion that they should do both. He and Kublai had often visited buildings inside the walls of Samarkand, and respect bordering on veneration had been shown to them every time. Every child in Samarkand knew the remarkable-looking man with the beautiful beard and the tall young Mongol by his side. Hundreds of Persians had experienced the wonder of being addressed in words which they understood by a grandson of the dreaded conqueror. And now they saw him bending over books written in Persian characters in their libraries and schools of wisdom. It was almost incredible that these two could be representatives of the Steppe . . . Thus it was that the Chancellor and Kublai found all doors open to them, and the invitation to visit the mosques of the city had come to Yeliu from Sheik al Islam himself, the highest spiritual dignitary.

An artificial lake lay in front of the mosque which the two were approaching. So it was that they saw the house of God twice—once silhouetted against the sky, a second time in the water, the surface of which was agitated by the huge fountains which rose at the sides of the lake. The reflection was no less magnificent than the building itself. The dome, covered with pure gold, on which the midday sun glowed, made a reflection in the water even more impressive than the original. Kublai saw the walls of the mosque, the pointed turrets and the wide porch with its curved, ogival arches broken a thousand times in the rippling surface of the lake, each part gleaming in a different shade. Kublai had often admired the brilliance of the palace walls made of thousands of little coloured stones placed together. Looking at the reflection of the mosque in the gently moving water, it became clear to him that some day an architect might conceive the idea that real walls, too, which would rise up in the light, could be covered with coloured scales.

The two walked over a graceful foot-bridge towards the mosque. The inside was even more magnificent than the outside, with its *ivans*, high aisles supported by pillars which bore sheaves of flowers in stone, and its *mihrabs* or praying niches with vaulted roofs. In these Kublai discovered ornaments which reminded him of honeycombs. They were the size of a hand and were made of jasper, alabaster, gold and shimmering blue enamel. But the most magnificent thing was the pulpit. A *'mimbar'*, the Persian who was guiding them called it, and he did not tire of praising the art of the master who had carved this *mimbar*. Full of pride, he showed them carpets which shone even in the half light, and he assured them that in each of these carpets there were as many knots as there were stars in the sky.

A *muezzin* hurried before them up the winding stairs of the minaret which Yeliu and Kublai were ascending. Half-way up there was a circular gallery, from which the *muezzin* called the faithful to prayer five times a day. From it there was a view over the whole city. Kublai was so overwhelmed by the sight of the numerous domes and towers, palaces and public buildings, that he remained silent for a long time. When Yeliu began to speak to him in Mongolian, the *muezzin* stepped back.

'There would be a field of ruins here as at Bokhara if you had let me down,' said Yeliu.

Kublai's eyes moved from minaret to minaret, and the domed buildings seemed to him like state yurts built of stone.

'Have Persians different kinds of hands from Mongols, that they are able to build all this?' asked Kublai, still spellbound by the brilliance which met his eyes on every side. 'Are there many other cities like this in the world?'

'There are many,' said Yeliu, 'and no matter how often cities are destroyed, new ones rise up again and again. No ravaging power can impress its seal upon the earth permanently. But,' continued Yeliu after a while in a subdued voice, 'these domes and minarets, too, are symbols of oppression rather than of peace and happiness.'

'I don't understand that,' said Kublai, looking inquiringly at Yeliu.

'Have you not seen the expressions on the faces of the people of Samarkand?' asked Yeliu. 'Have you not seen the grief in their eyes? I do not mean the *mullahs* and *cadis*, who are over the others—I am thinking of the masses who have built the palaces and mosques with the labour of their hands.'

'Did the Persians not like doing it?' asked Kublai, surprised. 'After all, it's their country which the buildings make so splendid!'

'Did you see their expressions?' asked Yeliu again.

Kublai now recalled the haze which made the eyes of all Persians seem so melancholy. He spoke of it, and Yeliu nodded earnestly.

'The Persians are an unhappy race,' he said. 'The desert has done them violence.'

Kublai pointed to the splendours in stone which surrounded them. 'Can the desert produce anything like that?' he asked.

'Once upon a time the Persians had many even more magnificent buildings. They were once a free people,' declared Yeliu, 'and they believed in a God of light. But then the warriors of Mohammed the Prophet came from the Arabian Desert and subjugated the Persians. Every Moslem is a *saffach*, a slaughterer, who believes that the more people of other faiths he kills, the more surely he will enter Paradise. Since Allah's warriors invaded the country there is a fountain in Persia which becomes red from time to time in order to remind the Persians that the heart of their old God bleeds.'

'And in spite of this they have built these mosques and minarets for Allah?'

'What else could they do?' said Yeliu. 'The conquerors, who came in the name of a merciless God, would not have hesitated to exterminate the whole race. The subjugated people tried in every way to placate those in power. They built golden domes, which caught the brilliance of the whole sky; they knotted their dreams of happiness into carpets; and many a one spent half a lifetime making one single vessel in order to turn the eyes of the invaders from himself and to soften the hearts of the oppressors. The Persians live in fear, and even when they raise their eyes to the minaret, they are reminded by it that they are at the mercy of an alien power.'

'Are minarets not praying-towers, then?' asked Kublai, who was not certain what Yeliu was alluding to.

'Only the lower half of the minaret is for Allah,' explained Yeliu. 'From half-way up the *muezzin* calls out. If he were to call from right on top his words would not be heard. The summit of the minaret is reserved for the Shah's soldiers. From up there signals are given which are picked up by the sentries on the next minaret. The Shadow of Allah has taken up quarters in the upper half of the minaret.'

'Now I understand you,' said Kublai. 'But soon there will no longer be a Shadow of Allah. Chepe will overtake him. And then . . .' Kublai did not finish the sentence.

Yeliu looked at him sadly. 'Then the upper half of the minarets will belong to the Khan's soldiers,' he said.

'Hasn't everything turned out for the best?' asked Kublai, on the defensive. 'Isn't the destruction at an end since the Khan sent messengers with white flags, promising mercy? Have we not freed the Persians of their fear?'

'You have seen how they look,' said Yeliu.

Kublai gazed in front of him in silence.

'I am not without hope,' said Yeliu. 'The Khan has admitted the great possibility of conquering a nation without shedding blood. Everything will depend on whether his horsemen will continue to tolerate the fact that the Persians are different from themselves, and will not crush the confidence which is beginning to spring up in their hearts.'

'You yourself know best of all that the Khan doesn't want to do that,' said Kublai. 'No one will dare to act against the Khan's wishes.'

'In that case it may be that the shadow will lift from this country,' said Yeliu, 'and that the heart of their own God will cease to bleed. We shall see that by the expressions which meet us.'

Kublai looked over the golden domes and minarets. His eyes searched on until they came to a white chain of mountains against the horizon. 'How long will Chepe have to ride?' he asked. 'When will he be back again?'

'I am thinking of Chepe too,' said Yeliu. 'I wish he was back.'

Suddenly Kublai caught Yeliu by the wrist. 'Look! Down there in the shadow of the mosque——'

'I've noticed him for a long time,' said Yeliu quietly. 'You should look after him a little more. He's too much alone since Chepe went away.'

'He's watching us,' whispered Kublai. 'I know he considers you a traitor, and me too.'

'That should not upset you,' said Yeliu. 'Arik also will be won over by the victory which is now ripening. It is certainly a slow victory; it needed much patience. But it is a victory in which there are no conquered. Therefore it will last. Come, perhaps more couriers have arrived from Chepe meantime. Much depends on the news which Chepe sends.'

By the time the Chancellor and Kublai came to the open space in front of the mosque, Arik-Buka had disappeared from beneath its shadow. The Chancellor and Kublai hurried to the Khan's yurt.

CHAPTER THIRTEEN

The Friend of the Persians

THE couriers whom Chepe sent brought good news:

In no town has the Shah a safe home any longer . . . The Shah's harem is in our hands; his own mother fled after him . . . His tent is in our hands; it was empty and pierced by the arrows of his friends. . . . His steed is in our hands. The Shah fled in a boat to an island in the Caspian Sea . . . The Shadow of Allah has been hunted to death . . .

Yeliu tried to move the Khan to order back Chepe, Subotai and the *tuman*. But the Khan wished them to go as far out into the west as possible as scouts, to feel out the unknown. He said to the Chancellor: 'Soon Chepe will be passing through provinces which no longer belong to the Shah's kingdom.' This prospect calmed Yeliu.

On his advice the Khan allowed the mayor and elders of the city, who came to pay their homage, to remain in office. The country was recovering. Grass began to grow over the scars caused by fire. Tributes and gifts piled up in the yurts. The Khan invited famous artists and scholars to visit him, and the Chancellor acted as interpreter when the Khan conversed with them.

The princes and *Orluks* murmured. Tuli acted as their spokesman. 'Your Chancellor behaves as if the Persians were brothers of the Mongols,' he said.

The Khan listened to the reproaches in great surprise. Then he said: 'Did we not march forth in order to make the West a part of our Kingdom? If this succeeds without our *tumans* perishing, so much the better. Should I blame Yeliu because thousands of my Sons of the Steppe owe him their lives?'

'Millions of Persians look upon him as their deliverer. He is counting on that!'

'I do not understand what you mean by that.'

'He gathers friends around *himself*, not around you. No one in the camp understands why you give that stranger so much power. He has entered your service, though he does not hate you any less than Tang Liweng did. But he will never rise up like an "ant" gone wild—he's too clever for that. He appears harmless, but all his aims are directed to making you his tool.'

The Khan smiled scornfully. 'You are too concerned about me,' he said.

'Do not underestimate his guile!' warned Tuli. 'He is sowing a peace of which the fruit will be revolution.'

'I know where I am with him,' replied the Khan. 'He has convinced me that while it is certainly possible to subdue peoples from the saddle, it is not possible to govern them from it. Yeliu understands the art of making authority last.'

'That remains to be proved,' said Tuli, looking angry. 'You shall see. One day all those with whom he has made friends will change into foes again. As soon as they have spied out enough from us they will attack. If we had kept to our custom we would have no surprise to fear. A dead enemy does not rise again.'

'If they dare to do so,' said the Khan, 'Allah's wrath will strike them and our *tumans* will become a fire to devour them.'

Tuli was not placated by this outburst. 'Our warriors will never again fight as they used to. They are no longer hungry wolves. They have learned to feast.'

'Don't worry,' said the Khan. 'My *Orluks* keep them well in practice. Boghurtchi has thought out new exercises: the "drill", the "whirlwind". Day after day Ogotai makes the earth tremble around Samarkand with his siege engines. Good music in the ears of Sons of the Steppe! They will never become unused to the saddle!'

'They are beginning to feel at home in the shadows of towns,' objected Tuli, 'in apricot and peach gardens!'

'Homesickness for the Steppe keeps them alert,' said the Khan.

Tuli said no more. He turned away muttering. The fact that his youngest son was cherishing bitter doubts did not escape the Khan. Of all his sons, Tuli was the one nearest to him.

'You should not begin to have secrets from me.'

Tuli looked up reproachfully.

'Say whatever you have to say!' the Khan encouraged him.

'What's the use,' complained Tuli, 'when you haven't the same ears you used to have?'

The Khan smiled.

Then Tuli burst out: 'The man whom you call your Chancellor is changing you, and you don't notice it. That is his way of conquering you. He tries to change all of us. But he does not succeed with us. Chepe remains Chepe, your arrow. And I, Tuli, remain Tuli, your mirror. You called me "Mirror" because the first object I grasped at was a mirror. I have become a mirror which is blind to everything except to you. This mirror bears your image in it, as you were before the moon darkener came. I'm a jealous mirror. And you ought never to forget that Tuli also means "shield". I am your shield which does not permit anything destructive to come near you. But you push the shield away and the destroyer has access to you.'

The Khan was silent and shocked. Then he said: 'I learn from Yeliu, yet I remain who I am.'

Tuli protested angrily: 'You called my four sons the four *gulug*, "Pillars of the Kingdom". He has already taken possession of one pillar.'

'Kublai, like all of us, is a Son of the Steppe,' protested the Khan, 'but he's more gifted than Arik and Mangu and Hulagu. Kublai and no other shall complete my work one day.'

Tuli continued in great agitation: 'Did you not notice, then, how Kublai was when he returned from his first campaign? All those whom he had killed seemed still to cling to him. He could not shake off the dead as every warrior does. He killed because Chepe and Arik dragged him off with them, not because he found pleasure in destroying enemies. He is no longer a panther, as Arik is. Your "Chancellor" has spoiled him. And once your warriors lose their confidence in killing——'

o

The Khan became thoughtful. 'I will consider your words,' he said, 'and I will speak to Yeliu about the matter.'

The very same day the Chancellor was told of Tuli's doubts. 'All my sons and the *Orluks* say that you are sowing a seed which is dangerous.'

'No one whom you have spared will provoke your anger. They did not love Mohammed, and they are about to cease hating you.'

'And my warriors are about to forget how to kill quicker than the enemy.'

Yeliu did not answer at once. But there was no uncertainty in his voice when he asked: 'Which needs more skill, to kill a tiger or a human being?'

'What are you driving at?' asked the Khan, astonished.

'In the woods south of here there are all kinds of wild beasts— bears and wild boars, panthers and tigers. Perhaps all the virtues of a warrior could be tested on them.'

'A magnificent idea!' said the Khan approvingly. 'And if I tell my rowdy warriors that it is my idea, they'll think it splendid.'

He immediately called the princes and *Orluks* to discuss the hunt with them. It was to be a hunt such as the world had never seen before. The Khan marked off a vast hunting-ground on a map which Yeliu had drawn for him. 'This territory is to be cordoned off by a chain of horsemen,' he ordered. 'The chain is to advance inwards and to multiply itself. Every ravine, every cave, every thicket is to be beaten through. Not a deer, not even a hare shall escape. I want noise to rejoice my ears, loud enough to reach the heavens! But the killing is only to start when I ride into the ring. For I want to see if my warriors have forgotten how to strike to the heart with their thrusts.'

For weeks on end the woods and gorges south of Samarkand resounded to the cry of the beaters and the rumble of the drums. The animals came out from their hides, driven by fear. The caves, into which Genghis Khan's warriors penetrated with torches, were empty. The hunted wild animals crossed brooks and swam rivers and tried to save themselves in abysses. The beaters stopped nowhere; there was no safe place. When this devil's corral became so packed that the animals were colliding with each other, the strongest ones tried to break out. They rebounded against the leather-covered shields and blunted lances with which the human wall was bristling, and attacked each other. As the beaters dared not wound any of them, enough remained. These forests had never before been combed through. When all the wild animals had been driven on to the open space, visible from a long way off, in the middle of which stood the empty throne of Genghis Khan, with a huge open cage beside it, innumerable animals of all kinds crowded on to the 'Table of Death'.

The Khan appeared. He made a sign. All of a sudden the noise and thundering stopped. The animals were seized with paralysing fear when, in the midst of an uncanny silence, the Khan and his retinue entered. The Khan was the first to kill. He fought with a tiger which had been driven into the huge cage. Then he allotted opponents to the princes and *Orluks*. He was going to chose a deer each for Kublai and Arik-Buka—they insisted on a panther. The Khan agreed, but he gave orders that they were to share a panther. Tuli stood beside the Khan as his youngest sons took aim. It was a short fight. The panther attacked Arik-Buka and, leaping at him, knocked him down. Even before it had time to use its paws Kublai directed a side-thrust at its heart. The panther had marked Arik-Buka's face and torn his shoulder. Kublai was untouched as he looked into the dying eyes. Then he raised his eyes to Arik-Buka, who had stood up with difficulty. Kublai could not help smiling, for Arik's face looked just as it had done after the fight between them at which the crazy camels had looked on.

'I'm only glad you had a little more on you than you had at Tundarik!' said Kublai, laughing. 'But you can be satisfied. It was you who got the panther; I only gave the thrust.'

Arik laughed all over his scratched face. For a moment it seemed as if nothing which could separate them had ever come between the two.

One warrior from each *arban* was allowed to enter the ring. Some were carried away wounded, as happened on the battle-field too. It was clear the Sons of the Steppe had lost none of their war-like ardour in the apricot gardens. The Khan was satisfied.

When all the dangerous animals had been killed, the Khan gave a sign for the hunt to be brought to an end. According to custom, the grandsons came up to the throne and knelt before the Khan to ask for the lives of the animals which still remained. Arik-Buka knelt beside Kublai, and now he felt the old feeling of ill-will rising up in him again. Little fault as he had to find with his brother while they were routing out the four-legged robbers and finally confronting the panther, he felt uncomfortable kneeling beside Kublai asking for mercy—even though it was only for animals. His inveterate distrust rose up. Clemency—that was exactly right for Kublai . . . Clemency was just what the white flag promised . . . Arik-Buka had not much time to brood. By a sign the Khan granted freedom to the animals which had escaped the blood bath. Then he ordered a feast which was to last nine days.

There was feasting and drinking around huge fires. The 'Table of Death' resounded with song. The very first evening Arik-Buka drank a great deal. When he was half drunk he began to express his anger against Kublai.

'It was a great piece of luck that a *kulang* stallion didn't come up against us!'

'Don't drink so much!' said Kublai.

'Oho, you old blood-drinker!'

'Don't dare to say that again!' said Kublai firmly.

'You think, do you, that I'll do what you tell me because you do what the other—that moon darkener—tells you!'

'Your mind is dark!' said Kublai angrily.

'That renegade,' Arik-Buka blurted on.

'One more word against him, and . . .'

'That friend of the Persians!'

At this Kublai stood up and said: 'You no longer know what you're saying, otherwise I would hit you in the face!'

'Let him alone!' said an old warrior. 'The panther has already done it for you.'

Kublai went off to sit down at another fire. Arik-Buka looked after him gloomily. The other warriors wanted to encourage him to drink, but he had lost all desire to do so. He stood up and went away to the other side.

'What has he against Kublai?' asked one of the warriors.

'He has something against the Chancellor,' said the older man.

'What has he against the Chancellor?'

'How do I know? Perhaps because he took Samarkand and took only Kublai with him and a couple of white flags—and because he did it without war.'

'But war won't be given up altogether because of this one man.'

'It would be bad if it was,' said the old warrior. 'Hunting is good fun, but nothing compared with war.'

Arik-Buka went searching about from one fire to another. No call and no face which turned to him held his attention. For he was looking for someone who was not there . . . He is on a hunt which is worth while, thought Arik-Buka. One which does not end with clemency . . . A hunt after my own heart . . . Arik-Buka went farther and farther away from the fires without meaning to do so. In the past it did not worry me a bit to kneel down and ask mercy for animals. But now, since our enemies are being spared too, I can no longer do it. I can no longer look at Kublai without thinking of white flags—I cannot look at him another day . . .

Arik-Buka had arrived unintentionally at the pastures on which the white-nosed horses were grazing. And he suddenly knew what he was to do. He caught two of the horses, swung himself up on one of them, and rode off towards the west . . .

Not until two days later was the Khan informed that Arik-Buka and two of the white-nosed horses were missing. The Khan was not put out of humour by the news.

'I should have sent him with them. In Arik's eyes we are no compensation for Chepe,' he said, laughing. 'Let him ride—he has a seat which is only happy in the saddle. He can change horses at any fortress occupied by our people . . . and the country is quiet.'

Early on the ninth day of the feast a solitary horseman came riding at a furious pace up to the 'Table of Death', from Samarkand. He was riding a horse whose legs and neck were bandaged, like the couriers' horses. The warriors saw with astonishment that it was the Chancellor. They had never before seen him on a horse. He asked at once to see the Khan.

'The Khan is asleep.'

'My news cannot wait. I was in Samarkand only yesterday.'

The Khan was wakened.

'You here? How did you come so quickly?'

'On a courier's horse,' said Yeliu.

'I had no idea that you could hold on to a horse. You look exhausted,' said the Khan, looking at him sharply. 'Is it from the ride?' he asked.

'There is news which changes everything.'

'What has happened?'

'The Shadow of Allah is causing unrest in the west.'

'I do not understand you,' said the Khan. 'Has not Chepe hunted Mohammed to death?'

'He has come to life again: his son Jelal-Addin has declared himself to be the Shadow of Allah.'

'So there will just be another hunting down,' said the Khan, his eyes sparkling. 'And since he has not got a safe house anywhere——'

'He has towns in which he is safe. The fortress of Herat, the fortress of Gurgendch, the fortress of Bamian, the fortress——'

The Khan interrupted Yeliu. 'You seem to have become forgetful,' he said. 'Mongol garrisons are placed in all those fortresses. In the most important of them there is a *minkan*—a thousand men strong.'

'All that has changed overnight,' said Yeliu. 'There is not a Mongol left living in Herat, Gurgendch or Bamian.'

At this the Khan stamped the ground. 'On your advice I spared all those towns!' he cried. Looking sharply at Yeliu, he continued: 'How is it that you know all this before I do? Have you spies of your own in your pay?'

'They come to me of themselves,' said Yeliu.

'Because they regard you as one of themselves, isn't that it?' The Khan walked up and down the yurt several times in his agitation. He stopped right in front of Yeliu. 'You know that my people would tear you to pieces if I did not hold my hand over you.'

'I know it,' said Yeliu. 'They look on me as a traitor.'

'Have you come to seek refuge with me from those who distrust you?'

'I have come to strengthen you against them.'

'Against my sons? It is they, not you, who are conquering the world for me.' The Khan looked at his Chancellor threateningly. 'They call you the friend of the conquered,' he said.

'You know I am that.'

'Your friends have turned into rebels.'

'I cannot understand how it can have come to that,' said Yeliu. 'Something must have happened which has incited them to renewed resistance and made them responsive to Jelal-Addin's prompting.'

The Khan became furious. 'Have you come now to defend them again?' he asked.

'It would be better to lay hold of the Shadow of Allah, no matter how often he comes to life again, than to plunder even one of your subjects.'

'Subjects, indeed! The whole Persian population is a brood of murderers. I will exterminate them.'

'If you do that you will turn the most fertile province in your domains into a desert.'

For a moment the Khan was struck with amazement. Then he said: 'You are a word-spinner who understands something of books and of the stars but nothing of the ways of the world. I have listened to you long enough! As long as there is still one rebel living I do not wish to see your face. I will burn to ashes the flags which you had carried before you, and the same will be the fate of the towns which I spared on your advice.'

The Khan suddenly stopped short, for he had noticed that someone else had entered. He turned round quickly. Kublai was standing in the doorway of the yurt.

'What do you want here?' the Khan asked imperiously. 'Do you want to ride behind white flags again? That is at an end for ever.'

Kublai stared at Yeliu perplexed.

'The seed which he has sown has shot up,' continued the Khan. 'You must forget that he exists; it is his fault that my men are being treacherously murdered. His counsel has cost the lives of thousands of Sons of the Steppe. Another man shall undertake the task of teaching you—your father. I know that in his hands you will be in the hands of one who does not corrupt.'

Kublai was white to the lips as he asked: 'Who has dared to blame Yeliu?'

'He himself!' cried the Khan. 'He has called himself a friend of the conquered.'

Kublai tried to speak again, but the Khan would not allow him.

'I wanted peace,' he said threateningly, 'but his friends have declared war on me in the midst of peace.'

'They have been led astray,' said Yeliu. 'Something must have happened which is driving them into the arms of the Shadow of Allah!'

Trembling with anger, the Khan shouted: 'Listen to the friend of the Persians! How he tries to throw the blame off them and put suspicion on our men!'

'Let the guilty meet your anger,' said Yeliu. 'I have come to plead for the millions of innocent ones.'

'Perhaps I should begin to "sieve" again?' asked the Khan scornfully. 'If only I had never "sieved"!' He looked darkly at Yeliu and then continued more quietly: 'You have given me much useful counsel. I forget nothing. Neither will you find me ungrateful. But how can I trust you for another hour if you make common cause with rebels? A voice within me warns me to be on my guard against you.'

'Yeliu will never raise his hand against you,' said Kublai indignantly. 'I vouch for him.'

The Khan riveted his eyes on Kublai. Then he said scornfully: 'I fear nothing from him, Kublai. He knows only too well that his life would end with mine. Therefore, he will never seek to harm me. But I am wont to demand more of my people. How can I rely on someone who never once takes it upon himself to do what the least of my warriors does for me?'

'What should Yeliu do for you?' asked Kublai.

'Kill,' said the Khan. He pointed to Yeliu. 'Ask him if he is willing to reduce the number of my enemies by even one single person?'

As Kublai hesitated, the Khan himself turned to his Chancellor. 'I was much surprised to see that you could keep your hold on a saddle. Now then, place yourself in the ranks of my warriors when we chastise the assassins in Herat and Gurgendch, and behead the rebels.'

'There are more effective means of decreasing the number of the enemy,' said Yeliu firmly. 'Patience will turn them into friends.'

At this the Khan's anger broke all bounds. 'You miserable wretch! You would dare to teach me how enemies should be treated! You weakling, who imagine you are somebody because your hands are white! They are already red with blood, only you are blind to it. The blood of those stabbed in the back is on your hands, for you have guided the hands of the rebels! Your accursed clemency has encouraged them to raise their heads. They were lying in the dust when I announced from the pulpit of the mosque in Bokhara: "I am the Anger of Allah!" I made the *muftis* and *sheiks* clean our horses' hooves. They were less than the dust before me. Only since we spared Samarkand do they count as anybody again. Allah's rod of chastisement shall now strike them for the second time and shall not pass over a single one of them. Go, and never appear before my eyes again as long as one of your friends still lives! Go!'

Yeliu went away. Kublai's eyes were fixed on the ground.

'Come over here to me!' said the Khan. And when Kublai was standing right before him he laid his hands on his shoulders and said: 'Look at me.'

'He is no traitor!' said Kublai.

'I know that,' said the Khan, 'but he is spoiling the war for me. He does not know the danger we are in. We have shown a weak spot, and our enemies have taken advantage of it. They have taught me a lesson: He who would establish the rule of the Steppe dare not spare the towns—not a single one of them!' The Khan shook Kublai. 'Never have I needed you, my warriors, so greatly as now,' he said. Then he whispered: 'You will not let me down, Kublai. I saw how surely you struck down the panther. You saved Arik's life. He carried you out of the ice, he and Chepe. Now both of them are in danger. They are far away in the west. I have had no news of Chepe for weeks. Now I know why that is so. The rebels intercept the couriers.'

'Let me ride,' begged Kublai. 'I'll get through to Chepe.'

'It troubles me quite enough that Arik is away,' said the Khan. 'We must divert the rebels from his and Chepe's *tuman*—drive them back to their lairs and set fire to them. If we succeed in that, the way will be clear for Arik and Chepe to return. It will be a battle for Arik—man against man, Kublai! And there will be at least twenty against each one of us!'

Tuli entered at that moment. His eyes were sparkling as he asked: 'What news did he bring?'

'The Shadow of Allah has come to life again!'

'Good news,' said Tuli, looking fierce.

'The Persians are flocking to the standard of Jelal-Addin!'

'Very good news,' said Tuli. 'So there will be plenty of fighting soon!'

'A great deal,' said the Khan, 'for there are many of them.'

'And this one here?' Tuli pointed to Kublai. 'What has my *Nilka* to say to it?'

Kublai flushed crimson. *Nilka* means 'the pampered one'.

'Do not worry, Tuli!' cried the Khan gaily. 'Kublai is burning to hew a way for Arik through the enemy jungle.'

Tuli pointed so contemptuously over his shoulder towards the door that the Khan knew at once whom he meant when he said: 'He will be better without *him*.'

'At least for a few months!' said the Khan. 'But Kublai will have a lot to tell Yeliu the next time he is in his yurt. And perhaps the stories your son will tell him will please him so well that they will make a warrior of him in the end. Now call my sons and the *Orluks* so that I may allot the rebels' lairs among them!'

Tuli went off at once.

CHAPTER FOURTEEN

A Streak of Light

DARKNESS enveloped the warriors' yurts which surrounded the space on which the fortress of Bamian had once stood. The *tumans* had been on the march longer than the Khan had reckoned on. But now they had done their work and had arrived at the pre-arranged mustering point—the western gate to that mysterious country, Tibet.

Only two *tumans* were still missing—the *tuman* of Subotai, which, having hunted the Shadow of Allah to death, had set out on a reconnaissance expedition beyond the Caspian Sea; and the *tuman* of Sigi-Kutuku, which was hunting down Mohammed's son in the hot country beyond the Indus. The Khan was impatiently awaiting the return of both *tumans*. Neither moon, nor watch-fires, nor sentries were to be seen. Genghis Khan's *tumans* did not need to be on their guard—there were no longer any enemies left in the country of the Shah.

It was cold. The heavens looked down with icy eyes. A sharp wind shook the yurts, which looked as though they were pressed, shivering, around the dismal embers which smouldered in the enormous heap of ruins in their midst. Ghenghis Khan had given a new name to this piece of ground. He called it Mobalig, the accursed spot. One of his grandsons, Moatugan, had fallen in the battle for the fortress of Bamian, and this had infuriated the Khan. Not one stone of Bamian now remained upon another.

There was not a stir in the lanes of the camp. The warriors were sleeping a death-like sleep. They had achieved titanic tasks —diverted rivers, razed towns to the ground, created deserts.

The face of entire countries had been changed by them. Now the Sons of the Steppe were lying on the dark, terrifyingly marshy ground into which so many of their comrades had sunk, never to mount a horse again.

The mast on which the nine-pointed *Tug* fluttered in the sharp wind stood out darkly. Beside it was a yurt which towered over all the others. It was long past midnight when a warrior emerged from a smaller yurt which stood not very far from the *Tug*. For a long time he peered around on all sides, then he moved away from the yurt and began to walk along the camp lane, which led south. He stopped at a yurt which stood a little aside from the others. A streak of light fell from this yurt.

The warrior lifted the door curtain. He saw a man sitting on the ground by the fire in the middle of the yurt. He could not see the man's face, but only the hair and beard. Both were turning grey. The horseman noticed the shoulders, which were hanging forward. And he noticed the hands. The firelight was playing over them; they were the brightest things in the yurt and did not show a trace of weariness. The hands were holding a strange stringed instrument, and seemed to be listening intently to the instrument at one place after another as the ear of a doctor listens to a patient.

The old man seemed so absorbed in his occupation that the young warrior hesitated to enter the yurt. But as he was about to let the curtain fall again the old man, without raising his head, said: 'Come in, Kublai!'

Kublai entered and let the curtain fall behind him. It was warm in the yurt, and Kublai felt comfort in the darkness which lay in every corner. This darkness seemed to have but one purpose— to make the fire in its midst more visible, and also the man's pale hands, which seemed to be there only for the instrument.

'Sit by the fire. It will do you good!'

Kublai sat down. Now he could see the face, too, and he noticed now greatly it had changed. It was Yeliu's face, but meantime many things had left an indelible mark on it. Kublai noticed the change with grief.

'Are you hungry?' asked Yeliu. He had not looked up even yet.

'I have had enough,' said Kublai brusquely, and the words 'had enough' sounded harsh, and hurt his own ears, making Kublai ponder: Of what have I had enough? Of the raw meat which we swallowed hurriedly between the battles; of the many fires, and the breached walls, and . . . Oh, I have had enough of so much!

Yeliu plucked a string of the instrument. It made a horrible sound.

'Someone threw it away when fleeing,' said Yeliu.

Kublai shut his eyes. How many had he seen throwing away something in terror when the breath of the pursuing horse had touched their shoulders . . .

'It didn't withstand the fall,' said Yeliu. He showed Kublai a crack on the body of the instrument. Then he searched for something on the ground. Kublai noticed that the grain of the wood resembled tongues of fire, magnificent static flames, and as Yeliu slowly turned the instrument over in the firelight, these flames seemed to leap to life.

'It has not lost its beauty,' said Yeliu, 'but it will never again sound as it used to. It is called a *yue kin*, a moon zither, an instrument which was used for the first time in China.'

And now Yeliu looked at Kublai. 'There has been much killing,' he said. But his eyes asked: What have you been doing—you were away so long?

Kublai said hesitantly: ' In the beginning I did it because I thought of Arik; he was in danger. Then I did it because I didn't want to be killed; and then because all the others were doing it. It was a fever which did not let me see reason. My father was always beside me, and before the attack he said: "As you ride forward lie with your stomach on the horse's neck, and the arrows will pass over you through the air!" Just as Chepe took care of me in the ice, now he looked after me. And when we had stormed the first town, he placed me before the others. And now he no longer called me *Nilka*, but cried: "Look at him whom the Khan has called *Gulug*—pillar! He has fought better than I have. Look at his hands! They have become horny from tearing down the accursed rebel walls. Now he has claws—my panther boy!"—And they all looked at me. And after that I fought because I wanted it to be like that always. When fighting I was seized with a frenzy which carried away all those who were with me too. In my eyes there was nothing more magnificent than the sight of walls in ruins.'

Kublai looked up. His eyes were smarting from looking at the fire. He saw Yeliu putting away the instrument and looking for something behind him. Only now did Kublai notice how many things lay hidden in the warm darkness of the yurt—chests, all kinds of receptacles, books . . . Yeliu produced a bowl. There was nothing special about it. It was a blue bowl, and Yeliu held it with the tips of his fingers.

'A little earth with a gentle breath of heaven on it,' he said. 'The bowl, like the instrument, must have been brought from the Kingdom of Chin into the Kingdom of the Shah. It has the colour *Chia Cheng*—sky blue after the rain, which a Chinese master potter sought at the command of the Emperor. He sought it twenty-seven years, until he found it.' Yeliu turned the bowl in his hand. Kublai noticed its wonderfully rounded form. Suddenly a hole gaped open in it. A piece had broken off the edge.

'You were with them in Herat, weren't you?' asked Yeliu.

'Why do you ask about that?' said Kublai, looking into Yeliu's face. 'I see that you know it already. Why, then, do you ask me? Ask me about anything else, but don't ask me about Herat!'

'It is better if you do not have to carry it around with you for ever,' said Yeliu. 'Tell me everything,' he begged. And he tried to fix in the broken piece which lay inside the bowl.

'The defenders of Herat fought more frantically than all the others,' said Kublai. 'They knew what awaited them. They had killed a whole division of a thousand men. My father said: "A thousand times a thousand have crept into the vipers' nest— for each one of our people we will make a thousand bite the dust."

'Four hundred naphtha mouths spat fire into the fortress. When my father thought enough of them had been roasted, he ordered our men to feed the breath of Hell into the lungs of the defenders of Herat. He had poison gas blown through long pipes over the walls, but only from windward, because the deadly whiffs were also harmful to the lungs of us horsemen. We saw many of the defenders tumble down from the walls. But there were still plenty left. Then my father sent thirty "waves" against the walls. None of our warriors were amongst them. We stood behind the prisoners lest they should flee. None of them thought of doing so. They tried to escape into the town, for in spite of the burning and the breath of Hell, they preferred to be in Herat than with the devils who had turned Herat into a hell. They did not succeed; the defenders did not understand their ardour, and let no attacker live. When the moats were filled level my father got the heaviest siege engines into action. And then the walls gave way at last. We were busy in the town for three whole days. There was no longer any fighting man against man. It was a hurried extermination of defenceless people. At the end of three days there were still some left living. My father gave the command: "It is enough, the remaining ones are dead even if they still walk about!" We withdrew. Then our baggage train was attacked. The "dead" had overtaken and encircled it. My father shouted: "Since dead men can come to life again I order you to kill the 'dead' once more!" And in spite of the double trouble he had the dead counted. He had been told that Persians secretly swallowed pearls to save them. My father had these pearls searched for . . . and many were found—a huge dish was filled with pearls. My father held the dish in front of his warriors and said: "These western people set their hearts so much on such things that before dying they have nothing more important to do than to eat them. Never shall you set your hearts on such useless things! For only such as do so can be conquered!" And he shook the dishful of pearls on to the sand, and made his horse dance on the spot which had been sown with pearls. "Thus shall we stamp upon the rebels until they are mingled with the earth!" my father cried. "The fire from our naphtha-pipes shall devour them! The water of diverted rivers shall drown them in their lairs! They deserve nothing better, for they have treated our ambassadors like burnt food. They rose against the lord whom the Eternal Blue Heaven had placed over them. They rally to the Shadow of Allah as if we had not hunted him to death. They treacherously kill the garrison—our brothers—and no one gave them the slightest cause——" '

Kublai stopped and stared into the fire.

'Why do you not continue?' asked Yeliu.

'Because I know why they rose up against us,' said Kublai. 'They had a cause.'

Yeliu looked up. He scrutinized Kublai and finally asked him earnestly: 'Was it Chepe?'

'Yes—and Arik,' said Kublai. 'It is since I came back that I know.' And now he blurted it all out. 'It was the first night we shared the yurt again. The nearness of Arik and Chepe had silenced all my doubts. They had been in danger, and I had helped to fight through and get them out of it—that was it. And we had punished rebels who had risen against the Khan without the slightest cause . . . It was late in the night when I heard Chepe and Arik whispering together.

' "Is it worry that keeps you from sleeping?" whispered Chepe.

' "I'm not worried," replied Arik-Buka. "I can't sleep with the thought that Kublai is with us again in the yurt and that he is just like one of us, one who is spoken of with admiration by the others, one who will never again enter the moon-darkener's yurt . . . that he has become a warrior—that's what keeps me from sleeping."

' "I was never anxious about him," said Chepe. "You know that."

'Arik-Buka now whispered so loudly that Chepe urged him to speak more quietly. "He would never have become like that," he said, "if he had not gone through the hell which you had set in motion." And now I learned of the plan which Chepe had concocted and put into operation after the Shadow of Allah had been hunted to death. I learned why Arik had ridden off to Chepe. He wanted to be there when they turned people into rebels. It was he, Chepe, who let Jelal-Addin escape in order that he would sow the seeds of revolt, so that there would be rebels to hunt down like wild beasts later. Chepe and Arik visited the towns which they were supposed to spare, and behaved in them in such a way as to bring about open revolt. They took the more important people as hostages, and said to them: "Take us to your hiding-places; we can find by ourselves the treasures which are in your houses!" They forced Persians to beat the war

drums, and then cut off their hands. They set parts of the town
on fire; only ghosts of trees remained standing in the gardens.
Above all, they gave their attention to "scholars and such-like
useless people". They ordered *mullahs* and *cadis* to pass judgement as judges on stones which had caused Mongol horses to
stumble. And so, by annoying the conquered people in every
way, they set hell going.' Kublai continued tonelessly: 'There
had been no danger for Arik and Chepe—they themselves first
created the danger. They had wished for and instigated all the
devastation long before . . . and yet their sleep is like a stronghold
into which none of the slain penetrates. How can that be, when
night after night the slain come to me, and all of them have the
face of Haltsundoriki, whom I killed because I thought Arik was
in danger?' Kublai groaned. 'O the rose gardens and the stone-
work marvels of the mosques, where are they now?' Kublai
gazed into the fire with wide-open, horrified eyes, as if he saw
something terrible, and whispered: 'O you domes, arched like
the heavens, I lament for you! O you minarets and pillars on
which the starlight sets its silver feet, I lament for you! O you
springs, eyes of the earth, out of which the depths shone, I
lament for you! You cheerful gates, you bridges which stretched
from bank to bank light as the wings of birds, I lament for you!
You richly carved *mimbars*, you niches with vases of onyx and
cornelian, you mosaics and carpets, woven like dreams by tireless
hands; you brocades, you metal vessels with golden veins, I
lament for you! O you hanging gardens, O everything ex-
quisite which we have trampled down, I lament for you! O you
dead——!'

P

Kublai did not take his eyes from the fire. His mouth was open and drawn with pain. Suddenly he grasped Yeliu's hand. In a changed voice he said: 'Is it true that I cannot turn back? For that is what they said . . . they said: "He has killed too many, now he is like us, and what was alien in him we have driven out—for he who had an ear for Yeliu is no more . . ." Is that true? Have I no longer a heart? For that's what they said.'

'Do not look into the fire!' said Yeliu. 'Look at the bowl!' He was still holding it in his hand, and as Kublai looked up he carefully stretched it out towards the fire and held it between the glowing embers and Kublai's face. And Kublai saw that a bird was gleaming in the bowl. 'Now look at him—the phoenix,' said Yeliu. 'There's not a bit of him broken—his picture is undamaged.'

'Feng Huang, is it?' asked Kublai, and he began to tremble with excitement. 'How can it be that he's there and I didn't see him?'

'The master himself has hidden his picture,' said Yeliu. 'He painted it on the inside of the bowl and then covered it over with *chia cheng*, the blue of the heavens. Only when the bowl is held against the light does Feng Huang appear. Then his picture penetrates heaven and earth. But he is always there, even when he does not seem to be.'

Kublai gazed spellbound at the picture of Feng Huang.

'What do they know of your heart?' he heard Yeliu saying. 'The great fire, against which it was held, has wakened it up from all blindness. And while your eyes were looking for a gap in the walls of the fortresses, for a gateway to destruction, your heart did not fail to notice the domes and minarets—or anything which pointed to heaven . . . The lament which you have just spoken over the fire was inspired by your heart, wasn't it? Your heart has led you into my yurt. It will give you no peace until you have taken the step which you are destined to take. For one day you shall no longer be a Son of the Steppe, but *Tien Tse*, Son of Heaven.'

'How can that be since I have murdered?' protested Kublai. 'The dead never leave me alone. Haltsundoriki never stirs from my side.'

'You could not find a better *anda*. He will worry you as the *anda* in the desert worried Robber Nameless until he became Thousand-Moon-Bear.'

'Am I to creep into a cave?' asked Kublai gloomily.

'Each one has a different road to go,' said Yeliu. 'You shall rule.'

Kublai looked up once more. His eyes were troubled as he said: 'I hear all your words. All your words are as beautiful as the bowl, and as the instrument in which the flames play; they are beautiful as your hands—but do you not see that my hands are blunt from war?'

'Is there anything that they have not tried to persuade you of?' said Yeliu. 'I cannot see that your hands have changed!'

'That may be,' said Kublai, 'but it's not hands that matter. Too much has changed in me! I have in me Herat and Gurgendch and Bamian—all the towns I helped to destroy. How could you grasp that? You have not disturbed one stone; in the midst of the immeasurable destruction you have even tried to save!' Kublai looked around the yurt. His eyes fell on vessels and a few chests in the warm darkness. Suddenly he heard someone groaning faintly behind him.

He jumped up. Yeliu held him by the wrist.

'Don't worry,' he said. 'It's a wounded man; he's still unconscious.'

'Why have you concealed from me that there's someone else here?'

'Would you have told me what was oppressing you if I had? He has not heard a word.'

Kublai peered into the face of the wounded man. 'Is he one of ours?' he asked.

'I did not ask.'

'And you dare to hide him in your yurt?'

'He needed me. Was I to leave him lying where he was?'

'You know that there's the death penalty for that,' said Kublai excitedly.

'When I saw him lying where he was, I did not think about that—and now it is too late. Look into his face!' said Yeliu gently. 'You can go close up to him; he won't waken.'

Kublai bent over the wounded man. In spite of his foreign

appearance, he had features which reminded Kublai of someone. At first he thought: He looks like Arik. Then suddenly he knew that this foreigner was very like himself. 'All those around him were dead,' said Yeliu; 'he alone was breathing. They had over-looked him, though he was still clutching a dagger.'

'Where is the dagger?' asked Kublai. And without waiting for an answer he continued: 'This man doesn't look like someone from Bamian.'

'No,' said Yeliu.

'You know the man?' asked Kublai, looking searchingly at Yeliu.

'How should I know him?' asked Yeliu. 'He was one of the many lying there—and he alone was still living. So I took him into my yurt.'

'To take one with you when a hundred thousand are dead—when millions are dead—is there any sense in troubling about *one* person?'

Yeliu listened to the breathing of the wounded man. 'There's hope that he will recover,' he said quietly, as if he had not heard Kublai's question. 'The fever is easing off . . . Only'—and now Yeliu looked up again—'he'll need a lot of care, and who will watch over him while I'm with the Khan?'

'*You* with the Khan?' asked Kublai, astounded. 'I hear from Chepe that the Khan does not give you a thought. He is only waiting for Subotai and Sigi-Kutuku, and when they are here he will set off on a new campaign at once. He's going to march through Tibet and invade China from the south-west in order to proceed with the Kingdom of Sung as he has done with the Kingdom of the Shah. It's to go on just as it has been going on.'

'He will call me, and it will be soon,' said Yeliu positively.

'How can you know that?'

'The stars indicate a great change. The Khan will turn back.' Yeliu lowered his voice. 'But before then his life will be in danger. He, who thinks that only his enemies are mortal, will be shaken with fear. He will look death in the face. The "Beast from Tibet" will meet him.'

Kublai gazed spellbound at Yeliu.

'It is called Kiotuan in the old folk songs and tales of the mountain folk who live here,' continued Yeliu. 'Other races have other names for it, and everyone has a different mental picture of it. To many it is perhaps just a shadow from which there is no escape. In Hindu Kush legend it is an animal with ruby-red eyes and a long, straight horn over the forehead. It can appear anywhere, and knowing all languages, can speak with anyone. And then it speaks about everything which a man has done in his lifetime.'

'Does the Khan know about it?' asked Kublai, his eyes wide with astonishment.

'He knows about Kiotuan,' Yeliu admitted. 'I told him about the "Beast from Tibet" when he asked me one time if an end would come to him one day.'

'And did he listen to you calmly?'

'Oh, no, he was not calm,' said Yeliu. 'He listened as if he wanted to know everything and at the same time did not want to know. And when he had heard everything his face was bloodless, and he forbade me ever to mention the subject again.'

'An animal with ruby-red eyes and one horn—how could one ever forget that?' said Kublai excitedly. 'And what a name—Kiotuan——'

'It will put a stop to the murdering,' said Yeliu positively. 'The Khan will meet with an accident, and he will hear Kiotuan's voice. The Khan will turn back.'

'His sons and the *Orluks* will never allow that!' said Kublai. 'They will say: "How can you thwart us, we who do everything for you? Will you scorn the command of the Eternal Blue Heaven and cease from making the whole earth subject to the Steppe?" They will stop the Khan's ears with their war-cry.'

'He will listen to the "Beast from Tibet" and not to them,' said Yeliu, 'for fear will overcome him. Then will be the time for us two to stand by him.' Yeliu bent over Kublai's face and whispered: 'Then will come the hour to save China, my beloved country, which you will restore one day to its position of Middle Kingdom. They will raise their heads like snakes, and their tongues will be cleft. But they will be powerless against us, if you listen to none but to your own heart.'

'No one shall influence me against you,' said Kublai. 'I know that your thoughts hit the mark—I still have your arrow in my quiver. And now I have seen from the bowl that your eyes see through to the heart of things.'

Kublai rose quickly and left Yeliu. 'I must get back before they notice that I've been away,' he said.

Yeliu raised the curtain. A broad streak of light fell on the camp lane.

CHAPTER FIFTEEN

The Meeting with the Unicorn

THE next morning Arik-Buka said to Chepe: 'He was away in the night.'

Chepe replied: 'It does happen that one has to leave the yurt in the night.'

'Kublai was over an hour away,' persisted Arik-Buka.

Chepe whistled softly through his teeth. 'Do you think he has been backsliding?' he asked.

'Where else would he have been?' asked Arik-Buka. 'Just remember: when we went to bed there was light in only one yurt.'

'We must keep an eye on him,' said Chepe, 'until there's so much doing again that he won't have time for foolish thoughts.'

'It's a good thing that it's the Chinese who are going to get it in the neck now!'

'Is it not all the same whom we are fighting?' asked Chepe.

'Not for Kublai. He has an account to square with the Chinese.' And half in scorn, half in anger Arik-Buka told Chepe the story of Haltsundoriki.

The very same day the two forgot their worries. A horseman, enveloped in bandages like his horse, arrived at the camp. He had set out from the shores of the Caspian Sea fourteen days before. It was Subotai. Chepe and Arik-Buka were wild with joy. They brought Subotai, who was hardly able to stand, straight to the Khan, who had a few of the *Orluks* and all his sons around him.

'Well, my old sharp-sighted hawk, what news have you to

give?' cried the Khan, after he had greeted Subotai affectionately.
'Is the West worth conquering?'

'We rode far,' said Subotai, 'over high mountains and
enormous pastures; our horses swam mighty rivers; we rode
round a whole sea. And it seemed again and again as if the West
was only beginning. We met people whose faces were not dark
like ours, but fair; whose eyes were not black like ours, but blue
like ice; tall, proud people, who know how to fight.'

The Khan became sunk in thought. At last he said: 'Your
brave warriors shall remain there with the enemy as feelers,
Subotai. But before we turn our attention, with all our *tumans*,
to those pale-eyed, proud people in the West, to show them that
the Eternal Blue Heaven has appointed us as rulers over all the
earth, it will be well to leave things in a safe state behind us. If we
go to the West without first paying the Southern people a visit,
they will feel safe and grow defiant.'

'Tang Liweng showed how easily they lose their heads,' said
Chepe.

The flaming flush which overspread the Khan's face showed
how the mere thought of the 'ants gone wild' put him in a rage.
'I trampled on him!' he cried. 'What's to prevent me from
dealing with all the other vermin in the same way? What are a
couple of million men to me!'

'Will that not hold us up too long?' interjected Subotai.

'No, not if we invade them from the south-west,' said the Khan.

'By a route which does not exist!' cried Chepe sarcastically,
and they all understand at once to whom he was alluding. And
the Khan said: 'Do not worry, my Prince Arrow! I shall only
seek the astrologer's counsel again when I have leisure to observe
the stars. And since the West is so vast, I almost fear I shall
never again have leisure to observe the heavens.'

Chepe threw Arik-Buka a triumphant glance, and both looked
surreptitiously at Kublai. His face did not betray a thing.

'As soon as Sigi-Kutuku has returned from beyond the Indus,
we shall ride off. And before we set off towards the frontiers of
the West, China will be added to the Empire of the Steppe!'

The Khan's yurt was shaken by wild shouts.

'Death to all rice eaters!'

'Death to the Chinese rabble!'

'Death to every Tang Liweng!'

Kublai stood there white as a corpse. Nobody noticed it, not even Chepe and Arik-Buka. They all had eyes only for the man in the midst of them who now was just as he had been in the year of the panther.

'We shall shorten the time until Kutuku's return by having a hunt!' cried the Khan in high spirits. He looked once more as he had looked in the hour when he had ordered the destruction of the Kingdom of the Shah—like one to whom nothing is impossible and who is proof against all dangers. 'You shall all be my guests at the Table of Death!' he cried.

'All?' asked Chepe slyly, and everyone knew who the question referred to. But the Khan said: 'Yes, everyone! No one is to be absent, not even the moon-darkener!' His eyes twinkled. 'Has he not shown that he can sit in a saddle? Now we want to see how he will behave with a deer before him!'

'Or a wild boar which is taking a friendly interest in him!' cried Jagatai.

'Or—behind an animal which does not exist!' scoffed Chepe, who understood that the Khan wished to have a hit at the wise man. At that moment Chepe noticed that Kublai's face brightened up. The hunting-fever has got hold of him, thought Chepe. But Kublai's thoughts were occupied with the puzzling animal of which Yeliu had told him in the night.

It was a real hunt, not a battue like the great hunt to the south of Samarkand. Whoever started a wild animal had it for his own, and no one dared dispute it. The hunt raged through the gorges of the Hindu Kush right up to the frontier of Tibet. Each man was bent on killing as much as possible, and no one had time to look round at his neighbour.

The Khan had given his bodyguard a holiday so that each one of his men might take part in the hunt independently. He allowed no one to remain near him except Tuli and Yeliu.

Yeliu rode unarmed. Before he set off on the hunt Kublai had offered him a bow and a quiver of arrows. Yeliu had refused with a smile, though he knew well that it was Kublai's intention to

steal away from the tumult as soon as possible in order to take his place with the wounded man.

'Take my thrusting lance,' the Khan had said to Yeliu as they rode off, 'if you don't know how to use a bow and arrow! You will not be quite so safe in the Hindu Kush as in your yurt.'

'You should not have sent away your bodyguard,' Yeliu had answered. The Khan had laughed in his face. 'So you can't stop giving me advice?' he said.

'Let Tuli at least be near you!'

'Very well,' the Khan had said. 'I shall share with Tuli the pleasure of seeing how you get on at a hunt!'

The Khan had soon come on a wild animal. His arrow had never missed. He had killed a wild yak steer with his thrusting-lance, and now he was galloping after a wild boar. Tuli had gone off some distance; he had another wild animal in front of him. Yeliu was galloping hard behind the Khan on a good horse. He saw the Khan standing up in his stirrups and raising his bow. He saw the arrow speeding off. And in that same moment he saw the Khan's horse shying and the Khan falling. The boar was hit. It turned round furiously. Threateningly it approached the fallen man. Its flanks were covered with foam. The Khan felt a piercing pain in his chest. He could not move. He stared at the animal, which seemed to become bigger and bigger the nearer it approached. The Khan saw the tusks—two terrible naked daggers which moved up and down. The whole of the monster was in violent motion. Suddenly it stopped three paces away from the Khan, and he could not understand why its tusks were not boring into his agonized body, to bury themselves right in his heart. But now the Khan noticed a hand calmly and quietly lifting up the lance which lay beside him. Then he saw the lance stuck in the boar's neck pointing towards the sky. A stream of blood which almost touched his face spurted out, forming a broad red track between him and the animal. And the Khan heard Tuli shouting: 'A jolly good thrust, Moon Darkener! The boar is dead, it's finished!'

And now the Khan saw a beast walking up to the spot where the boar had just been—a beast which looked at him with red eyes. It was taller than the boar, and of a green colour like the grass around them. And just as the lance had stuck out from the boar's neck, so a long horn, straight as an arrow, pointed up to the blue sky from the forehead of the strange animal. The animal had a head like a horse, and now its nostrils moved and it spoke: 'Do not worry, the danger is past!'

The Khan could not escape from the eyes which glowed like rubies.

'Does it hurt very much?' asked the unicorn.

'Oh! You can speak!' stammered the Khan.

'But all animals can,' said the unicorn modestly.

'What do you want of me, and who are you?'

'I am called Kiotuan,' replied the unicorn promptly. And he added in a jocular way: 'Oh yes, I do exist!'

'I have never seen your like before,' said the Khan.

Now the unicorn lowered his voice. 'You were never before so near to—taking the step.'

'What step?' asked the Khan, alarmed.

'Oh!' said the unicorn, in a tone of surprise. 'Now you speak as if the pain in your chest had not been a clear enough sign. There were two signs besides—the fall and the raging boar.'

Almost inaudibly the Khan asked: 'Must I die?'

'Not at once,' said the unicorn. 'I have come to speak to you about that matter.'

'Am I really going to die?'

'It is time to turn back.'

The Khan groaned.

'It is time to look behind you,' said the unicorn, in a gentler voice.

When the Khan groaned again the unicorn placed its head nearer the Khan's ear, the narrow, straight horn pointed towards the West, and the 'Beast from Tibet' said: 'Is the grave which you have left behind you not yet big enough? How many more times will you die in order to fill it?'

'Am I already dead, then?' asked the Khan hoarsely.

'How many people have you killed?' said the unicorn, in the voice of one answering.

The Khan felt his leather jerkin becoming wet inside, and he began to shiver. 'Am I bleeding to death?' he asked in a whisper.

'It is only fear,' said the unicorn, 'though you have not yet made a grave of one-quarter of the earth. How will it be one day if . . .?' The unicorn broke off in the middle of the sentence. The Khan made a painful effort to prop himself up, and cried: 'No!'

'How well you understand me!' said the unicorn, and raised its head. 'So you will not trample beneath the hooves of your horses that mysterious country from which I, and you also, if I remember aright, originate?'

'No!' said the Khan wearily.

'And what about China, the country of nine times a hundred thousand gardens?'

'No!' groaned the Khan.

'And when your sons grumble and your *Orluks* roar, you will not forget that instead of two ugly tusks, two rubies suddenly stood before your eyes?'

'No!' answered the Khan tonelessly. And suddenly, instead of the 'Beast from Tibet' nothing but dazzling light met his eyes.

'Father!' said Tuli anxiously. 'Father! Why do you keep on saying "No"? To whom are you speaking?'

The Khan looked at him with an expression which was quite new to Tuli.

'Did you not see it, then?' asked the Khan.

'Whom should I have seen?' asked Tuli suspiciously.

'The beast,' said the Khan.

'It is dead,' Tuli assured him. He pointed to the boar, which was lying in its blood. 'It was a good thing that at least Yeliu was near you.'

The Khan now looked at Yeliu, who was standing silent and motionless beside him.

'But surely you saw it? You saw it, did you not?'

'No,' said Yeliu, 'but I saw from your face that you had seen it.'

'And you did not see it, either?' asked the Khan, disconcerted. 'Well, perhaps it was not there at all, then?'

'It was there, but only for you. It was you who had had an accident, not I,' said Yeliu. '*You* were near enough to . . .'

'Speak no more!' the Khan interrupted him. Turning to Tuli, he said: 'Sound the bugle and call the hunt off at once. Let no more animals be killed—not a single one. Have me carried to the camp and call the princes and *Orluks* around me.'

'Will you not wait until you are feeling better? You are too exhausted,' objected Tuli. 'The whites of your eyes are covered with red veins.'

'I have never seen so clearly as I do now what is yet to be done,' said the Khan.

'You should allow yourself some rest and not decide on anything too quickly,' Tuli warned him urgently.

'The Chancellor is to remain by my side in future,' continued the Khan, undeterred. 'He is to have first voice in the Council as he had before Samarkand.'

Tuli now looked into the face of the man who had saved the Khan from certain death, and his look was full of hate.

At that same hour Kublai was bending over the face of the wounded man in the Chancellor's yurt. He had long since come to know this narrow face off by heart. When he shut his eyes he saw it distinctly in front of him, and if the eye-slits had been a little bit more slanting, Kublai could have believed that he was looking into a mirror and had his own face before him. Nevertheless, he had the feeling that this face had never divulged anything to him hitherto. It seemed an extremely candid face; but had not Kublai once thought that about Genghis Khan's face too—in the victory yurt, when the Khan had replied to the Caliph's ambassador and Hulagu had told him that that was merely the Khan's way of dissembling . . .? No face betrays everything, pondered Kublai. What may not be hidden behind this face, which is so like my own and yet is such an enigma? It began to dawn on Kublai that a face can look inwards as well as outwards when the eyelids are closed.

The wounded man's mouth was slightly open; it had willingly and with increasing eagerness drunk the medicines and strong beverages which Yeliu had left ready with exact instructions. 'He may regain consciousness during my absence,' Yeliu had said. Kublai waited for this more and more impatiently. Hour after hour he watched to catch the first look from those eyes before they should fall on him . . .

It was a glance which flickered out like a butterfly—moist, groping, astonished, helpless, incapable of freeing itself and fleeing. But it did not remain so for long. It hardened, gained lustre, tried a few capers, and then flew to Kublai's eyes and fixed itself so firmly on them that after a while Kublai tried to free himself from it. How different the face seemed now. All of a sudden all weakness had disappeared from it. The mouth had closed—now it was a taut line over which the arches of the lips were stretched. The temples and forehead and the whole face seemed to be illuminated by a reflection from within. Kublai saw thoughts written on the face of the wounded man, but he could not read them.

And now the wounded man whispered something. It was no confused murmuring, every syllable was clear, yet Kublai could not understand a word . . . He listened with all his might, and a look of distress came over his face because he would have liked so much to have understood at least a word. And then the wounded man began to smile, and this smile was quite easy to interpret. It meant: I thank you for being near me . . . The expression of the mouth ceased to be hard, the eyes left Kublai's face and began to search around. Kublai pointed to the glass in which was something to drink. The eyes of the wounded man smiled and kept on searching. Kublai took up a bowl which was filled with fruit. The wounded man smiled and turned his head aside. What was the fluttering glance seeking? Suddenly it swept farther out like the wings of a bird of prey; it stopped as if ready to swoop. Claws seemed to emerge from it; it fixed itself on something narrow which was glistening on top of a chest. Kublai stood up. The glance directed his hand. His hand found a dagger, a weapon with an unadorned hilt, and its blade hidden in an unadorned sheath. Kublai perceived that the eyes of the wounded man never left his hand now; they coerced Kublai in an inexplicable way until they forced him to lay the dagger on the breast of the wounded man. The man whispered a few words, and his smile translated the unintelligible whisper as: I am happy, you see; now all is well . . . Summoning all his strength, the wounded man felt for the dagger, and hardly had his hand clasped the hilt than the light vanished from his face and he sank back into a profound sleep.

Kublai gazed utterly perplexed at the enigmatical face—that face which had suddenly become so different and now was so like his own once more. And as he looked at the dagger he asked himself how it was that a weapon could suddenly be lying there.

There was an uncanny silence in the yurt. Kublai noticed that the small sand-glass, which Yeliu had set up to mark the intervals at which the wounded man should get his medicine, had run out. Kublai poured a dose of medicine into the man's mouth.

Soon afterwards the sound of horses' hooves was heard approaching the camp. Kublai listened: it did not sound like the noise of a merry hunting party returning home. Kublai listened in vain for the laughter and jesting which was usual at the end of a hunt, and though he had lost the sense of time while watching the wounded man, it suddenly seemed to him that it was too early for the return. It was not yet dark; Kublai did not want to be seen outside the Chancellor's yurt ... The sound of footsteps made him start up.

As Yeliu entered, Kublai at once read on his face that something unusual must have happened. Yeliu did not say a word; his eyes sought the wounded man, and Kublai noticed that he looked alarmed.

'Do you think he's bad?' asked Kublai. And then he saw that Yeliu's eyes were fixed on the dagger and not on the face of the wounded man.

'He was conscious for a few moments,' Kublai explained, 'and he wanted it—I don't know how I came to do it ... Should I not have given him the dagger?'

Yeliu forced a smile and said: 'Now I'm not anxious about him any longer.'

'As soon as he had the dagger,' Kublai reported, 'he fell asleep again.'

Yeliu bent over the wounded man. 'It's a different kind of sleep now,' he said. 'Listen to his breathing—now he says with every breath: I shall recover.'

Kublai looked at Yeliu intently. 'Aren't you glad?' he asked.

'I am not thinking of *him* now,' said Yeliu, in a tone which made Kublai listen still more attentively.

Q

'What has happened?' he asked. 'They didn't come home as they usually do from a hunt?'

Then, with deep emotion, Yeliu drew Kublai close to him and told him everything that had happened to the Khan before his eyes. 'The injury which he incurred when he fell is more dangerous than he himself believes,' concluded Yeliu. 'He lost consciousness while they were carrying him back to the camp. Now he's lying in his yurt like this man here. The Khan, too, will free himself from the hand of death, for in his inmost heart he is just as sure of what he wants as this man is.'

Kublai started up. He had heard the wounded man moving. He looked over and noticed that the movement had made the dagger come out of its sheath a little. A sign glistened on the blade which sparkled blue like ice, and when Kublai looked more closely he recognized it as the claw of a golden eagle. What a strange sign, thought Kublai. And what a strange man!

'When shall I watch with him next?' asked Kublai gently. I must get to the bottom of this, he thought to himself. There's danger here, and Yeliu does not know . . .

Then Yeliu said: 'It's better for you not to come to my yurt again until the Great Council has met.'

'And who will be with him while you're with the Khan?'

'The wounded man is out of danger,' said Yeliu so firmly that Kublai looked down, embarrassed.

CHAPTER SIXTEEN

The Great Council

IT was not until three weeks later that the princes and *Orluks* assembled for the Great Council which the Khan had pro-claimed at the end of the hunt. They had been awaiting the day with impatience. While the Khan had been confined to his bed he had had the Chancellor called to him so often that it seemed as if he expected counsel and help towards recovery only from him. Now the hour of decision had come. The princes and *Orluks* had resolved to banish the false vision which the moon-darkener had evoked to come between him and them. They were sure of themselves. If the Khan looked into their faces and read in all of them that he and they were 'of the same kidney', he could not act otherwise than 'as the Steppe commanded'.

Now the princes and the *Orluks* were standing around him, their heads raised.

The Khan was not yet able to hold himself erect; he was sitting on his throne, bent forward. But the sparkle in his eyes was undimmed as he announced his decision not to march on Tibet but to return to the Steppe over the Arai Pass, across which the main body of his *tumans* had come.

A grim silence followed this declaration.

'Do you not wish to return home to the Steppe?' asked the Khan.

'It is too soon as yet to do so,' said Tuli. 'Has not the Eternal Blue Heaven ordained that we shall rule over all nations?'

'You are right,' said the Khan. 'But have we not been going the best way about robbing ourselves of all the peoples?'

'There are too many of them!' said Jagatai, violently.

'You seem to wish to be lord over depopulated deserts rather than populated countries,' said the Khan.

The astrologer can be heard behind every word he says! thought the *Orluks* and princes, enraged. The Khan continued calmly: 'I was about to set off for China to deal with that immeasurable country just as I had done with the Kingdom of the Shah. I was blind. I saw the southern people as ants which are good for nothing but gnawing and squirting poison.'

'Is that not what they do?' asked Chepe angrily.

'Is it surprising that they live in fear that we may trample them underfoot some day?' The Khan searched for words. 'Are they not more like a swarm of bees which industriously gathers gold for us?'

'What do we want gold for?' asked Juchi ill-humouredly.

'They produce many useful things,' continued the Khan, undeterred. 'Their engineers make guns and siege engines for us; they have built the bridges by means of which we crossed the rivers. The silk shirts with which they supply us do not tear, but glide into our wounds with the arrows and make it easy for us to remove the arrows. They have doctors who make our wounded men well again.'

At this Tuli lost all control of himself and interrupted the Khan: 'And they have astrologers who contrive to confuse the mind of our Khan! What do we want of these "useful people"? Were we less feared, perchance, before their stink enveloped us? We need but you alone. Was not our Khan our *Sutu Bogdo*, our confidant of heaven, whom *Menke Kuku Tengri* listened to when he spoke with him in our name? Was not our Khan our wolf with the burning fur who set our hearts on fire and even had a road found when *Kohinar Salkin*, the confuser of horses, spread icy darkness around us? Of what use is one who speaks of roads which do not exist? Because you are our soul the mountains bow before us! O my beloved father and our Khan, were you not our panther who broke forth from the water of the marshes and did not tire of felling the enemy so that they lay like rotting trees? Of what use is this man, who speaks of beasts which do not exist?' Still more vehemently Tuli continued: 'I was present only one pace away from you and *I* did not see the fabulous beast!'

In the silence which followed Tuli's words, the Khan said: 'I have spoken with the Beast from Tibet. I promised it I would spare China. I have never yet broken my word.'

'A phantom cannot demand a promise! That "Beast from Tibet" was nothing but a devilish trick. And I saw the devil standing beside you—he was on the spot!'

'The Beast itself told me its name,' replied the Khan with restraint.

'The Beast, indeed! That charlatan stood behind you and whispered the name to you! I came up just in time to hear it!'

'And where were you when I was in danger?' asked the Khan scornfully. 'Very well, then,' he continued, 'if Yeliu applied a charm, his charm saved my life. The wild boar would have killed me. I was defenceless—was I not lucky that Yeliu cast a spell on it?'

'Cast a spell?' shouted Tuli, pale with rage. 'He stabbed the animal in a perfectly normal manner, just as any of us kills a wild boar. It's true, I'd never have believed it of him. He is extremely skilled in killing! And he can hold on to a horse too! What surprise has he yet in store for us?'

A threatening murmur ran through the row of *Orluks* and princes.

'I do not fail to perceive that you are all concerned about me,' said the Khan. 'But your objections are difficult to understand. First of all you suspect Yeliu of devilish magic power, and in the same breath you express your doubts as to whether he is capable of making use of that power. But he actually did cause the wild boar to stop just three paces away from me.'

Tuli looked at the Khan sullenly. 'Very well, I believe that he has powers at his disposal of which we know nothing. Why, then, if he was able to cast a spell on the wild boar, did he not, with his powerful glance, keep you on your horse when it shied? Why did he let you fall?'

Thereupon the Khan cried indignantly: 'Your mouths are distorted with suspicion. I did not call you together to pass judgement on my Chancellor.'

'What do we want with a "Chancellor"?' shouted Juchi. 'As long as he was not at your side, you saw no spirits!'

The Khan ordered silence by an imperious motion of the hand. 'I saw Kiotuan, the Beast from Tibet,' he declared firmly. 'And you also, my sons,' he said, in a voice which made everyone shudder, 'and you, my *Orluks*, shall one day see the Beast from Tibet—when you are as near to death as I was. It will stand in front of you, as it stood before me, with ruby-red eyes and a horn pointing to the Eternal Blue Heaven . . . And it will speak to you; and all of a sudden you will be able to look behind you without turning your head . . .'

The Khan had raised himself up with difficulty, and now he spoke in a tone of voice which none of his sons knew in him: 'It is said that the land is surrounded on all sides by water . . . I have been riding sixty years, and I have never come to the end of land —and I thought I could measure with my horse's hooves all the land that exists. But now I know that I shall never see what I have so ardently yearned to behold—the great waters . . . I have thrown away my years like chaff——' The Khan's eyes gazed far beyond them all, and his sons and the *Orluks* saw tears running down his face.

Then Arik-Buka walked up to the Khan, threw himself down

in front of him and embraced his knees: 'O, Father of all of us,
do not speak thus! You, our *Tug*, our standard, that joins
heaven and earth with each other! You, without whom we are
nothing! You are lord over all things, and the great waters shall
hasten towards you once you are in the saddle again. You exist;
the "Beast from Tibet" does not. There are millions of people,
and none of them has ever seen it. Not a single one!'

The Khan stood upright, listening, but it could be seen that
not a word of what Arik-Buka said had reached his ears. For
a moment the sons and *Orluks* thought that the Khan's mind
was confused, but then they noticed that strange brightness
which always lit up the Khan's face when anything threatening
was on the way. . . . Everyone began to listen. The sound of
horses' hooves rapidly approaching broke the silence. And
now an officer of the watch entered and announced: 'Sigi-
Kutuku!'

A triumphant gleam passed over the faces of the *Orluks*. Sigi-
Kutuku! Jelal-Addin's pursuer! He had come just at the right
moment to announce that the Shadow of Allah had been hunted
to death for the second time . . . The *Orluks* waited eagerly for
the vanquisher of the son of Mohammed to appear . . .

A man staggered in. He had black spots on his face. No one

recognized him as Sigi-Kutuku. When he reached the middle of
the yurt he stopped.

'Permit me to stand here, O Khan!' said the man with the dis-
figured face. 'It is better that the breath from my mouth should
touch no one.'

Now they all recognized him by his voice, and the *Orluks*
looked at him with unconcealed horror.

'Step aside!' ordered the Khan. Sigi-Kutuku did not move.
The Khan came down from his throne and walked towards Sigi-
Kutuku. He greeted him, as he did all his returning *Orluks*, by
placing his hands on his shoulders. Kutuku tried to step back.

'I bring death,' he said, 'nothing but death! I have become the
death of my ten thousand. O my *tuman*, whom I have murdered
in the swamps of India!' he stammered on. 'O my warriors, now
I have the same face with which you looked at me after I had
driven you to destruction!'

The Khan said: 'You have done what I ordered you to do.
Our women have but to bear sons once more and our mares to
drop foals once more, and your *tuman* will have come to life
again. Kutuku, my faithful one, you have done what I commanded!'

'I have murdered,' said Kutuku obstinately; 'you will soon
admit that I am right.' And with a voice which made everyone
listen tensely he confessed: 'I knew what was coming.'

'How could you have known that?' interjected Tuli.

'You are imagining something after the event,' said Chepe to
comfort him.

'If only that were so!' cried Kutuku despairingly. 'But it was
beforehand that I saw it, and I did not heed the words spoken to
me.'

'What did it say?' asked the Khan; and Kutuku felt the hands
which were still holding his shoulders beginning to tremble. 'Tell
what it was like.'

Then Kutuku whispered: 'It was night and we were lying on
the open field. Suddenly I woke up, and there it was over me.
At first I thought it was the darkness of the night—but it was
another darkness. There suddenly seemed to be a hole in the sky.
Many of the stars were no longer to be seen; they were covered by

a great wall of shadow. And this wall spoke to me in an audible voice and said: "Turn back and murder no more! You see that your people are falling although the enemy are running away from them. Already half your men are dead. Turn back!" I heard it, but I shut my ears. I saw the speaking wall of shadow, but I tried to imagine it was only a product of my feverish, overheated brain. But the wall of shadow was there, and it was right. It told me to look behind, and I did not have to turn my head. At one glance I saw my whole life. The wall of shadow promised to leave me and to come back to me again only when I had returned to you.'

Sigi-Kutuku's eyes became glassy. 'There it is!' he cried. The *Orluk* freed himself from the Khan's hands. 'There! Now it is whispering again—and now it is swaying and falling over me . . .' Sigi-Kutuku held his clenched fists before his eyes and staggered. The *Orluks* and princes were paralysed with fear. Yeliu arrived too late to hold up Kutuku. He laid him down on the carpet. He closed his eyelids and loosed his clenched fists which were covered all over with spots.

Chepe thought to himself: He is not afraid—it does no harm to him. And Tuli thought: He was standing just like that beside the Khan when the Khan saw his apparition. He is a raiser of spirits . . .

Yeliu stood up. Then he himself began to stagger; and he fell forward noiselessly. The Khan and Kublai caught him as he fell.

The following day, after he had consulted with Yeliu, the Khan proclaimed that at the end of nine days the whole army would return to the Steppe, and that they would build a town with stone walls in the midst of the Steppe as a sign that the time of anger had come to an end.

CHAPTER SEVENTEEN

The Conspiracy

IN the days which followed, the Khan took counsel with his Chancellor. The princes and *Orluks* had orders to work out the plans for the return march. As they left the Khan's presence the faces of all of them were equally impenetrable; and when they put their heads together in Tuli's yurt the words of all were inspired by the same hate. He has wrested every weapon from our hands, they thought. But if he thinks we will give up the struggle because of that——! Their thoughts ceaselessly followed the one man, looking for a weak spot in him . . .

Kublai alone was absent from these meetings. The Khan had given him the task of deciphering secret documents which had been captured.

Of all of them Arik-Buka was the hardest in his judgement on Kublai. 'The grey devil has been at work on him. Kublai is no longer one of us,' he said.

They were all agreed on one thing—that as long as they were in this 'accursed place' it was no use trying to do anything. But once the breath of the Steppe blew round the Khan again he would waken up from his bad dream. The Steppe would remind its greatest son what he still owed it. The return, against which they had all murmured at first, now seemed to them the only way back to the heart of the Khan and to new 'fields of fame'.

The ninth day dawned. The princes and *Orluks* assembled at the usual hour in Tuli's yurt. There was only one thing different —Chepe was missing. He did not arrive until an hour later, and they all noticed at once that he was labouring under great excite-

ment. As they surged round him with eager faces they saw how
his eyes flashed like those of a beast of prey which is sure of its
victim. Lowering his voice to a hoarse whisper, he said: 'He has
played his last card!'

Tuli grasped Chepe by the arm. 'Have you finished him off?'
he asked.

'He's still alive,' said Chepe, 'but he won't be for long.'

When the others looked at him inquiringly he admitted: 'I
went to his yurt, and though he was with the Khan, I found
someone there before me.'

'I can well imagine who it was,' said Arik-Buka bitterly. 'Did
you at least identify him?'

'It was not Kublai.'

Then the eyes of the others began to sparkle too.

'Who was in the yurt?' asked Arik-Buka.

'A man who lay in a deep sleep . . . a wounded man . . . but
not one of ours.'

'An enemy in his yurt?' asked Tuli hoarsely. 'There's the
death penalty for that.'

'It's even better than that,' said Chepe. 'I found this on the
sleeping man.' He pulled a dagger from beneath his tunic, and as
he drew the blade a little out of its sheath they all saw the sign:
the claw of a golden eagle. Arik-Buka noticed that a tremor of
terror passed through the others, and he asked: 'What does that
sign mean?'

'It is the sign of "The Old Man of the Mountain",' explained
Chepe. This told Arik enough. The 'Old Man of the Mountain'
was the ruler of the assassins, Lord of Alamut, the 'Eagles' Nest',
an impregnable fortress far away in the West. He sent out his
fedavi, men fanatically loyal to him, to assassinate people in high
positions. These *fedavi* shrank from nothing; they courted death
in carrying out their tasks. For only by so dying, they believed,
would they enter paradise, of which they had once had a foretaste.
The 'Old Man of the Mountain' got possession of them in a
devilish way. He caused novices to sink into a deep sleep and had
them brought to a palace in which every pleasure was available
to them. After a certain time the *fedavi* was again lulled to sleep,
taken from the palace and back to the 'Eagles' Nest'. And when

the *fedavi* woke again he had but one desire—to die in carrying
out an order of the 'Old Man of the Mountain'. Before sending
him out, the 'Old Man of the Mountain' burned on the *fedavi's*
breast, just above the heart, the name of the person whom he was
to kill. To each of his emissaries he gave a letter addressed to the
'Guardian of Paradise' instructing the latter to open to him and
grant him what was promised in the letter . . . Arik-Buka
thought of all this now, and without a moment's hesitation he
demanded: 'Give me the dagger!'

'I have put him into a still deeper sleep,' said Chepe.

For a while a satisfied silence reigned in the yurt. Then Juchi
asked: 'How did he come to be wounded, do you think?'

'I can only suppose that it was this way. Apparently during
the tumult at Bamian he was going to try, but he didn't succeed in
pushing his way to the victim the first time.'

'To whom?' asked Arik-Buka, for the idea which came into
his mind at that moment seemed too monstrous.

'Such a man is always sent to the most important person,'
Chepe informed him.

'And you're sure that Yeliu knew whom he had in his yurt?'
asked Jagatai.

'I even maintain that he called him,' said Chepe. 'Otherwise he
would not have taken him in and kept him hidden so long; for he
certainly knew what the penalty was.'

'Give me the dagger!' repeated Arik-Buka. 'I shall strike him
down before the Khan's eyes.' Chepe looked sharply at Arik-
Buka. 'You shall have the dagger,' he said, 'but not for yourself.
I have chosen another to strike at the heart of the traitor. I care
too much for Kublai,' Chepe concluded in a trembling voice.

'He will never do it,' said Arik-Buka.

'I have good news for you, Arik,' said Chepe. 'Kublai has
doubts about his—teacher.'

'How do you know that?' asked Arik-Buka.

'I overheard a conversation they had before Yeliu went to the
Khan. Kublai offered to watch with the "wounded man". He
pleaded in a tone which betrayed that he had already asked this
several times in vain. There was suspicion in his voice. Yeliu
refused firmly. The wounded man was no longer in danger, he

said. Kublai went away, not without resentment, so it seemed to me, and . . .' here Chepe lowered his voice, 'now, if ever, is the time to try to win him back.'

'He's not worth it,' said Arik-Buka. 'I used to be the nearest to him, and I know that he's lost to us.'

Chepe took hold of him. 'You're going to give him up? You who carried him out of the ice! Go to him and bring him this as well as the dagger. He's already busy deciphering secret writing!'

Chepe produced a small locket beautifully chased. 'I found it in the wounded man's clothing. I expect it contains the letter to the "Guardian of Paradise". Go and make your brother ashamed, but don't give him up! No one is to be left to the traitor.'

Arik was just about to go when Juchi said: 'All that you have told is too terrible, Chepe, but we must believe you. You have proof that it is a *fedavi* who is lying in Yeliu's yurt. . . . Only, I am just wondering why Yeliu has been caring for the would-be assassin of the man whose shadow he himself is?'

'He wants to be more than a mere shadow,' said Chepe, and his eyes flashed. 'That grey devil believes he is strong enough to gain mastery over the Khan. There is no doubt but that he is in league with our enemies. Was it not through his influence that the Persians—his friends the Persians—were allowed to continue governing in the Kingdom of the Shah? The people with influence always manage to make off in good time—they have a better chance than the simple folk. Nobody troubled about Yeliu while the battles were raging. Who knows who was going in and out of his yurt, since he could hide a *fedavi* without anyone having the least suspicion? I have not yet got any proof of the extent of the conspiracy he has been hatching. But why does he keep the chests in his yurt locked? I tried to open them; not one of them gave way. What reason has he to lock his chests—and even from Kublai?'

Chepe pulled the blue bowl from inside his jerkin. He held it out to the others. 'Is there anything special to be seen in it?' he asked expectantly. 'A writing or a sign, perhaps?' Before their surprised eyes Chepe held the bowl up against the light. And now they all saw the red bird, and burst into cries of consternation.

'If only we could burst open the chests!' exclaimed Chepe, fling-ing the bowl away contemptuously.

Arik-Buka stuck the locket as well as the dagger inside his jerkin. 'Where can I find Kublai?' he asked.

'He went off towards Bamian,' said Chepe, 'and as there's nothing left there to obstruct the view, you cannot miss him.'

'When the conspirator returns to his yurt, watch out lest he tries to escape; and as soon as he's there shoot an arrow with a red streamer on it up into the mast of the *Tug* so that I can see it from afar,' said Arik-Buka.

'And what about the Khan?' asked Juchi. 'Without his know-ing it, shall we . . .?'

'He will know soon enough that the snake which was going to bite him has been trampled on. We promised him that we would reduce the number of his enemies—the astrologer is his worst one. When the hour of our departure comes he will no longer be alive.'

So, without further delay, Arik-Buka set off to look for Kublai.

He came upon Kublai unnoticed. Kublai was sitting in the midst of a field of ruins, on the remnant of a wall, sunk in thought. He was staring in front of him, and when Arik-Buka looked over his brother's shoulder he saw that Kublai was staring at a poisonous adder. Obviously he had smashed its head with a stone.

'A good omen,' said Arik-Buka. Kublai turned round, and for a moment his face had a frightened expression.

'I mean that,' said Arik-Buka, pointing to the dead snake and the stone. As Kublai looked over at it, Arik-Buka continued: 'A good hit! But your ears used to be better.' He tried to laugh. 'In the past it wasn't so easy to come on you unawares, especially from behind,' he said.

'I don't know what you're driving at,' said Kublai, who had recovered his composure. Arik-Buka sat down beside him on the ruined wall. 'As far as I know the Khan has instructed you to de-cipher secret documents. If you are willing to accept a similar commission "from another side" too, here is such a document.'

Arik-Buka drew the locket from inside his jerkin. 'We can be certain that at most only three people have seen it before.' Arik-Buka held up to Kublai the opened locket, out of which a little roll of paper appeared.

'Where did you get that?' asked Kublai.

'You don't know it, then?' asked Arik-Buka, in reply. And when he saw by Kublai's face that the locket was unfamiliar to him, he said: 'I'm relieved to see that you don't know it.'

'How would I know it?' asked Kublai.

'It's a good thing that you don't know it,' repeated Arik-Buka; and he drew the little paper out of the locket and unfolded it. 'What's written on it?' he asked.

Kublai saw at once that it was written in a language he did not know. 'I cannot read it,' he said, and Arik-Buka knew by his voice that he was telling the truth.

'Do you think that your teacher can decipher it?'

'It's possible,' said Kublai. 'He knows many scripts.'

Arik-Buka rolled up the paper, stuck it into the locket and pushed this back inside his jerkin.

'Where did you get it?' asked Kublai again.

'Do you not know that either?' asked Arik-Buka, and he fixed his eyes on Kublai's face. Arik-Buka's hand held the dagger.

'You were in Yeliu's yurt, were you?' asked Kublai.

'So you recognize the dagger?'

'Yes,' said Kublai.

'So you also know that there's a man hidden there?'

'I know that Yeliu is caring for a wounded man in his yurt.'

'And he hasn't told you what kind of man he is?'

'No,' said Kublai. 'He doesn't know that himself.'

Arik-Buka drew the dagger a little out of its sheath and pointed to the golden eagle's claw. 'Have you seen that before?' he asked.

'Yes,' said Kublai. 'I saw it when the man who is lying there let the dagger slip a bit out of the sheath when he moved in his sleep.'

'You know what the sign means?'

'No,' said Kublai.

'And what about your—teacher? Does he?'

'It's possible that he knows the meaning of that sign. He knows the meaning of many signs—but I'm not certain whether he has even seen that sign.'

'Indeed?' said Arik-Buka. 'You mean he has not yet had sufficient time to do so. How long has he had that man in his yurt?'

'Since the battle of Bamian. He found him amongst the dead, and when he saw that he was still alive——'

'Indeed?' said Arik-Buka, with assumed carelessness. 'So he took *him* in when there was only a spark of life left in him did he?'

'That is quite certain.'

'The man doesn't look as if he had been fighting in the battle on *our* side,' said Arik-Buka pointedly.

Kublai made no reply.

'You know the penalty for hiding an enemy!'

'Yeliu didn't want to hide him. He did so only to save his life,' said Kublai.

'That man is dead. Chepe has put an end to him,' said Arik-Buka.

'Why did he do that?' asked Kublai, with unconcealed horror.

'You seem to take an interest in that man,' said Arik-Buka scathingly.

'I have been looking after him,' said Kublai, embarrassed.

'Indeed!' said Arik-Buka. 'And you really don't know what kind of man he was?'

'No,' said Kublai.

'Well, I'll tell you. The golden eagle's claw is the sign of Hussein, the "Old Man of the Mountain". The man with the dagger was one who had been sent out to murder—he was a *fedavi*. You know that it is always the most powerful person in a country whom a *fedavi* is sent out after.'

All the blood left Kublai's face.

'You know all that, don't you?'

'Yes,' said Kublai.

'You knew neither the man nor the sign on the dagger, did you?'

'No,' said Kublai, no less firmly.

Arik-Buka's features became distorted with hate. 'But *he* knew it!' he said.

'No, he didn't,' protested Kublai. But now his voice did not sound so sure as before. 'No, no—it's unthinkable that he knew it. He has no eyes for weapons. I never saw this dagger in his hand. He didn't take it out of its sheath. He didn't see the sign!'

'Very well,' said Arik-Buka. 'It's possible that he doesn't take an interest in daggers. But—he does understand something about wounds, doesn't he? Didn't he want to make the man well?'

'Yes,' said Kublai, 'that's what he wanted.'

'And no doubt he examined the man all over for wounds.'

'Certainly he did,' admitted Kublai—and at the same moment such a fear passed over him that he grasped his breast.

'That's exactly the spot,' said Arik-Buka, his eyes flashing. 'The "Old Man of the Mountains" burns the name of the victim right above the heart. You know that! I can see by your face that you do. And your—teacher *must* have seen the name.'

Kublai stared over the ruins. His lips whispered continuously: No, no, no . . . But his brain thought: Why did he not want to let me into his yurt any more? Why did he refuse my request again and again? Why did he never let me have a look into the chests? 'He's not capable of such a thing——' stammered Kublai.

'Oh!' scoffed Arik-Buka. 'He has shown that he's capable of many things. When no one thought he was capable of such a thing, he suddenly arrived on a horse—an expert horseman. He suddenly struck down a wild boar—an expert hunter; and if Chepe had not been quicker than he, he would suddenly have seen the Khan lying in his blood—an expert conspirator! One could learn from him! No one could have contrived it more skilfully! He's a master in his domain. First of all he moves heaven and earth to worm his way into the Khan's confidence. Then, right in front of the Khan's eyes, he dissociates himself from the rebel Tang Liweng in order to divert all suspicion from himself. Then, by favourable auguries and eagerly accepted advice, he makes himself indispensable. Then he gets the Khan's grandson on his side, so that he will have a weak-minded tool who will rule later as he wishes. Then he hires a murderer, and when this plan fails, he strikes the blow himself.'

Arik-Buka seized Kublai by the arm. 'He is a devil who has secret powers at his disposal. He is a creature of darkness who can spread darkness over others. He knocked the Khan off his horse without having to stretch out his hand to do so—never before had the Khan fallen. He made the wild boar stop in order that the Khan's fear would turn into terror; for only in the terror of death could he cause him to see the "Beast" . . . He has power over the powers of darkness. He is a snake; his tooth is full of poison and his tongue is cleft.'

Kublai shut his eyes in despair. He remembered and saw the split arrow before him. The gaping halves were like the open jaws of a snake. . . .

'The Khan would never have seen the "Beast from Tibet",' continued Arik-Buka, 'if that conspirator had not been at his side to influence his thoughts in a moment of weakness. You must admit that yourself. Could he have invented a more suitable animal? The unicorn hit the Khan in the heart. The "evil eye" took a living form and shook the Khan's splendid mind. In this way Yeliu was able to influence the Khan so much as to make him wish to imprint on the Steppe, his mother, the brand of infamy— a town! We are to become cage-people! He wanted to put the Khan a prisoner in a stone cage!—— Could a more ignominious death be devised for the greatest Son of the Steppe?'

Kublai looked before him disconsolately. Only ruins met his gaze. He struggled desperately against believing—but there was his brother beside him, holding out tangible proofs to him. Kublai, agonized, looked at Arik-Buka. 'Why do you only go an indirect way about it—through me?' he asked.

'*I* would not have come to you,' said Arik-Buka, harshly. 'I had given you up because I considered that you also were a traitor, one who had let his soul be broken by that one. But Chepe sent me. The dagger came from him too. You have to thank him for it, not me.'

Arik-Buka held the dagger out to Kublai.

'Thank him for what?' stammered Kublai.

'With the *kulang* stallion and with the panther you showed how

surely you could strike to the heart,' said Arik-Buka, looking at Kublai with astonishment. 'We swore on the middle summit of the Holy Mountain that we would never part from each other,' he whispered. 'You have broken that oath, and I would have had to kill you if this hour had not come in which you can make amends for what I have suffered for you. Take vengeance on him who divided us! Strike down the man who has hung himself like a shadow over our *Sutu Bogdo*! Smite down the Shadow of the Khan!'

Kublai perceived the wounded love in Arik's eyes. He took hold of the dagger.

'I shall track him,' said Kublai tonelessly. 'Not even the shadow of his words shall escape my ear; and my eye . . .'

'Look over there!' said Arik-Buka. And he pointed to the *Tug*, on the mast of which a red rag was fluttering. 'That is the sign. He is in his yurt. He is back earlier than usual from the Khan. He is in a hurry. See to it that he is not present when we assemble before the Khan to receive his orders for the departure.'

Side by side Kublai and Arik-Buka sought a way through the ruins of the fortress which the Khan had called Mobalig, 'Accursed Spot'. When they came within sight of Yeliu's yurt they separated and Kublai went up to it alone. In his left hand he held the locket which Arik-Buka had given him; it was in his clenched fist. The dagger was hidden under his jerkin. It knocked against his heart at each step . . . That is Arik knocking, thought Kublai; he is ceaselessly reminding me: I—am—with—you——you—must—do—it . . .

When Kublai arrived at the yurt he felt such a violent pain at the place against which the dagger was pressing that he drew it from inside his jerkin and threw it away. For a moment he stood there overcome by a terrible sense of desolation. He felt just as much cut off from Arik as from Yeliu. Thrown back completely upon himself, he was neither capable of entering the yurt nor of turning back. At this moment he heard Yeliu's voice.

CHAPTER EIGHTEEN

The Last Instructions

'COME in, Kublai!' It sounded no different from that night when Kublai had secretly left Chepe and Arik and, torn by doubts, sought refuge with Yeliu.

He has recognized me by my step, thought Kublai. He raised the curtain and stepped inside. As soon as the yurt curtain had fallen behind him, he had the unmistakable feeling that besides Yeliu and himself there was a third, an invisible presence, there. After he had cast a hurried glance at the *fedavi* Kublai was quite certain that it was not the dead man who caused him this feeling of uneasiness. Yeliu was sitting by the fire with the same calm demeanour as usual. Kublai feverishly examined every corner with his eye, yet he could discover nothing which could have awakened his suspicion.

'Sit down with me at the fire; it will do you good!' The same words as then, thought Kublai, though not quite—that time Yeliu did not say 'with me' ... How can he say 'sit down with me' now, and behave as if everything were not finished, and the dead man not dead, and the conspiracy not broken up, and the avenger not standing in front of him, even though I have thrown away the dagger? ... Have I not hands which are blunt as paws ...? Or has this incomprehensible man, who is sitting there so calmly at the fire, got such power over me even yet that he was able to take the dagger from me without moving a finger ...? One doubt after another tortured Kublai's brain—and at the same time he felt a certainty in his inmost being that these thoughts were utterly absurd and far-fetched. He searched his mind desperately for one thought that could stand up to Yeliu's look.

For Yeliu had now raised his eyes and was looking at Kublai. With a smile which seemed to show that he knew all Kublai's worries, he said: 'What are you torturing yourself about? You are looking for something which does not exist, are you not? My talent is that I am without fear—that is all.'

His smile did not disappear as he continued: 'It is too late now to do what you intended.'

Only now did Kublai see the great change which had come over Yeliu's face, and it dawned on him whose the third presence was.

The shadow of death lay upon Yeliu.

Kublai was so utterly aghast at this sudden realization that he looked round for something to hold on to, and sat down. He could not take his eyes off Yeliu's face, though it caused him immeasurable shame to look upon that countenance devoid of all cunning and transparent in all its features, which regarded him across the airy veil that shimmered over the flames.

'I have been expecting you,' said Yeliu, and he smiled again. 'When they sent you they certainly could not foresee that in doing so they were giving us the opportunity for the one thing which now remains for us to do. How would I have been able to fetch you to give you the last instructions which still remain to be given?'

A violent pain in the region of the heart prevented Yeliu from continuing to speak. The frail body became taut, but the pain was so great that its effect could soon be seen—a fleeting pallor passed over his face.

'Before we begin,' continued Yeliu, after a brief pause, 'I must ask you to forgive me for an offence.' Yeliu cast down his eyes. His glance sought Kublai's left hand, which was closed over the locket, and haltingly, as if deciphering a secret writing, he said in the voice of one reading aloud: 'And an emerald palace shall be opened to you, and forty slave-women shall serve you, when you have destroyed him who is a thorn in my eyes—Genghis Khan.' Yeliu looked at Kublai. 'You see, I knew it. And even before I had read the letter to the "Guardian of Paradise", I had come across the branded name. Still I kept it from you. How could I initiate you, the grandson of the Khan, into that frightful secret? What else could I do but keep you away from the zone of death as soon as the "One who had been in Paradise" was again in a fit state to raise a dagger?'

Then Yeliu said with emotion: 'Fate spared *him* to me from amongst thousands and thousands of dead. Could I cease to see in him a wounded man, after I knew that he had come to murder? He was blameless, indeed he must have believed that he was favoured by being chosen, and he could not know that he was being misused in the most frightful way! Could I have killed him, I who do not believe that anyone has a right to kill? Could I have delivered him up, I who do not see that anyone has a right to deliver up another? And yet I saw that through this man, whom I had torn from the jaws of death, I was bringing danger to another. The knowledge that there was no way out of this predicament has consumed my heart. I did all that was in my power to save him, yet at the same time I hoped that it might be in vain. . . . Spare me from hearing who killed him.'

He died by the dagger with which he was going to kill, thought Kublai.

It was as if this thought released new pain in Yeliu's breast. He pressed his elbows against his sides. With difficulty he continued: 'I am being warned that there is no time to lose. There is still much to be discussed. In the chests you will find some things which I thought it advisable to write out for you, for instance, about the computation of the calendar, and the casting of bells, and the efficacy of the roots of *tshirimsha* grass which are a cure when someone is attacked by *ʒinga* and the limbs swell, the teeth loosen and all the blood goes from the hands . . . There's nothing else locked up in the chests but writings of this kind, about which I talked to you while we were on the journey. I have had time to ponder many things. Whoever looks at a thing long enough comprehends it at last. In this way it is also possible to get inside the meaning of words. Listen to how it fared with me regarding the word "Mongol". Mongol means weak river . . . the beginning of a river . . . a river which still has its course before it. Mongols: horsemen riding off. Sons of the Steppe, still unspoiled by desires such as are felt by those who dwell in palaces; simple people who sing over *argal* fires the songs which they learn from rustling grasses; who greet the water, and the rocks, and who carry on their breasts their *eigas*, their wooden bowls. Mongols: a rising river which promises life . . . and it has become a raging river, and it is called Genghis Khan, destroyer of cities, and Anger of Allah . . .

'I could have gone—he had expelled me from his yurt. Yet I remained. *Po yen*—patience a hundred times, I whispered, as I sought some lone survivor in the fields of ruins. *Po yen*, as the rice farmers of my country whisper when the Yangtse has over-flowed its banks and swallowed up millions of human lives. *Po yen*, whispers the rice farmer when the raging storm kills his father; *Po yen*, he whispers when contagious disease kills his brothers—Patience a hundred times, when famine kills his sons . . . and he gnaws the bitter bark of trees, and at every bite he whispers: Patience a hundred times! And he does not curse the river, nor the sky which made it break forth and swell . . . And when the waters of horror have subsided he returns to his field and gropes under the mud for the rice shoots . . .'

Yeliu lowered his voice. 'I returned to Genghis Khan,' he said, 'although I was against him. Only by consuming myself in his service could I overcome him. For see, he listens to me now! One of his own kin comes to my yurt and seeks counsel with me. You, his grandson, will no longer be a stranger to the peoples who tremble before him. O Kublai, I have no more strength to remain here any longer. I have already died with too many others. And each one took a breath of my heart away with him.' Yeliu looked over at the *fedavi*. 'It is time for me to set out on the journey if I am to overtake him. I have taken it upon myself to look after him. As long as he could still hold a dagger he felt too much under the eyes of the terrible one who sent him. In the new place perhaps he is no longer deaf. I must try to catch up with him . . . And I shall certainly stay there a while. But I will come back again and again in order to live completely the one thought which animates me. Do not grieve: we shall meet again.'

With a touch of gaiety, Yeliu continued: 'Oh, I know well how I shall have to manage that we do not miss each other. When you are riding by the rice-fields, and there is no longer a clanking of weapons behind you—I, an insignificant peasant, shall be treading to turn the water-wheel so that the rice-shoots do not thirst, and you, glancing at my withered features, shall not be in doubt for a moment . . .

'And again, you shall recognize me from afar in the fisherman fishing with cormorants and putting exactly the right rings round the birds' necks so that the biggest fishes remain in the basket . . .

'As a beggar I shall look out from the shadow of a gate on the same day when you inspect it to examine its strength . . .

'At a review of officials it shall be I who will direct your eyes to the wrists of those whose hands are crooked from constantly "holding them open behind their backs".

'But I shall also draw your attention to that brave fire-watcher who saved the child and did not receive the reward which you had ordered should be given to him.

'And I shall step on to the arena before you as that horseman who, with invisible reins, subdues the rearing horse so skilfully as to merit your praise.

'And likewise from the face of the robber whom the judge has had stretched out on a bamboo-field that his body may be cruelly bored through, until he dies, by the bamboo shoots which burst from the ground like the tips of spears—even from his eyes I shall look at you, and you shall let clemency prevail. As if they were all your children you shall rule alike over those of the North who are onion-eaters, merry fellows, industrious and turbulent; and those of the South, who are spoiled by much eating of lotus-seeds and birds'-nest soup. And for all of them you shall offer the great sacrifice, as in ancient times, on Tai-chan, the greatest of the Five Holy Mountains. You shall cast off hurry; for the world shall finally belong, not to the horsemen who know nought but the hunger and passion of riding, but to the ploughman. You shall come to understand that there are five points of the heavens —North, South, East, West and that point which links all together, the Middle. In the middle you shall find yourself as one who strives for wisdom—for the strength to share the sufferings of others. Should you find in yourself thoughts which darken the heavens, you shall order the armies to march against you. And if you think you can spare yourself from self-chastisement, then your Prime Minister will sacrifice his life in the public square to remind you before the eyes of all that you are the Son of Heaven and not the son of darkness. You shall be patient a hundred times, and Arik's hate will be worn blunt upon your patience. All this has had to be said to you, at whose heart the bird Feng Huang pointed with his beak when I saw you for the first time.'

Up to the last Yeliu had spoken with a smile. Now he pointed to a bamboo flute which lay on one of the chests, and said to Kublai: 'Give me the flute! I will try to play it. You know that Feng Huang loves music—perhaps I shall succeed in moving him to come.' Yeliu began to play, and tones of a strange sweetness were heard. Kublai listened spellbound. And suddenly his eyes perceived the Phoenix. His wings were spread; he was rocking in time with the music. His capers made Kublai feel merry. Feng Huang seemed to be conjuring up the notes from the ground with his steps. Then, buoyantly and airily, just as he had floated in, he disappeared again through the wall of the yurt.

Only when he was gone did Kublai perceive that Yeliu was dead.

CHAPTER NINETEEN

The Hour of Departure

ARIK saw the dagger at once when he arrived at Yeliu's yurt. He picked it up and pushed it under his jerkin. Then he listened. There was nothing to be heard. He's not speaking any more, thought Arik-Buka; he no longer has any breath to do so; he's dead . . . And suddenly he felt frightened about Kublai. Perhaps he did it with his hands, he thought, and the other defended himself, and had a sword? Arik pulled the curtain aside. And then he saw Yeliu lying there lifeless, and Kublai kneeling beside the dead man. Arik-Buka did not look at Kublai. He feasted his eyes on the sight of the hated Yeliu, who was lying there and would never be able to rise again. This alone was important to Arik. What does it matter to me how Kublai has done it? he thought . . . And the fact that he's overcome by it, well, that won't bring the enemy to life again! He's been executed, and he will never stand in the way again, and he will not be present at the hour of departure . . .

Arik-Buka remembered that he had been sent to fetch Kublai to come to the Khan's yurt for the assignment of orders. He went up to his brother from behind, and despite his excitement, there was a perceptible note of solicitude in his voice as he said: 'Come! The Khan is waiting for us!'

Kublai stood up. A strange timidity prevented Arik-Buka from looking his brother in the face.

The two walked silently side by side to the Khan's yurt. When they entered, the Khan had already begun to give his orders. He was just saying: 'As there are many things to be deliberated with the Chancellor on the way, he shall ride beside me.'

Arik-Buka was unable to contain himself any longer. 'Listen, O Khan!' he cried. 'Listen, all of you, his sons and his *Orluks*! The traitor is dead! Kublai has killed him!'

Everyone turned round and stared at Kublai and Arik-Buka. The Khan fixed his eyes steadily on Kublai.

'Yeliu is dead!' Kublai confirmed.

The Khan stammered: 'What do you say? Yeliu dead? . . . Was he not here with me only an hour ago?' And then he looked at Arik-Buka. 'Who dares to speak of a traitor?' he said.

'There are two men lying dead in his yurt,' said Chepe bluntly. 'I killed the second one.'

The Khan turned pale. 'Who dares to kill someone whom my Chancellor had in his yurt?' he said.

Arik now went up to the Khan and pulled the dagger from beneath his jerkin. He drew the blade far enough out of the sheath for the golden eagle's claw to be seen. 'The man whom the Chancellor had in his yurt was carrying this dagger,' he said.

The Khan saw the sign. He looked at Arik-Buka, utterly dismayed. Then he looked at Chepe, and at his sons and the *Orluks*, one after the other. He saw the same gleam of triumph in every eye.

Are those my sons and my *Orluks*? the Khan asked himself, bewildered. That is what conspirators look like when their plot has succeeded.

At this point Chepe said: 'The fact that it was Kublai who killed him speaks for itself!'

The Khan looked at Kublai searchingly. 'You killed him— you?' he asked.

'No,' said Kublai. 'But I am guilty; I intended to kill him.'

The *Orluks* looked at each other, baffled, and Arik-Buka said: 'He is too much overcome; he does not know what he is saying.'

The Khan went up to Kublai and took him by the shoulders. 'Tell me, is it true that he is dead?' he asked.

'He is dead,' said Kublai tonelessly. 'And I was going to kill him—to kill him who died for you a thousand times—day after day, all the years he was in your service.'

'The man who had a *fedavi* hidden under a cover!' cried Tuli indignantly.

'We shall see what he has in his chests!' cried Chepe.

'Kublai shall speak, and no one else!' ordered the Khan. He had made a discovery which had suddenly caused the shouting of the others to sound empty. For as he looked closely into Kublai's face it struck him how like the face of Yeliu this face had become. The Khan did not take his eyes off his face while Kublai was speaking. Kublai disclosed to the Khan that an inheritance such as no Chancellor had ever before left to his sovereign was awaiting him in the chests. He told of the *fedavi* and of the predicament in which Yeliu had been on his account. With a calmness which dumbfounded everyone Kublai then went on to tell of the shadow of death which he had perceived the moment he had entered Yeliu's yurt. The princes and *Orluks* stared in front of them while Kublai was speaking. Arik-Buka alone never took his eyes off him. And now he, too, saw what the Khan had discovered in Kublai's changed face . . .

Yeliu is not really dead at all, thought Arik-Buka, horrified. I still hear him speaking. . . He always spoke like that when he stood before the Khan . . . It is *his* look which the Khan sees in Kublai's eyes . . . Why does not the Khan's face turn dark with anger? Does he not notice that Yeliu, the inscrutable one, has slipped into that circle which his sons and *Orluks* have drawn around him . . .?

When the Khan let go of Kublai's shoulders and went back to his throne his face was as it had been before Arik-Buka had shouted: 'The traitor is dead!' The Khan continued his instructions. He took them up at the point where he had been interrupted and, as was his custom when he wished to emphasize a sentence particularly, he repeated: 'As there are many things to be deliberated with the Chancellor on the way, he shall ride beside me . . .'

And the eyes of Genghis Khan indicated Kublai.

Yeliu's obsequies delayed the departure, but the distance to be covered each day was strictly maintained, and a few months later the *tumans* marched over the Arai Pass, towards the Steppe.

R

Arik-Buka rode beside Chepe. He had hardly spoken at all during the whole journey. Now Chepe pointed to the white chain which cut off the view to the South.

'I wish we had stayed there—he and I,' said Arik-Buka gloomily.

Chepe shook his head.

'We have lost him in the worst possible way,' said Arik-Buka.

Chepe rode on silently.

'I want to know what you think about Kublai,' persisted Arik-Buka, after a pause.

'I am not thinking of him,' said Chepe. 'My thoughts are with Yeliu.'

'You should not soil your lips with that name!'

'I am no longer certain that he was a traitor.'

Arik-Buka stared at Chepe, horrified.

'He was different from us,' said Chepe thoughtfully, 'but . . .'

'Did he not change the Khan into someone I could no longer recognize?' interrupted Arik-Buka. 'Did he not break the Khan's soul? And did he not do the same with Kublai? Has he not deprived the Khan of the will to take possession of countries by trampling them beneath the hooves of his horses and putting his foot on the necks of the conquered?'

Chepe looked far in front of him. He saw Kublai riding beside the Khan.

'Kublai will rule one day,' said Chepe calmly.

'May *Menke Kuku Tengri* preserve him from that!' exclaimed Arik-Buka, and there was a threat in his voice.

Chepe looked at him intently. 'I don't understand you,' he said.

Arik-Buka rode on. His face was hard and inscrutable.

'All you sons and grandsons of the Khan are destined to be rulers,' said Chepe.

'*He* is not,' said Arik-Buka bitterly. 'He alone has forfeited the right. The heritage of the Khan will fall to Sons of the Steppe—and the task of completing what the greatest Son of the Steppe has begun. Kublai is no longer a Son of the Steppe. He may decipher writing and tend wounded men; he may collect fragments and pass the night getting beyond the stars with measuring apparatus. As long as he does those things I will not even stop to remember that he still exists. But if he, who has so intolerably much of that other one in him—to whom that other has even given his face—haven't you noticed it?—if he dares to aspire to the sceptre of rulership, I will oppose him. For how could I allow that one to rule? And if he tries to mount one of the thrones which have been swept empty by the Sons of the Steppe he will find me standing before it, and my hand will not be empty! I will remind him that he has broken an oath with which we bound ourselves to each other as we looked over towards the South from the middle peak of the *Tobu dolo gam*, when the sun was playing on the Desert as on a mirror and turning to fire over the sands of the Gobi . . . Then Yeliu shall fall!'

Chepe noticed how distorted with rage Arik-Buka's face was, so he refrained from saying what he thought. His heart was filled with sadness.

Arik-Buka's eyes sought the two horsemen at the head of the procession. He noticed that the Khan was bent forward. Kublai was sitting upright in his saddle. He rides like a victor, thought Arik-Buka. He rides with as much assurance as if Yeliu were not dead, or as if he had a guarantee that he would rise again one day . . . But I will see to it that that never happens! Never!

Son of Heaven—Son of the Steppe

'I WANTED never to allow that to happen,' concluded Arik-Buka, who had been taking the lead more and more in recalling their story. And he looked at Kublai unrelentingly. 'But I was not watchful enough. Otherwise you would not be here now in this luxurious tent of ermine. It was too late when I marched against you.'

Kublai looked silently in front of him. He had seen with dismay how lightly Arik-Buka had passed over everything which could unite them, and how eagerly he had snatched at everything which could separate them. Now he heard Arik-Buka saying scornfully: 'What did you expect to come of our holding up to each other how things used to be between us? I could find nothing in that mirror which would prevent me from marching against you again tomorrow if only I were free.'

'I ask myself,' said Kublai, 'whence you get the right to take your brother so severely to task, even though his way and yours were not the same.'

'Brother!' cried Arik-Buka bitterly. 'Do you not know, then, that you have lost your face and have long since looked like that other one? In striking you I wished to strike Yeliu.'

Kublai smiled. 'It may be that something of him has entered into me. But I believe, rather, that there was something already in me which he brought out. However that may be, you overlook the fact that Genghis Khan, whose heir you consider yourself, was not against Yeliu in the end. He had a town built in the Steppe, as his Chancellor had advised him to do.'

'The town was very practical as a central depot for the

tributes!' interjected Arik-Buka. 'And you will admit that it was
not Yeliu's methods which Genghis Khan used in his later years
to collect those tributes. And was it, perchance, in the spirit of
Yeliu that Genghis Khan ordered that the whole population of
Hia should be sacrificed at his tomb, and that everyone whom
he met on his last journey should be slaughtered?' Triumphantly
Arik-Buka continued: 'And it didn't stop by any means at this
one "reversion to the customs of the Steppe"—Oh, no, indeed!
May I remind you of a few more things? Think of our father,
Tuli, the destroyer of Herat and other nests of rebels! Think of
how he sacrificed his life for Ogotai, the first successor of Genghis
Khan and the first heir to his Empire and to all the nations which
were yet to be subjugated! If I am not mistaken it was a year of
the hare when he marched against the rebellious Khitats. And it
was at the Khabkyal Pass, where we had overthrown the Khitat as
Kohinar Salkin, the icy wind, overthrows a forest of rotten trees,
that Ogotai was seized with an illness from which he lost his
speech. And the *shamans* saw at once that he was possessed by
spirits, and they held sheeps' shoulder-blades into the fire in order
to inquire of the oracle which sacrifice would free him from them
—whether people, or herds, or silver. But the leaps of the burning shoulder-blades showed that the demons, lords over the slain
and ravaged in the Khitat country, demanded the sacrifice of one
of the same blood as Ogotai. Whereupon Tuli, without the least
hesitation, spoke thus: "Our father has chosen you, Ogotai, like
a gelding, and has fondled you like a sheep, and has set you upon
his exalted throne, and has ordained that all the peoples be foot-
stools for your feet. Shall the great Mongol nation be plunged
into mourning? I have been created to be your shield, and to
guard you from all harm. Therefore I will drink the water of
exorcism, and my soul will be like a sponge which will draw the
demons into my body until my body falls in ruins. I will divert
hell from you and draw it upon myself so that you, Ogotai, may
live and may not leave the great Mongol nation without a father!"
—And Tuli drank the water and danced the dance of exorcism
until he fell down dead, and Ogotai rose from his couch, cured!'

Kublai raised his hand to silence him, but Arik-Buka would
not be silenced. 'He was faithful to the Law of the Steppe,' he

said, his eyes flashing. 'He testified by his death of sacrifice that only *one* can be Lord, and that the throne of the supreme ruler of the world is in the Steppe. And our brothers, too, remained Sons of the Steppe. Think of Hulagu, who knew no boundaries to the claims of the all-conquering Steppe! For three years he assaulted Alamut—after that there was no longer an "Eagles' Nest", nor an "Old Man of the Mountains", nor a Paradise of Hussein, nor any *fedavi* . . . Hulagu trampled Hussein like a worm. And how magnificently he dealt with the Caliph! That pious ruler of the Moslems thought a lot of his treasures. So, after Baghdad had been trampled to dust Hulagu left the Caliph to starve in his gold vaults, and when he began to whimper, our brother Hulagu held a lump of gold up to the Caliph and said: "Here! Eat this!" What a great idea! Mangu, too, remained simple and hard. He didn't hesitate an hour when he discovered that his cousins and nephews were opposing the choice of him as Khan. He had his opponents exterminated to the very last man. There was one difficulty, however. For the *Yassa*, the Law of the Mongols, forbids the shedding of a relative's blood. But Mangu was not long at a loss for a way out. He had his nephews and cousins shaken to death in carpets! He had one *tuman* after another combed through until there was no longer one unreliable man left in the ranks of the horsemen; not one who cherished any doubt but that only one mighty in the Steppe should occupy the throne of Genghis Khan. You see! They all trod the way which I trod— you alone chose Yeliu's way!'

'Yeliu was mistaken,' said Kublai, who could hardly bear Arik-Buka's glare. Arik-Buka pricked up his ears expectantly.

'*Po yen*,' continued Kublai, 'patience a hundred times has not sufficed to make you see how things look to me.'

'You speak with his voice,' retorted Arik-Buka, 'and you have his face. But I can hear through all his words, and I have seen through you long ago. You want to conquer me as he tried to conquer the Khan—with that gentleness with which water wears the edges off a hard stone. You want to have all the power to yourself!'

'I want nothing but to keep you,' said Kublai. 'Every office which I have to dispose of is open to you.'

At these words Arik-Buka's eyes became cold as ice. In a scathing tone he said: 'If you were to say to me: "Take half of my kingdom," believe me that, eager though my hand is for power, it would not grasp it, for I cannot share with a traitor even the air which I breathe!' Arik-Buka laughed a harsh laugh. 'What would I do together with you, anyhow? You who think only of fields, and canals, and bridges, and houses for the sick and aged and other useless people?'

'You could take over the protection of the frontiers.'

'As your *Chao-Kuri*—Subduer of Rebels?' interrupted Arik-Buka contemptuously. 'What do you want to make of Genghis Khan's youngest grandson? A frontier guard to whom every frontier would be a challenge to cross it? You can spare yourself the trouble of mocking me. *I* have not forgotten what *Menke Kuku Tengri* charged the Mongols to do: to conquer the whole world, or nothing! For me the Steppe is the beginning and the end of the world!'

'Then return to the Steppe!' said Kublai calmly.

Arik-Buka looked at Kublai distrustfully. 'You are letting me free, then, are you? I may go?'

'Wherever you wish to,' said Kublai. And neither his voice nor his face betrayed how much those words cost him.

'I will muster new *tumans* against you,' Arik-Buka assured him. 'I will march against you again and again until your throne is trampled in the dust!'

Kublai smiled. 'I know that it is not your way to give up,' he said, 'but I fear you will not succeed in making me your enemy. It is possible that you may trample the Dragon Throne underfoot. If Heaven so wills you may destroy my armies on the frontiers, my rice farmers and myself . . . But even if Heaven should will it, you shall never destroy my love for you! My love for you will outlive me. It will be the door in the wall of your hate; and it will not cease to stand open and to remind you that there is a way in. Long ago you carried me out of the ice when my strength gave way. How could I dare, then, to cease from seeking a way out for you from the deadly coldness which envelops your heart?'

Arik-Buka searched Kublai's face. He found nothing in it

which attracted him. Every feature reminded him of Yeliu. When he lowered his eyes he saw Kublai's outstretched hand. Haltsundoriki's silver band glistened on the wrist.

He has cast off everything else, thought Arik-Buka; and he felt a bitter taste in his mouth. Everything but that band! The estrangement between us started with him. Haltsundoriki was the first to separate us—not that he wished to do so—it was Kublai who always held fast to everything that was separating us . . .

'There is too much standing between us,' said Arik-Buka, without looking up. 'May I go?'

'You are my brother, not my prisoner,' said Kublai.

'I will come back,' said Arik-Buka threateningly. 'Then it shall be seen which is the stronger, the Son of Heaven or the Son of the Steppe!'

Saying this, he turned away.

Kublai watched the rugged shoulders disappearing as the ermine door-curtain fell. Then everything swam before his eyes; an endless, oppressing whiteness enveloped him. Kublai shivered. He felt a pain in his heart just as at that moment long ago when Bosa's ear-shell had closed for ever. But the pain was sharper now. Arik! cried Kublai's heart, though his lips were closed. Arik! And the soundless cry cut through him more deeply than the icy breath of the white-nosed steeds on the Roof of the World.

With only a few faithful followers Arik-Buka returned to the Steppe. But he did not get so far as to muster more *tumans* against his brother. For in that same year his hate consumed his heart, and like Genghis Khan he was laid to rest on the Burkan-Kaldun.

Kublai, too, returned to the vast country of the tall grasses and the yurts. When he died he was buried, in accordance with his last decree, beside Arik-Buka. But that was not until thirty-four years afterwards.

During those thirty-four years Kublai ruled the Middle Kingdom as 'Son of Heaven'. The period of his reign is recorded in the books of the Chinese historians as a happy epoch.

When Kublai Khan ascended the Dragon Throne the Chinese countryside had been laid waste with fire and sword and many

towns were in ruins. Out of a hundred million Chinese, forty
million had fallen victims to Genghis Khan's hordes from the
Steppe. The survivors were miserably housed, tortured in the
day by hunger and at night by dreams of fear. Tshe-Tsu freed
them from hunger and fear. Thirty thousand of the poorest were
fed every day from the Imperial kitchens. Those who had been
driven from their land were given land, seeds and cattle. The
orphans and the sick were taken care of. The Emperor had the
great canal finished. And he built roads on which goods from
Persia and Egypt, India and Mongolia were conveyed in safety.
Chinese junks sailed around the coasts of Africa and Arabia and
into the Pacific Ocean. The Emperor Tshe-Tsu regulated the
calendar, erected schools and observatories, and patronized
artists and scholars. His Prime Minister was Yao-Chi, a man

whose wisdom won admiration even beyond the frontiers of the Yellow Earth. Tshe-Tsu protected all religions and all peoples in his Empire, and was a father to many races. The peasants were able to set their rice shoots in safety, for this 'Son of Heaven' held the People of the Steppe within their own frontiers.

Tshe-Tsu built Peking, the mighty walls and gates of which awaken wonder even to the present day. Hangchow, the city of a million inhabitants and a thousand bridges, was favoured by him and completed in his reign. His summer residence, Changtu, was in itself a dream of beauty. The rarest trees in all Asia were carried to Changtu on the backs of elephants, together with their roots and their native soil. Camels arrived there laden with birds and with living wild animals, and evening after evening courier horsemen arrived with fruits which had been plucked in the South, normally twelve days' ride from Changtu, only on the morning of the previous day. In Changtu there were fountains, ornamental bridges, fish-ponds with copper railings round them and pleasure pavilions with roofs of gilded bamboos supported on pillars ornamented with dragons' heads. Tshe-Tsu went to the hunt on a magnificent throne drawn by elephants. His huntsmen carried cheetahs and gerfalcon on the cruppers of their horses. The Emperor rested in a tent made of panther skins, lined with ermine, and held by a hundred silken ropes. Every year on his birthday he made a sacrificial offering of milk; and the milk which he spilled at this ceremony came from spotless white mares of which he kept ten thousand in his studs.

In the middle of his huge fairylike garden the Emperor kept a special bed in which grass from the Steppe grew in earth which had been brought from the heart of Mongolia. And the water with which it was watered came from the Rivers Onon and Kerulen.

Chronological Table

2250 B.C.	The famous Chao music comes into existence under the Emperor Shun, in China.
213	Shi Huang Ti ('the first Emperor') completes the Great Wall of China, to protect the Middle Kingdom against the warrior horsemen of the Steppe.
A.D. 937	The Yeliu family in Northern China founds the Liao dynasty.
1115	Following a victory over the Liao, the Chin dynasty is founded.
1126	The Liao prince Yeliu-Tashi founds the Kara-Khitan Kingdom in Turkestan.
1135	Kabul Khan, grandfather of Genghis Khan, invades the Kingdom of Chin.
1162	Temuchin is born.
1175	Temuchin's father, Yessugai, dies.
1188	Temuchin gains a victory over Targutai and the Taichutes.
1194	Following a victory over the Tartars Temuchin is named Chao-Kuri, 'Subduer of Rebels,' by the Chin Emperor.
1206	Temuchin, having conquered and united all the Mongol tribes, becomes Genghis Khan, 'The Great Khan'.
1207 and 1209	Genghis Khan marches against the Tanguts.
1211–16	Genghis Khan wages war against the Kingdom of Chin.
1215	Peking falls. Yeliu Ch'utsai enters the service of Genghis Khan.
1219–22	Genghis Khan wages war against the Shah Mohammed of Persia.
1223	Genghis Khan returns to Mongolia.
1225	His eldest son, Juchi, dies.
1227	Genghis Khan dies.
1229–41	Ogotai, his third son and first successor, rules.
1232	His youngest son, Tuli, dies.
1235	The great *Kurultai* takes place in Mongolia. At this War Council of the Steppe four wars are decided upon:

against the Kingdom of Sung, against Korea, against Asia Minor and against Europe.

1236–42   Batu, son of Juchi and first Khan of the Golden Horde, conquers Russia and invades Poland, Germany and Hungary. On the 9th April 1241 the Battle of Liegnitz in Silesia is fought. After this the Mongols turn back although Germany lies open to them: the news of Ogotai's death has reached them, recalling them to the *Kurultai* in the Steppe.

1242–46   The dispute for the succession continues.

1246–48   Kujuk, son of Ogotai, rules as second successor to Genghis Khan.

1251–59   Mangu, eldest son of Tuli, rules as third successor to Genghis Khan.

1255   Hulagu, second son of Tuli, marches into Asia Minor and becomes the first of the Il-Khans.

1260–94   Kublai, third son of Tuli, reigns on the Mongol throne as fourth successor to Genghis Khan, and on the Dragon Throne of the Middle Kingdom as first Yuen Emperor of China.

1263   Arik-Buka, fourth son of Tuli, dies after having tried in vain, as 'Son of the Steppe,' to overthrow his brother Kublai, the 'Son of Heaven.'

The West first learned of Kublai Khan through Marco Polo, son of a Venetian merchant, who was an intimate friend of the Emperor for seventeen years, and who later, whilst in prison in Genoa, wrote a book which earned him the nickname of 'Marco Millions', because his descriptions of Kublai's kingdom seemed like fairy-tales to his contemporaries. But actually they were true.

The above particulars are given as showing the historical background on which the story, *Sons of the Steppe*, is based. But they are not meant to convey the impression that *Sons of the Steppe* aspires to be an account of the Mongol period which can be assessed by scientific standards.

In order to acquaint myself with the vast field covered I have, it is true, looked up all available sources and obtained much inspiration from Mongolian, Chinese, Persian and European sources. I am indebted to a number of well-known historians. For instance, Hoelun's Lament in the fourth chapter of Part I is largely identical with a passage in *Yuan chao pi shi*, 'The Secret History of the Mongols' of the year 1240.

It was in Russia in the winter of 1943 that I first conceived the idea of writing a book on how Genghis Khan was ultimately overcome. When I was a prisoner in France, living in a garden hut of maize straw, my plan matured. Finally, in June to December 1953, I got down to writing the story. Owing to the historical circumstances of the time, this was only possible in freedom.

Hans Baumann